Enigma of Fire

Marilyn Leach

D1379787

This is a work of fiction. Names, characters, places, and incidents either are the product of the author's imagination or are used fictitiously, and any resemblance to actual persons living or dead, business establishments, events, or locales, is entirely coincidental.

Enigma of Fire

COPYRIGHT 2016 by Marilyn Leach

All rights reserved. No part of this book may be used or reproduced in any manner whatsoever without written permission of the author or Pelican Ventures, LLC except in the case of brief quotations embodied in critical articles or reviews.

eBook editions are licensed for your personal enjoyment only. eBooks may not be re-sold, copied or given away to other people. If you would like to share an eBook edition, please purchase an additional copy for each person you share it with.

Contact Information: titleadmin@pelicanbookgroup.com

Cover Art by *Nicola Martinez*

Harbourlight Books, a division of Pelican Ventures, LLC
www.pelicanbookgroup.com PO Box 1738 *Aztec, NM * 87410

Harbourlight Books sail and mast logo is a trademark of Pelican Ventures, LLC

Cover photo of church (c) Lilian Harris

Publishing History
First Harbourlight Edition, 2017
Paperback Edition ISBN 978-1-61116-527-2
Electronic Edition ISBN 978-1-61116-526-5
Published in the United States of America

Dedication

To all those who have served or are serving their country with honor in military service, and to my family who are among them: Ace, Jason, Stevie, Floyd Jr., Blaine, and Melvin.

Other Berdie Elliott Mysteries

Candle for a Corpse
Up from the Grave
Into the Clouds

What People are Saying

Leach's careful attention to detail brings the English countryside to life. ~ Amanda Cabot, author

I love Marilyn's voice, and I hope there are MANY more books to come. ~ LA Sartor, bestselling author

Prologue

The wife and mother swept the floor in easy draws, the sound of the straw against the tile punctuated by the noise of her children playing.

"Get the children away from the window," her husband commanded. The man jerked his hand from right to left and back again.

"What?"

His eyes flared and she could see the veins in his neck bulge as he stretched it forward. "Get the children away from the window. Now!"

"Children, come here." She stopped her sweeping and motioned them to her.

The little boy pulled his sister's toe in a silly game they played, and they both broke into voluble giggles.

"Children," he screamed, "go to your mother!"

Both children started and eyed their father.

"What's wrong?" She watched her husband move along the wall in a stealthy manner. "What's wrong?"

"Shh, listen." The man swallowed as he braced his rigid fingers against the door and put his ear close. "Can't you hear them? Listen. They're coming near."

The little girl left her brother drawing finger circles on the floor and stepped close to her father. "Who's near, Daddy?"

He grabbed the little girl's jaw with his hand and squeezed it. She grimaced and tried to pull away, but he clung on all the tighter, and then laid his face nearly on hers. "Quiet," he spoke in a hiss.

His wife drew a quick breath. "Oh no, God, please." Her prayer was short. The broom clattered as she dropped it to the floor and hurried to her daughter, putting her arms round her. "Yes, yes, we'll be silent," she assured her husband.

The man released his grip. "Stay low and stay alert. Find cover. We can't let them know we're here." He spun round and went toward the bedroom.

The mother bent down and pulled her daughter to her. The child leaned into her body and whimpered.

"Quiet, my love, you must be quiet." The mother stroked her little one's soft hair. "You must be a brave little girl."

She felt her hands begin to tremble as she came to her feet. Gripping her daughter's hand, with her other arm she scooped up her son, who sat quiet with wonder on the floor. Both children in hand, she darted her eyes cross the room. What now?

Her husband reentered the space. She gasped.

He gripped a gun braced against his side. He said nothing but moved determinedly along to the window. She could see the alarm in his eyes, his face skewed with fear, as if destructive possibilities screamed out a warning.

She felt tears spring to her eyes.

"What's Daddy doing?" her son asked in a tiny voice.

"You must be Daddy's brave little boy," she whispered and watched a tear trickle down her daughter's cheek, red from her father's clench.

The woman could feel the icy fingers of panic grip her heart. Holding her children's hands, she ran from the room into the kitchen where she grabbed a table knife.

She spied the back corner behind the wooden table. "Come along, children," she encouraged. She crouched low, urging her precious little ones with her as they crawled along the floor under the table to the corner.

She could hear her husband bark unrecognizable slurs to those who threatened beyond.

"Are we playing army?" her little girl asked.

"Yes, yes, we're playing army. We must obey orders and stay quiet."

Her daughter's eyes were filled with bewilderment, and a single sob slipped from her tiny lips.

The woman maneuvered herself round and placed her back against the wall, her legs pressed against her chest where she hid the knife. She clutched her children, pulling them against the sides of her body. "We're going to stay right against the wall and close to each other." She could feel her heart pounding. "Remember Daddy loves you very much," she murmured as they huddled together in the dark corner. She tried to hum a calming lullaby, though her voice quivered. A single tear escaped and slowly slid down her hot cheek. "He loves us very much."

1

"Sometimes it feels the sweeping hands of that clock are wrapped round my toes and squeezing."

The kitchen aroma of a well-prepared meal tickled Berdie Elliott's nose as she placed decorated picnic ware in the ample food hamper, whilst aching feet reminded her that she hadn't had a sit-down since early this morning.

"I tell you," she said to her friend, Lillie Foxworth, who added folded linens to the plates, "sometimes it takes all one possesses to keep up."

"True," Lillie mumbled.

"When I followed my dear Hugh into the pastorate after his military retirement"—Berdie took a deep breath—"and I came with the same commitment of faith and service, mind you, I hadn't reckoned that I'd be a hostel hostess in a small English village, racing the clock to feed the five thousand at Whitsun."

"Oh, but remember, Berdie," Lillie ribbed with a large grin and hazel-green eyes dancing, "to be hospitable at all times is a grace. You could be entertaining angels unawares."

Berdie waggled a fork toward her friend. "Night wanderings, unwelcomed pets, demanding diets: if the guests staying here are angels, I should think their halos have slipped slightly."

"Come now, Berdie." Lillie took the fork from

Berdie's hand. "I've not noticed five thousand, just nine people at last count, and it's a picnic al fresco at the lake, not the village fete."

"You're such a stickler about minor details."

Lillie put the fork next to the others in the utensil basket and surveyed the situation. "There's no room in the hamper for the main dish."

"You see? Stickler for details." Berdie chuckled and Lillie joined her. "Take out the jar of pickled onions to make room. It's quite clear, Lillie, where our nattering gets us."

The sound of the vicarage front door chime sang out its plea for attention.

"Oh bother," flew from Berdie's lips.

"Ah, angels have come knocking. The word's out all cross the heavens," Lillie shouted as Berdie left the kitchen. "There's a room going spare at the vicarage and food to be had."

Berdie chortled while she hustled through the front hall.

She arrived at the pub mirror, placed just alongside the door, and glanced at herself. Middle age had been kind to her, but she hoped her brown eyes didn't appear as tired as she felt at the moment. She pushed an errant piece of her red-brown bobbed hair to its appropriate place, adjusted her tortoiseshell glasses, wiped her hand cross the ditsy designs of her apron that covered her more-pudgy-than-lean body, turned with steady mind for whatever may greet her, and flung the vicarage door open.

There before her stood Milton Butz, the inevitable dots of maturing adolescence decorating his fourteen-year-old face, and behind, his tall, ginger-haired friend, Kevin McDermott. Hardly heavenly beings.

"Milton, Kevin, hello," Berdie greeted.

"That big dog is running all over the village again, Mrs. Elliott." Milton released a slight pant.

"He's been digging in Mrs. Hall's herb garden, again." Kevin's round eyes held an element of panic as he took a deep breath. "And he's scary."

Berdie wanted to shout, "That annoying canine escape artist is more trouble than he's worth, and seeing as he belongs to retired Leftenant Commander Cedric Royce, just one of our 'angelic' guests, the commander can ruddy well chase about after it." But instead, she offered a more refined response that was in line with her position and wouldn't shower the boys with her displeasure. "The dog's name is Sparks, and he's quite"—Berdie searched for a constructive word—"energetic for an animal his size and difficult to contain."

"He doesn't seem very friendly either," Kevin added.

"He's not a lap dog, no."

Milton's barrel chest rose and fell—the boys had obviously rushed. "Do you want us to collect him?"

"Milty." Kevin's eyes grew wider, and he kicked the back of Milton's shoe.

"He's just a dog." Milton's demeanor was fearless.

"Thanks for the offer, lads, but I believe Leftenant Commander Royce is at the Upland Arms enjoying a swift half. Perhaps you could fetch him and let him deal with the beast."

"Beast?" Kevin's cheeks flushed under the freckles.

Milton looked slightly disappointed. "Are you sure you don't want us to try to collect Sparks?"

Kevin's eyebrows knit into a deep frown.

"Thank you for the offer, Milton, but the dog listens best to the commander." *In truth, the commander is the only one he listens to.*

"Yeah, OK, Mrs. Elliott. We'll fetch your guest."

"That dog isn't very friendly," Kevin reiterated.

The redhead stood at least six inches taller than Milton, but you could see who possessed the gravitas.

"See you then." Milton turned to go, while Kevin finally smiled, offered a hearty wave, and followed after his pal.

"God go with you," Berdie called after them.

And God help anyone who should try to corner that animal apart from Cedric.

In his stay with them so far, Sparks, the oversized black Labrador, didn't appear especially mean as Kevin described him, but he certainly wasn't approachable either. Mr. Braunhoff, the very capable churchwarden, had set up a portable sheep enclosure in the vicarage back garden for the creature when he arrived with the commander, but the dog seemed to find unfathomable ways to escape. Though he had dug up the vicarage peonies, eaten his own body weight daily in dog food, and urinated on the garden furniture, he seemed very loyal to Cedric. Hopefully, the boys would find Commander Royce, and Sparks would be contained again soon.

Moving her slender figure forward with grace, Lillie arrived in the hall. Short, loose curls of ebony-colored hair surrounded her tawny face. "Who was it?"

"That dog's jumped ship."

"Not again?"

"I haven't time to chase after the silly thing."

"What would you do with it once you found it anyway?"

"Should I dare say? I sent Milton Butz and Kevin McDermott to go fetch Cedric from the pub."

"Excellent plan, though that means the commander will be late for the picnic."

"He'll be in good company unless we push on."

"Now, now. I've got the meat pie snugly in its proper place, and we're ready for the off."

"You're a godsend, Lillie." Berdie still marveled that her husband, Hugh, had his first parish assignment right here at Saint Aidan of the Woods Parish Church in the very village, Aidan Kirkwood, where her dearest friend lived. She and Lillie had been chums since university, some thirty years ago.

The three and a half years she and Hugh had spent here seemed but a minute. And now she had only minutes before the lunch was due at the lake.

Upon reentering the kitchen, Berdie was in command mode. "Let's take the food hampers first and then the drinks chest. They're all going to be very hungry."

"And weary, aching, plus wet through, I shouldn't wonder."

"Most likely." Berdie grabbed the jar of pickled onions. "And they'll relish every throbbing moment of it, mark my words."

****

"Here we are." Berdie espied the scull with four oarsmen the moment she parked the car at road's edge. It moved along with rhythmic oars in the sun-reflective waters near the shoreline of Bampkingswith Hall's Presswood Lake. Though Colonel and Mrs. Presswood now resided in their London flat the lion's share of time, they had allowed a small rowing club to let their boathouse, using the lake and its grounds as they would.

"Man the hampers," Lillie jibed.

Berdie and Lillie made way to the water's edge where Berdie caught sight of Hugh's silver-white hair. She watched his back expand then constrict while his middle-aged legs pushed a steady rhythm in chorus with his comrades. The sound of the crew's verbal labors met her ears as they forced their oars through the water.

"Keep it steady," Hugh called out.

Though he wasn't wearing his naval-captain shoulder amulets of his past military career, nor the clerical collar that was his current badge of office, his leadership was evident.

"Nice release, Chad," Hugh commended the young and very fit bowman, who possessed dark, handsome features.

"Always, Captain." Chad's voice was buoyant.

"Good pace." Hugh grunted and inhaled. "We're on a promise to take it all, men. What say?"

"I can row or I can chunter, but I can't do both at the same time." Rollie, a fellow Hugh's age but not quite as in trim, worked to get the words out.

David, the reserved and ever-thoughtful fourth crewman, chuckled.

Berdie adjusted her sunhat and waved to Hugh. "Lunch's arrived."

"Right on time or close enough," he shouted.

The other boatmen cheered heartily.

"Land ho," Hugh directed his crew.

Lillie shielded the sun from her eyes with her hand as she observed the men. "They seem to be in high spirits."

Berdie nodded. "That'll be the endorphins running amuck. We'll see if they are still jaunty round eight this evening when painful aches and sore muscles set in."

By the time the crew reached the shore, settled the boat in its proper place, and considered the times of their runs, Berdie and Lillie had the hampers emptied and food laid out on the portable table they set up near the edge of the lake, several yards from the road.

Berdie was pleased with her table. Chicken-and-ale pie, which had found a place in the hamper, was joined by country ham and piccalilli sandwich rounds, spicy sausage rolls, cucumber pickles, Scotch eggs, peach cup crumbles, and homemade lime cordials: a fine picnic by anyone's standards.

"I want this picnic to be special," Berdie said. "Hugh's worked so very hard, not only to assemble this crew, but he's tireless in all his service to the church."

"Then we must add this." Lillie held up some Union Jack bunting, a string of vibrant triangles, to Berdie's view.

"Perfect."

While Lillie draped the decorative bunting across the table edge, the men approached.

Hugh led the lively crew to the luncheon table: former Leftenant Chadwick Meryl, the youngest, whose rowing gear clung to his well-built body; gray-headed retired Captain Rollie Lloyd, who kept the chaps in good humor despite muscle aches; and sun-kissed David St. John, shy but kind, who left the Navy as a young chief petty officer to work as an IT specialist. This was the St. Aidan of the Wood Church crew that was to race in the Whitsun Regatta sponsored by multiple parishes across the county. It wasn't the first time they teamed with one another, they had served together in the same naval intelligence unit, and were now all chums together. And in three weeks Monday, the bank holiday, they would row their hardest to vie for the winning trophy.

Hugh made introductions to Lillie and then began unfolding garden chairs he fetched from the backseat of Rollie's car, Dave helping out.

"Hugh said we'd have a picnic at the lake. I didn't realize it would be a banquet." Chad ran the back of his hand over his forehead, his deep-set brown eyes focused on the laden table. "This meal, in and of itself, makes coming to Aidan Kirkwood worth it all."

"Mrs. Elliott doesn't do things by halves." Rollie grinned and nodded to Berdie.

Berdie smiled in return. Rollie and his wife, Joan, had recently moved to Timsley, the nearby market town. And although they were longtime friends, she and Hugh were just getting reacquainted with the Lloyds again. "Your Joan would do nothing less."

Dave unfolded a chair. "We have a fine boathouse here, but no café. It's a small club, and I rather prefer it that way."

"This lot beats a café," Chad rebutted. "Al fresco suits me."

Hugh brought more chairs and set them round. "That's the lot." He sighed. "We're missing Busby, of course, but he's off visiting family in Canada."

"Ah, Busby. I'm surprised he didn't fly in just for the meat pie," Rollie teased.

"Indeed." Hugh rubbed his hands and stood tall, every ounce of his six-foot frame at attention. "I believe grace is in order."

Berdie watched Rollie and Dave bow their heads as Chad glanced round, apparently unaccustomed to such a thing, and then dipped his chin.

"For what we are about to receive, we are truly thankful, Lord. Feed and refresh us. Amen."

"Amen," Berdie, Lillie, and Dave responded.

"And God give us the grace to rise from our beds in the morning without the aid of a large hoist." Rollie rubbed his arm.

Berdie served the fellows their cordials.

"I should think a toast to absent friends is appropriate as well." Hugh held up his drinks glass. "To absent friends."

All repeated, "Absent friends."

Chad respectfully added, "To Ennis Wolf."

"To Ennis," the men repeated and took a swallow of lime cordial.

"Tuck in," Berdie invited, and the crew set to.

As she helped serve, she became aware that Doug Devlin and his daughter, Tillie, two of the "angels" currently staying in her home, had arrived by cab at the road's edge. They were making the lengthy trek cross the wild, grass-anchored soil that led to their picnic table.

And trek it was. Tillie gripped her father's wheelchair handles with tight fists, her slim twenty-something body calling upon all her weight to push. Tillie's long blonde hair fell forward as she leaned to thrust with her anchored legs, churning slowly across the soft earth.

Moisture appeared along Doug's blond hairline, his broad chest and muscular arms engaged as he worked to push the wheels along with his hands as well, angling and dipping as they went.

Though they had already been guests at the vicarage for nearly a week, Berdie had prepared and placed the picnic without any real thought to Doug's circumstances. She watched Tillie struggle. Doug used his leg to awkwardly balance while his other trouser leg lay empty below the knee.

Berdie felt suddenly negligent. "Dear Lord," she whispered.

Though Chad was the first to come to Tillie's aid, all the fellows set their plates aside to assist.

"You old sea dog, Devlin," Chad chided his pal.

"Chad Meryl, when did you arrive?"

"Just in time for a good thrash round the lake and a grand tea," he answered. "And this isn't the last you'll see of me. I'll be staying at the vicarage as well." Chad took control of the wheelchair as Tillie released her grip. "Let me help."

"Very kind," she responded in between breaths.

"Doug"—Rollie stepped lively to his friend—"good to see you."

Doug stuck out his hand. "Rollie, how's retired life?"

The men heartily clasped hands and shook.

Hugh and Dave stamped their feet in an obvious attempt to compact the soil and create an even track for the wheelchair to the table.

"My, his daughter is dedicated to take that slog on," Lillie noted to Berdie.

"She is indeed. Dedicated to the bone." Berdie once again felt a pang of guilt and bit her lip. "I never thought about access."

"Nonsense. He wants to be here with his Navy mates," Lillie reminded. "He'd probably wheel himself across the Sahara in a sandstorm to spend time with them."

Berdie watched as the men, and Tillie, made way to the table. "I'm sure he wishes he could be rowing again with his team. Still, at least I can give him a tasty meal for all his work."

"That's right. You've done a splendid job here."

Lillie was right. Being host to four guests, one of whom had special considerations, was just like her role as village vicar's wife. Berdie took it on as it came, learning as she went along.

"Wonderfully laid, Mrs. Elliott." Tillie reached the table where her darkest blue eyes took it all in.

"Did you enjoy your morning at the Timsley History Museum?" Berdie asked.

"A bit taxing for Dad, but yes," Tillie answered.

"This is grand." Doug cheered while Chad placed him at the table and set the wheelchair's brake.

"I'll fetch a plate for you, Dad," Tillie offered.

"You know what he likes best." Berdie once again felt she had overlooked an obvious need.

Doug eyed the eggs. "You know, I could fill the plate with Scotch eggs alone and be completely satisfied."

Berdie brightened while Lillie gave a casual laugh.

"Now, Dad, you need to think of your health. There's plenty of other good food. No Scotch eggs."

"My daughter doesn't let me get away with much." Doug grinned.

While Tillie filled a plate, Lillie leaned close to Berdie. "How old is she?"

"She's not yet twenty-five."

"Quite young to be the parent."

Berdie nodded. "Perhaps she had to be." Berdie spoke softly. "Her mother left Tillie and Doug several years back."

"I see."

"I've made a subtle attempt, since she's been here, to introduce her to some young people her age."

"Subtle, that's a new tactic on your part."

"I sent her to a party at Matthew Reese's home last night. I made a promise to keep Doug safe and sound. She got in late. Positive sign. This morning, she said she had enjoyed herself."

Berdie directed her full voice to the young woman. "I'll give what you've dished up to your father, and you can fill your own plate."

"Thank you, Mrs. Elliott, but I've got it." Tillie's smile was pleasant.

While everyone tucked into their food, Berdie heard the arrival of another guest, one who was not invited. She recognized that bark anywhere now.

Sparks, on a lead, thank heaven, made way to the picnic table with Cedric on the other end, who indeed was invited. Sparks actually grew quiet and stood to heel of the commander, who tugged lightly on the lead.

"What's he doing here?" Chad's loud words didn't sound rhetorical.

Hugh raised his eyes to the approaching silver-haired friend and smiled. "Oh, the commander takes Sparks most everywhere he goes now. He's staying with us too."

"I don't mean the dog," flew like bullets from Chad's mouth as he sprang from his chair. "What's *he* doing here?"

"Cedric? I invited him, of course, to come cheer his fellows on, to watch the regatta." Hugh's tone suddenly had a guarded edge.

"Cheer his fellows on?" Chad's face grew dark at the sound of the words. "You can't be serious."

Berdie watched Cedric make way toward the table, cheerful, it seemed, until he caught sight of Chad. He appeared stunned, almost frozen. Then his lips pursed, his fair skin flushed red round his neck, and he lifted his chin. "Good day, men," he called, took a deep breath, and stood his mature body ramrod-straight. "Hello, Leftenant Meryl."

"Hello, Leftenant Meryl?" Chad's jaw set. "Is that all you can say after what you did?"

Everyone stared at Chad, then the commander. By the surprise registered on the faces of those eating, Berdie wasn't the only one who stood amazed to see the interaction between the two men.

The commander made no comment, but Sparks gave a low growl.

"Gentleman, we're gathered round to celebrate a reunion." Dave motioned toward the table.

As if Dave had said nothing, the commander's eyes were fixed on Chad. "I shouldn't have come if I knew you would be here."

"Oh, I'm here all right. If I had any idea you were anywhere near, I'd have been better prepared to take you on." Chad's hands, at his sides, went into fists.

"Chad, steady on," Hugh cautioned.

Dave rose from his chair. "Whatever the problem, we're all friends here."

"Friends with you lot"—Chad nodded toward the group round the table—"yes." He stabbed an index finger toward the commander, shaking with rage. "Not him. Never him."

Berdie could feel Chad's caustic words sweep any civil discourse into the lake depths.

"Let's calm down." Hugh now also rose. "This can all be sorted."

The commander slacked the lead and Sparks lunged to the fore, showed his teeth, and began a barking tirade bent to protect.

Berdie looked round and took everyone in. Lillie appeared ready to run, Rollie's mouth gaped, Dave was anguished, beads of perspiration dotted Doug's forehead, and Tillie's fork was wrapped in her fist, tines poised as a weapon.

It was then Berdie caught her breath at the possibilities that could unfold with an angry man pitted against a defend-to-the-death canine. She found the commanding words flying from her mouth. "Will you please restrain your dog, Cedric?"

The former officer tightened his grip on the lead. "Down, Sparks. Heel." The dog responded to the command and pulled back, but his ears were on high alert, edgy feet eager.

"You may have a vicious beast to hide behind this time, but you've not heard the last of me." Chad grabbed his full plate from the table and thrust it to the earth, splattering food all over the celebratory bunting that fluttered round the table. His eyes flared; his whole body tensed. "You'll rue the day our paths crossed again."

The sneer on Chad's face made Berdie prickle.

Chad spat onto the soil, turned, and stampeded for the road. Even though he gave a wide berth to the commander and his pet, Sparks raised the alarm, barking as if to say, "Good riddance."

Tillie abruptly stood.

"What are you doing, Tillie?" Doug gripped the wheels of his mobile chair.

"Someone needs to go after him."

"She's right," Dave replied. "I'll go."

Dave moved quickly, while Cedric patted Sparks, who seemed pleased with himself that the threat had retreated.

Tillie wistfully watched Dave approach Chad whilst she sank into to her seat.

Cedric reached the group, chin jutted, shaking his head. "I'm sorry you all had to be privy to such conduct." He stood firmly, shoulders back, flushed. "If you will please excuse me, then I'll go now and let you eat in peace."

"Cedric"—Hugh's voice was clear—"we really would enjoy your company here. Dave will see to Chad. Consider it nothing more than a youthful moment of indiscretion."

Youthful moment? Indiscretion? Berdie couldn't believe her ears. There were threats made.

"We can put all this behind us and move on."

Tillie eyed Hugh.

"Please, Cedric, join us." Hugh waved his hand toward the laden table.

"Come now, Commander, it takes more than a few harsh words to keep you from enjoying good food," Rollie joked. "None of that military grub here."

"Well…." The commander stepped forward while Sparks lifted his nose to what Berdie assumed was the tantalizing scent of her chicken-and-ale pie. She hoped the commander kept Sparks on a short lead.

Cedric's eyes were steady. "If you're sure, that's very kind."

"Here's your plate." Doug held an empty dish toward the gentleman.

"Thank you, Doug. And a good afternoon to you,

Tillie."

Tillie smiled and nodded.

Hugh glanced at the shaken Lillie. "Commander Royce, this is Miss Foxworth, our choir mistress at St. Aidan and a dear friend."

He gave a polite nod her direction to which she offered a weak smile.

"Well, we can't have tasty food go to waste," Hugh announced.

Berdie knew he was trying to turn a difficult situation into a salvageable gathering.

While Cedric filled his plate, Berdie watched Dave St. John in the distance speak with Chad, who was now at his vehicle. Chad's shoulders appeared less tense as he conversed with his teammate, but when he pounded his fist into his palm, it was clear Chad's antagonism had not subsided. Dave handed Chad a set of keys, perhaps to his flat in nearby Kingsbridge. At least Berdie hoped so. She certainly couldn't see Chad and Cedric dwelling under the same roof of her much-loved vicarage. Not even in the same village for that matter.

While the fellows round the table worked at light conversation and Sparks rested at the commander's feet, Tillie ran a fork cross her piece of chicken-and-ale pie, and then pushed her entire plate aside.

Chad stirred dust on the road as he roared off in his car.

"I often have pickled onions with ham," Rollie offered rather absently.

"You know, some pickled onions wouldn't go amiss with these sandwich rounds. Do we have any?" Hugh asked Berdie.

"Didn't I set them out?" Berdie scanned the table.

"I know I packed some in the car."

"I'll get them." Lillie was out of her seat like some jack-in-the-box.

"Do you know where they are?" Berdie called after her.

Lillie didn't acknowledge Berdie's question. She simply carried on to the vehicle.

Berdie put her plate on the table and caught up her friend.

"Those two fellows. That was certainly a display," Lillie piped.

"Wasn't it just?"

"It put me off my food altogether. And my bunting's ruined. What's between Cedric and Chad?"

"No idea." Berdie reached the rear of the auto and pulled her car keys from her skirt pocket, gave them a shake, and considered what had just taken place. "And I'm not sure anyone here really knows either. Or if they do, they're being unusually quiet."

"Must be something quite awful. Chad was spectacularly angry."

"The commander wasn't exactly gracious either."

Lillie opened the front passenger door and looked inside the vehicle to the backseat. "No, not here."

"In the boot, my dear." Berdie pushed a button on her key fob and the tailgate of her sedan popped up, revealing the jar of treats in a back corner.

"Do you suppose it has something to do with a problem they had in the military?" Lillie stepped to the car boot.

"Chad's been out for two or three years, I believe, but the commander retired only a few months back." Berdie tapped the fob against her chin. "It's hard to say, but it wouldn't be entirely unlikely."

"I can see your nose twitching," Lillie teased. "You're dying to know what it's all about."

"And you aren't?"

"I can tell when your former-investigative-reporter nose raises to sniff out the whys and wherefores."

"Well, the truth is, at the moment, besides all my usual church responsibilities, I'm too busy keeping a house full of guests fed, clean, comfortable, and in an amiable state of being. And that's besides the dog. I've no time to sniff about."

Lillie took up the onion jar and faced Berdie. "I'll give you twenty-four hours before you start digging." She raised her brow. "Now tell me, why did the commander bring Sparks with him to the vicarage on this visit?"

"I'm not entirely sure. He's staying a fair amount of time. Perhaps he couldn't find anyone to look after Sparks." Berdie dropped her chin. "I do know that Cedric's wife died just a year back."

"Did they have children?"

"A daughter. But from the little Hugh knows, she and Cedric had some kind of rift and they've not had contact since."

"What about his wife's funeral?"

Berdie shrugged and returned the key to her pocket. "Hugh attended, not I." Berdie glanced toward the commander. "I suppose the dog is a companion of sorts."

"That's a companion? Bit sad, isn't it?"

"Yes, well, I think that's why Hugh invited him to stay with us. I guess he's been a bit down. It seemed the perfect opportunity to invite him to visit with the Whitsun Regatta coming, especially since the crew is made up of members from his old unit." Berdie sighed.

"Well and good, but my dear husband told him that he could bring the creature with him, and bring him he did."

"You mean Hugh didn't ask you about taking in the canine guest?"

Berdie cocked her head. "He didn't ask me because he knew what my answer would be, I should imagine. But it's a moot point now."

Lillie clutched the pickled-onion jar with both hands. "Still, I wonder what may have transpired between Chad and the commander if the dog had not been here."

"That, my dear, is hopefully something that will forever be left to the imagination."

"Berdie," Hugh called from the table, "did you find the onions?"

Berdie nodded. "Just coming." She closed the boot. "Whatever's between the two men, our plate is full with other goings-on. The regatta and all the preparation for it, Whitsun days of prayer, the children's Tea Time Club with the St. Matthew's youth, all clamoring for our time and energy."

Berdie and Lillie began walking back to the group.

"Hugh's taking the church primary school youth group over to St. Matthew's in Mistcome Greene today?" Lillie inquired.

"Today and every day, apart from Sunday, until Whitsun. He ferries them from school in the church people carrier at the end of classes."

"But it's Saturday."

"Even so, he's picking up the children from the school at the same time for a special dinner at St. Matthew's, a hotdog roast for the kiddies."

"Then we need to return to Aidan Kirkwood

soon."

Berdie released a quick breath. "There's that clock again, demanding we push on." She squeezed her lips together. "And then there's what we've witnessed here today, Lillie. I'd say there's a great deal of unanswered animosity between those two fellows. And as we all know, animosity never leads to good."

2

Berdie could scarcely believe that Hugh would be leaving to fetch the village children in less than ten minutes. The picnic, despite the incident and uneasiness that followed, had lasted far longer than planned, with not a word spoken of the episode. Berdie put it down to a bit of shock. Now the late afternoon became a scramble.

She placed fresh linen in the airing cupboard, reserving two fresh white pillowcases, and turned to enter the master bedroom where she could hear the blow dryer emanating its ferocious clamor. Hugh had apparently already finished his shower.

Berdie entered the bedroom. "That was quick," she quipped to Hugh, who stood handsomely in gray trousers and a crisp shirt with clerical collar, styling his hair with blow dryer in hand.

"What's that?" he yelled.

Berdie just shook her head and closed the door. She wanted to ask Hugh what he knew concerning the confrontation that had taken place at the picnic. But certainly not when trying to compete with the blow dryer, especially since the commander's guest room was one door down.

At the same moment Berdie began to change a pillowcase, Hugh put the hairbrush on the chest next him, took a final look in the gold-framed mirror, and turned off the deafening implement.

Berdie wasn't sure how to approach him, but she decided to just come out with it. "Hugh, that was a rancorous display today. Do you have any idea what the problem is between Chad and the commander?"

Hugh cleared his throat as he ran a finger over his silver-white hair. "Is it really for you to know?"

Berdie held the pillow against her body and moved closer to him. "Let me put it another way. Is there anything we can do to bring a resolution to Cedric and Chad's conflict?"

"We?"

She watched Hugh's left eyebrow rise, which meant her words had displeased him.

He turned toward her and looked her in the eye. "No matter how you put it, it's between the two of them." Hugh put his hands on her shoulders. "Berdie, I know how you love to get everyone's ducks in a row, but it's their problem to sort."

"Well, they don't seem to be doing a very good job of it."

Hugh turned back to the mirror and put the slightest touch of gentleman's fragrance on his palms, then lightly tapped his lower jaw. "If one of them would just get past their pride and take the first step, they could work it out, I'm sure."

"So you do know what's between them."

"Let it go, Berdie."

There was a light rap at the bedroom door. Berdie stepped cross the gracious room and gently pulled the door open.

"Oh, sorry, Mrs. Elliott," Cedric apologized. "I didn't mean to interrupt."

"No, that's fine, Commander."

"I was hoping to speak with Hugh."

"Of course, Cedric." Hugh gave Berdie a nod that said, "We're done with this particular conversation," which she alone could understand.

"Can I have a word with you out here?" Cedric stood solidly in the hallway.

"Of course." Hugh moved to the door and out, but kept the door slightly ajar.

Berdie glanced out the bedroom window that faced the back garden. Doug was sunning himself, relaxed in his wheelchair, a lime cordial in one hand whilst petting Sparks with the other. He carried on a conversation with the large and extremely-capable-of-fixing-anything Mr. Braunhoff, who worked at escape-proofing Sparks's pen. Tillie was out. She had gone to Bearden's Creamery, after trying every possible means of convincing her father he needed to come with her. But Doug begged off, saying the picnic had taken the best of his energy. So she promised him his favorite ice cream, strawberry, and nothing but organic, if he agreed to take a nap. He had assured her he would do, but it looked as if relaxing in the back garden suited him best at the moment.

The house was rather quiet for once. Berdie wanted to be respectful of Cedric's privacy, and at the same time she could just make out the commander's words.

"Hugh, I'm terribly sorry for the goings-on at the picnic. I feel such regret, yet I feel justified at the same time." His voice took on a slight tremor. "Chad's life is in ruins, and my hand is behind it, but there's little I can do now to change that."

"Let's go to your room, Cedric."

By the sound of the footsteps and the closing of the

guest-room door, they did just that.

"Chad's life in ruins. At Cedric's hand," Berdie whispered to herself. She inattentively wrestled the pillow into the pillowcase. "Lord have mercy."

Like an electronic bolt, the vicarage phone rang out its bleating rhythm and interrupted Berdie's thoughts. Despite the telephone in the bedroom, she felt it more discreet to go downstairs to the hall phone. She threw the half-stuffed pillow on the bed and descended the stairs. "Vicarage," she answered, louder than was prudent.

"I need the vicar. We need the vicar." The voice wasn't familiar as it wailed into Berdie's ear with an urgent sense of panic.

Berdie could hear some kind of disruption happening in the background. "The vicar's engaged in a weighty conversation at the moment."

"I don't care if he's speaking with the bloomin' queen—get him to the phone."

Berdie thought she heard shouting.

"We need him," the caller yelled, fright in the voice.

"Yes, please be patient. I'll fetch him."

Berdie ascended the stairs with a slight panic of her own. She didn't like the idea of Hugh possibly putting himself in harm's way. She knew him capable of looking after himself, but she didn't like it. Berdie rapped on Cedric's door. "Hugh," she called, "so sorry to disturb. There's an urgent call."

The door sprang open. "Berdie, we're in a serious conversation." Hugh lowered his voice. "And I've got to fetch the children in five minutes."

"I know, but the caller's insistent."

"Who is it?"

Berdie shrugged. "They're in great distress, and sound desperate."

Hugh turned to his guest. "I'm sorry, Cedric. Can we continue our conversation later this evening?"

Cedric's voice was calm. "Yes, of course, Hugh. Tend to your flock."

Hugh all but ran down the stairs, Berdie on his heels. And mid-stride, the doorbell rang.

"Not more angels, please." Berdie whisked past Hugh, who was now at the phone, and flung open the door.

"You've got a delivery, yeah?" Mr. Raheem's young nephew stood at the door, his dark eyes cautious. "Yeah?" he repeated in his London accent with a Punjabi twist.

"Oh, yes, thank you, Sundeep."

She tried to half listen to Hugh's conversation on the phone. Something about imminent need.

The fellow stared at Berdie. "Put it where?" He shook the box.

Berdie pulled herself back to the delivery. "In the kitchen." She pointed down the hallway to the intended room.

Sundeep entered the hall. He started as Hugh shouted into the phone, "Calm down and tell me where you are."

"Something horrible could happen. We need you." The terrified shout filled the hall.

"Blimey." The young man raised a brow. "Is your husband a vicar or a policeman? My uncle told me I left this kind of craziness behind in London. Really? And this a country vicarage and all."

"They just need Hugh's help." Berdie decided getting the London lad away from the conversation was probably a good idea. "Come along, Sundeep, I'll show you into the kitchen." She waved her hand for the young man to follow her.

Once in the kitchen, Berdie heard the plodding of what she assumed was Cedric making his way down the stairs to the front hall from his bedroom.

"There." Berdie pointed to the sink counter. "I'll sort it later."

Sundeep slapped it down. His thick black hair played with the edges of his eyebrows. "Two boxes, yeah?"

"Two boxes? Oh, yes, it was a big order."

"I'll just fetch the other one then."

"I'll walk you back to the door."

Sundeep was a new arrival to the village, currently living with the Raheems. She sincerely hoped the young man wouldn't form an opinion that this pleasant home was a bit madcap. Although at the moment, perhaps it was.

When they reached the front door, Hugh was off the phone. He and Cedric looked to be in concerned conversation.

"I realize it's a bit of a cheek." Hugh was flushed. "But seeing as you've gone with me the past three days and know the way…"

"Think nothing of it, dear man. I'd be glad to do it," Cedric said.

Sundeep glanced at the commander and then opened the front door. "Van's just here," he said to Berdie and stepped out.

She could see the delivery vehicle with the crisp green letters *Raheem's Greengrocer* painted on the side. She also observed another vehicle park right behind it. A woman and two small children exited the well-worn hatchback and quickly made way to her door.

When will it stop? Berdie realized her bedroom moment of reflection was short lived.

She recognized the female, who looked to be grandmother to the two young children. She had visited church last Sunday and brought the little ones with her. What was her name? She introduced herself and said she was new to the area. Mrs. Limb, yes. Berdie remembered how she thought at the time that the visitor's gray hair, pulled into a rather severe topknot, only embellished her somewhat angular body movement and made the dear woman appear stiff and rather wooden. Ah, yes, Mrs. Limb.

Hugh came alongside at the open door. "Our car keys, please."

Berdie dug into her pocket and dropped them into his open palm. "Be careful, Hugh."

He gave her a quick peck on the cheek. "Don't worry."

Berdie ran her hand down his arm. "And the club children?"

"Cedric's fetching them from school and will take them to St. Matthew's in the people carrier. I'll meet him there after."

"And there's plenty of petrol?"

"Over a half tank as of yesterday evening when I returned from St. Matthew's. And it hasn't been used at all today."

"Ring me when you've finished your call and get to St. Matthew's?"

Hugh nodded.

"God go with you."

Hugh tipped his head to Mrs. Limb when they passed at the front step.

Berdie smiled. "Hello, Mrs. Limb. My husband has an urgent call he's attending to."

"I see." The woman looked after Hugh. She seemed rushed and not at all relaxed, perhaps even more stiff than she had been Sunday. "Will the children still be going to Tea Time Club?"

"Yes." Berdie glanced at the little boy, who held the petite girl's hand. They looked very much to be brother and sister, both with similar features including large brown eyes. Berdie guessed the girl to be five or so and the little boy approaching seven. "Commander Royce will be taking them."

"It's just that Max and Emmy had a dentist appointment"—the woman's jaw seemed to barely move when she spoke—"and I didn't see the point of taking them back to the school first since the church was closer. I hope it's not a problem."

Berdie fumbled for words. "Well...no, not a problem."

"Good. I'll leave them in your care until they go. I must get on."

"Bye, Nanna," Max called to the departing woman. Emmy leaned against her brother and looked as if she would cry any moment.

"I'll fetch you when you return from club." She was already halfway to her car.

"My, Max and Emmy," Berdie piped, "your nanna seems in a bit of hurry."

Max nodded whilst his sister just stared at departing Nanna.

Berdie bent low to speak with them. "Now, Commander Royce is going to take you in the people carrier to the school where he will fetch the rest of your friends."

"Tony will be there." Max's eyes grew bright.

"Your chum?"

Max nodded.

"Very good." Berdie turned to see that Cedric had moved on. "Let's go get aboard."

As she and the children took first steps, Berdie noticed the opened door at the back of the delivery vehicle. Sundeep was undoubtedly trying to find the rest of her order.

She took Max's hand. He still clung to Emmy, and they walked together toward the distant church vehicle.

"Pastor Elliott had to park the people carrier out on the edge of the church property yesterday evening, so it's a bit of a walk."

"Why?" Max asked.

"There were so many good things happening at church last night, we had bucket loads of people and their cars here. So he parked it out of the way."

Just as the words left her mouth, a furry flash rushed past, then circled back. "Sparks," she growled under her breath. He danced around Max and Emmy as if taunting them to chase after him and frolic about.

"Sparks is accompanying me to the vehicle." Cedric came up to Berdie from behind. "He's actually fine with children. He can ride along."

"Can he?" Berdie worked at keeping her suspicious tone curbed.

"Are you going to the Tea Time Club?" Cedric asked the little ones.

They nodded. Emmy actually smiled. Berdie got the sense that the little one liked the commander, or more likely, his dog.

"This is Commander Royce," Berdie introduced.

"He's driving today. Commander, this is Max and Emmy."

"Well, Max and Emmy, come along with me and Sparks and be our first passengers," Cedric coached.

Berdie had to trust Commander Royce's assessment of the dog's temperate nature with young ones. Sparks actually seemed pleased to be in their company, she had to admit. She released Max's hand. He and Emmy gladly walked onward with the commander, Sparks appearing delighted.

Berdie turned to make determined steps back to the house where fruit and veg, still on her sink counter, had to be sorted. Then there was the evening meal to prepare for seven, including ever-faithful pen-mender, Mr. Braunhoff, and his wife, Barbara, who was to arrive any moment. Barbara Braunhoff was always a great help in the kitchen. It would have been for eight, but it appeared Chad wouldn't be staying with them—and good thing too. She wondered how he was faring.

Her mind tumbled with Cedric's words. *Life in ruins, my hand behind it, nothing I can do.* It sounded dreadful and the only help she could offer was prayer on their behalf.

"Wait." Doug's voice sounded out from the back garden. He straightened in his wheelchair; his arms gripped the handles. He seemed to be calling to Cedric.

"Mrs. Elliott," Cedric cried out.

Berdie turned.

"Could you take the children for just a moment longer please?" Cedric had already sent the little ones moving toward her.

She squinted and peered. That daft dog had decided to rest itself right on the drive in front of the people carrier.

"Bother," Berdie breathed. Cedric would now have to coax Sparks into the vehicle, and it would cost him valuable minutes. But why send the children back to her?

"Cedric, no," Doug yelled.

Mr. Braunhoff halted his work on the enclosure and took stock of the goings-on.

Berdie could see Doug's face was beetroot red, his eyes intent, as he ran his hand through his blond hair, then tried to maneuver his wheelchair across the back garden toward her.

Berdie took both Max and Emmy by the hand.

"I'm sure it's nothing, Doug." Cedric's voice sounded almost lyrical.

"Hurry, Berdie, quickly," Doug yelled. "Keep moving." There was alarm in his tone.

"Hurry?" Berdie walked toward the vicarage with the children, a slight increase in her pace. *Why hurry?*

"Cedric, don't chance it. Please." Doug's voice trembled as he shot out the command.

"Don't what?" Berdie asked herself as much as Doug.

"Down, Mrs. Elliott." Doug's eyes wide, his breathing was short and rapid for the toil of making his wheels go toward them as fast as he could manage.

"Down? What are you talking about?"

Berdie suddenly experienced a jolt to her body that propelled her to the ground with such force it left her breathless. A stab of pain coursed through her while the reverberation of full-on colliding trains penetrated her ears. The horrific ache that shot through her knees focused her senses as she tried to gather her thoughts. Grass etched itself into her cheek, making it itch. Then the smell of acrid smoke assaulted her nose.

She worked to catch a breath of air. *What's happened?*

Berdie became aware of a little head pressed against her waist as she lay stomach-down. She could hear sniffles. Working to rouse herself, she was cognizant of the fact that a small child was next her. Berdie placed her hand on the small back. "It's OK, love." Berdie lifted her head to see Max just beyond her, flat out on the grass, rubbing his eyes.

"Nanna?" he called.

"Max, you're OK," Berdie said in a voice she hoped didn't sound as uncertain as she felt. Though her ears were ringing, it was then she became aware of that unmistakable sound: crackles of vigorous flame.

As she pulled herself up to a sitting position, she turned to look in the direction of the people carrier. Fire licked the vehicle; black char littered the bonnet. "Cedric?"

Mr. Braunhoff, who must have flown to the vehicle, fought against the flames to retrieve Commander Royce. It didn't look good. Doug, several yards away from Berdie, had his cellphone to his ear. Sparks lay motionless on his side, still in front of the vehicle. Berdie felt a shiver cross her shoulders. As she took stock, shock was wrapping its fingers round her.

Emmy's whimpers became a wail. Berdie instinctively took the child into her arms and brought her to her chest. Emmy wrapped her tiny arms around Berdie's neck and buried her head in Berdie's shoulder.

This was her most important task at the moment. Mr. Braunhoff and Doug were seeing to the disaster. She must comfort Emmy and Max even while working to pull herself together. *They mustn't see the vehicle.*

She willed her body to rise. Her legs quivered, shortness of breath made her lungs labor, vertigo swirled her world into a blur, but she managed to get to her feet, bringing Emmy, who still gripped her neck fiercely, with her.

She staggered to Max, who was now on his knees, eyes wide with bewilderment. Berdie stood behind him. "I know you probably don't feel so good, but is there anything that hurts terribly?"

He shook his head.

She reached down and pulled him up with her free hand, letting him rest momentarily against her legs. "Good lad, Max. Do you think you can walk OK?"

"I think so. What happened?"

"A big bang. Now, we're going to go back to the vicarage." Berdie continued to keep him in front of her, holding his hand, as she shielded him from the frightful scene behind them. "Let's go get some nice hot tea." Slowly, one step at a time, they moved forward.

"What a brave little soldier you are, Max."

Emmy's grip now made Berdie's neck ache, her arm strength waned, and she used her hip to help carry the little girl's weight.

Someone was running toward her. Berdie blinked.

"What's happened?" Tillie's words were breathless. Her hard grip of the ice-cream container turned her knuckles white. She looked over Berdie's shoulder at the destruction.

"Tillie."

"Where's my father?" Her blonde hair swirled as she searched about. "What's happened?"

"Cedric." Berdie barely got the word out.

"Cedric?" Blood drained from Tillie's face. "In there?"

Berdie gave a terse nod.

"No." She scrutinized the flaming vehicle. "How did...?" Tillie dropped her container of ice cream and took off running toward the scene.

"Tillie," Berdie heard Doug call out.

"Dad." Her voice was shrill, filled with disbelief.

Berdie watched Tillie run to her father, fall down on her knees, and wrap her arms around him.

"Daddy, it's the commander?"

Doug nodded. Tillie laid her head on his shoulder and hugged her father tightly.

"I tried to warn him." Doug's face was dark, eyes wet.

"Warn him?" Tillie took Doug by the shoulders. "How do you mean, warn him?"

Doug choked.

"Dad, I'm sure you did all you possibly could." She stood and took in the sight. Shaking her head, she turned her gaze away and then released a loud sob. "I can't believe..." She wiped her hand cross her eyes as if to push weeping, along with the fiery vision of what she had beheld, away. "This can't be happening. We've got to get you away from this horrible mess."

"But, Tillie."

The young woman set her determined grip on the handles of the wheelchair and began to push Doug toward the back garden. "You know it's best."

Berdie felt her arm wanting to give way beneath Emmy's weight when she became aware of a hand on her shoulder.

"Mrs. Elliott, let me help you."

Berdie turned to see the imposing figure of Barbara Braunhoff and sighed.

"I just arrived." Mrs. Braunhoff grasped

whimpering Emmy in her sturdy arms and cradled her close to her shoulder. "There, there," she purred and rocked Emmy, stroking her head.

Berdie let out a long, slow release of air. "Bless you, Barbara. Your husband is…"

"Yes, I see," Barbara said.

Berdie still clung to Max's hand and still shielded him with her body. "Max, Emmy, and I are going to have some hot, sweet tea at the vicarage." Berdie raised her brows and nodded toward Max.

"Oh my, doesn't that sound just the thing."

"Aren't we going to Tea Time Club?" Max's question sounded so innocent amongst the rubble.

Berdie swallowed.

"We've a bit of a problem, love." Mrs. Braunhoff's deep voice was soft. She began to move forward, grasping Berdie's elbow with her free hand, towing her with. "The sooner we get to the kitchen and get the kettle on, the better."

Berdie moved along with Mrs. Braunhoff in mindless motion. She became aware she was almost squeezing Max's hand. She eased her grip.

"Is the doggy coming with us?"

Max's words brought an unexpected wetness to Berdie's eyes.

"He's taken up with other things at the moment," Mrs. Braunhoff said. "Do you like sweet tea, Max?"

"Nanna sometimes fixes toast and honey to go with."

"Now doesn't that sound tasty." Mrs. Braunhoff eyed Berdie. "Wouldn't you agree, Mrs. Elliott?"

Berdie blinked and found the words. "You know, I believe I've got the very thing in my larder."

"There, you see, Max? The very thing is in Mrs.

Elliott's larder. Doesn't that sound grand?"

By the time they reached the back garden and opened the kitchen door, Berdie heard the *we-wa* of emergency vehicles.

Inside, she knew Doug and Tillie were heading upstairs when the sound of the electric stairlift, which Doug took to get there, hummed.

Despite cracks in the kitchen window above the sink, the children were seated at the small kitchen table away from any danger. Mrs. Braunhoff put the kettle on and chattered on to Max and Emmy, engaging them in as normal a dialogue as she could manage.

Berdie escaped momentarily to the sitting room where, in the quiet of the space, the hallway station clock's rhythmic ticks revived a sense of unreal normalcy. She looked out the window to see Doc Honeywell's old car whisk past. Dave Exton, the editor of the *Kirkwood Gazette*, dashed madly toward the scene, and she observed what she knew would happen sooner or later. People were gathering in the vicarage front garden, pointing, discussing, with hand-to-mouth astonishment. The moment she turned to go back to the kitchen, the front doorbell rang.

Dear Lord, give me strength. Instead of going to the door, she found herself sinking into a nearby armchair. In an instant she heard the front door open and someone enter.

"Berdie?" Lillie's call sounded anxious.

"Here," Berdie squeaked.

Lillie entered the sitting room, her eyes focused on Berdie. "I heard…"

Berdie wasn't entirely sure what her face wore. She knew she was trying to sort what had happened, attempting to regain normal body function, whilst longing for Hugh. She looked at her friend and felt a wet trickle on her cheek.

"Berdie, my dear Berdie." Lillie swooped to her and gave a gentle hug, then took the chair next to Berdie and placed her hand on Berdie's own.

The warmth of Lillie's hand was comforting against the shiver that crept across her body. Her shoulders relaxed, as if a favorite blanket had wrapped away the chill.

"Poor Cedric." Berdie abruptly felt a dam burst within her. She brought her free hand to her mouth and tears began a trickle down her face.

The extra squeeze of Lillie's hand upon hers brought reassurance of her friend's care and understanding. She didn't have to be a stoic force—she could be vulnerable at this moment and it would be OK.

Berdie removed her hand from her face and sniffed. She finally gave space for the thought that agitated the back of her mind to come forward into focus. She could barely speak it. "Lillie, it could have been Hugh."

3

While window repairs filled the kitchen with the sound of hammer and saw, Berdie's head felt like it took every blow of the heaving tool. Her entire body begged for a quiet respite in a comfortable chair. She had her moment with Lillie but was now back in harness, as some would say, despite her aching body. Her dining-room table had been police commandeered by Constable Albert Goodnight.

She carried a tray laden with two brimming teapots, sugar bowl, and jug of milk into the hall where she took the few steps necessary to enter the dining room. "Time to tend the masses" barely eked out Berdie's lips.

Lillie came behind, holding a tray stacked with a dozen mugs of various designs. "The investigators are hardly masses; it just feels that way at the moment."

The large one-hundred-year-old, rectangular dining table had momentarily become Aidan Kirkwood police headquarters, despite the fact that beautiful antique candlesticks, handed down from Hugh's grandparents, sat gracefully upon it. Ivory candles adorned the holders, and a vintage-fabric table runner lay beneath. Hardly a police command center. Still, Albert Goodnight, who knew the undersized bedroom-cum-office in his police-house home wouldn't do this time, sat at the head of the table, in charge of this investigation. Well, in theory anyway.

Berdie and Lillie set the trays down and began serving those present.

"Now, I want an account of what happened at the crime scene from all of you."

Mr. and Mrs. Braunhoff looked at one another.

He caught their glance. "I mean when Mrs. Elliott and Miss Foxworth finally stop flitting about." Goodnight's grandiose, unkempt mustache matched the size of his midsection, where his police-issue shirt peeked through small gaps in his uniform jacket. "Now where's the wheelchair fellow? Wasn't he present when all the to-do took place?"

"Doug's resting upstairs. Tea, Constable Goodnight?" Berdie asked.

He gave a terse affirmative nod.

"You don't want my account, because I wasn't here when it happened." Lillie had mugs placed before each person. "It's been established, it is a crime scene, not an accident? It wasn't just a stray spark that got to the petrol tank, damaged wiring, anything like that?"

Goodnight blew out a puff of air. "No, it's definitely a crime scene. Now, someone needs to roust the wheelchair fellow out."

"His name is Douglas Devlin, and he served our country well. Milk, Constable?" Rather agitated, Berdie poured milk into Albert's cup.

Goodnight knit his bushy brows. "Mrs. Elliott, let everyone serve themselves to their bits and pieces so we can get on here." He pulled his head back, as if trying to find the proper place for his eyes to settle, and put pen to paper. "Douglas Devlin," Albert repeated as he wrote. He nodded toward his cup. "Three sugars if you please, Mrs. Elliott."

Apparently, "everyone serving themselves" didn't include him. Berdie bit her tongue and simply placed a reasonable teaspoon of sugar in his cup.

Goodnight cleared his throat and eyed the spoon. "Not much going spare, then?"

Berdie pasted a half-smile on her face and heaped a mountain of sugar onto the utensil, dumped it into his cup, and another, as requested. When she poured his tea, while the others "served themselves," Berdie wondered if perhaps she should just fetch a bottle of sweet cough syrup from the medicine chest for Goodnight, and be done with it.

"I need everyone's statements before the big boys from the Yard get here."

"They're here." Mr. Braunhoff eyed Goodnight as if the officer had somehow missed seeing the several vehicles, workers, lights, and miles of yellow police tape that surrounded the scene outside, and had done for over two hours.

"I said the *big* boys, Mr. Braunhoff. That lot out there are just the worker bees."

"Big boys?" Berdie asked.

Albert took a sip of his syrup and ran a finger along the bottom of his crowded upper lip. "Specialists."

Berdie finally sat down with a sigh and saw to her own cuppa.

"What kind of specialists?" Lillie clipped.

Berdie's mobile phone rang out her current ring tone, "Rule, Britannia!" from the sideboard where she had set it down. When she arose to get it, Goodnight rolled his eyes and ran his tongue over his top teeth. "Like herding cats," he mumbled.

"Berdie, love." Hugh's voice at the other end of the

line was somber. "I'm at hospital."

"Are you all right?"

"Yes, but there's good and bad news. Cedric is alive, though just."

Berdie brought her hand to her mouth with a small gasp. "I thought..."

"As we all did," Hugh completed her sentence. "But I'm afraid he's not expected to make it through the night."

"We've a mustard seed, Hugh. By God's grace, we've a mustard seed of hope."

Hugh went on. "Ivy Butz has initiated a telephone call to prayer. She's mobilizing the congregation to pray on Cedric's behalf."

"My prayers go with them as well."

"I need to somehow reach his daughter. Frankly, I don't even remember her name. I've no idea where she is, how to contact her."

"Leave that to me, Hugh. I'll work on it—you just watch over Cedric."

"Yes." Hugh sighed. "Poor fellow."

"Constable Goodnight is here doing an incident report. He's expecting some specialists from the Yard to arrive soon."

"I expected as much from the sound of things. Which brings me to say, Berdie, these specialists are highly qualified individuals who know their onions. And clever as you are, they don't need your investigative aid."

"Hugh, this happened at our door."

"Indeed. And that's why our duty is to tend to our hurting community. We must support and comfort."

"Yes, I understand what you're saying. Now, do you want me to come to the hospital?"

"No, continue to man the ship there. Loren's on duty here tonight. He's already been up once to call."

Dr. Loren Meredith, a pathologist at Timsley Hospital who worked with the Timsley police, was a dear friend and Lillie's love interest.

"Good, I'm glad he's there." Berdie took a deep breath. The flash of flame that could have sent Hugh to the hospital with only a seed of hope flashed across Berdie's mind. "I love you, Hugh," she whispered.

"And I, you, love."

"Don't ring off." Albert Goodnight's boom cut into the tender moment.

Berdie jumped.

"Give me the mobile. I need to speak to the vicar," Goodnight blasted.

"Did you hear?" Berdie asked Hugh.

"Indeed. Hand me over."

Goodnight was at Berdie's heel.

She gave the constable her mobile and resumed her seat. "Cedric's alive, though just," she announced.

Mr. Braunhoff clasped his hands together, eyes wide, and he shook his large head side to side. "By the grace of God."

"That, plus your quick and incredibly brave actions in pulling him out," Berdie declared.

"Indeed." Lillie lifted her teacup to him as in a toast.

Barbara Braunhoff wore a gentle smile. Her cheeks even went slightly pink as she placed a hand on her husband's broad shoulder. "My Carl is a good man."

Carl Braunhoff scratched the back of his neck, obviously uneasy with the praise. "I should be helping our Carl Jr. get that window fixed in the kitchen."

The couple's eldest son was nearly the size of his

father. "Your Carl Jr. will do a fine job, I'm sure, even without your capable hand." Berdie had a brand-new admiration for the valor of this large man. "More tea, Mr. Braunhoff?"

He grinned and nodded.

Berdie poured liquid refreshment into the shy man's cup.

"Is that right?" Goodnight's voice boomed as he continued to speak with Hugh on the mobile, though it appeared all were trying to ignore him.

"Sparks." Berdie plunked the teapot down. She just now thought of the poor creature.

"Doc Honeywell checked the dog after the ambulance took Commander Royce off." Mr. Braunhoff sighed. "He put the canine in his car."

"Sparks is dead?"

"I should have thought so, but then I thought the commander had breathed his last."

There was a vigorous knock at the back kitchen door, so loud everyone at the dining table heard it.

Lillie jumped to her feet. "I'll go."

As Lillie left the room, Goodnight glanced at her and continued his telephone conversation at the sideboard.

"Max and Emmy are with their grandmother now." Mrs. Braunhoff sipped her tea. "She was quite shaken that all this had taken place, but she certainly didn't linger to discuss it."

Berdie circled her spoon in her cooling cup. "Thank you for seeing to them, Barbara. I didn't even have Max and Emmy's last name, let alone parental contact information."

Lillie reentered the dining room. Two men accompanied her. "These two fellows are Scotland

Yard investigators come to speak with you."

While Lillie took her seat, Berdie stood and set her eyes on a very familiar face. There he was. She would know that brown weathered coat, trilby hat, and slight stoop forward anywhere. "Chief Inspector Kent." She smiled. "Pleased to have you in my home. Would you and your colleague like a seat?" She waved her hand toward the table.

"Berdie Elliott." Chief Inspector Jasper Kent returned the smile and rubbed his chin. "I wondered the moment I heard an incident had taken place at a church in Aidan Kirkwood if it might not be you." The fellow removed his hat, revealing his short, close-cut hair, and tipped his head her direction.

"Brice"—he addressed the tall young chap with a notable square jaw—"we are in good company. Mrs. Elliott and I have worked together in the past, unofficially of course."

"A vicar's wife?" Brice balked.

"She has a real nose for sniffing out the truth. She was formerly an investigative reporter."

Goodnight, still on the mobile, frowned as his eyes strayed to observe the men.

"How kind of you to say." Berdie delighted in the chief inspector's good word. "However, at this moment, I'm afraid my detecting antenna has taken a real knock."

"Must go, Vicar," Goodnight bawled. "Yard's here." He clapped the mobile on the sideboard.

No goodbyes then. Berdie was as equally displeased by Goodnight's coarseness as she was pleased to see Chief Inspector Kent.

"Albert." Kent glanced at the constable.

"Chief Inspector," Goodnight returned with little

gusto. "I just got some valuable information on this crime."

Goodnight appeared to be making an attempt to be seen as so very important to this case, for Kent's sake.

"I see." Kent eyed the mobile. "Let me introduce my colleague." Jasper waved his hat toward the fellow with him, who held an iPhone in hand and dressed much smarter than the chief inspector. "Inspector Peter Brice."

"Take a pew," Goodnight instructed and then laughed. "This being a vicarage and all."

No one joined him in his humor as the two men sat.

"Tea?" Berdie asked.

The young man shook his head no.

"Please, yes, thank you." The chief inspector helped himself to a mug and the brew. "We've got some general questions. Then we'll be interviewing each witness separately."

Goodnight ran his tongue over his top teeth and rocked toe to heel, hands clasped behind him. "That's fine," he said, as if giving permission by his stamp of approval. "Any point of origin yet for the vicar's phone call? Important, that. Must get to the bottom of this."

Kent and Brice exchanged a quick glance. "Yes, Albert, I look forward to your full cooperation in all matters, as you have ours. But no, no point of origin as yet."

Goodnight lifted his chin and sported his not-so-pleased unibrow that occurred when his forehead wrinkled in a scowl.

"Mrs. Elliott, I need…" Tillie, dressed in a simple T-shirt and denim shorts, long hair pulled back in a ponytail, stopped her forward progress into the room and looked from face to face at the table. "Excuse me, I didn't realize."

"It's OK, Tillie," Berdie assured and plopped down into her dining-table chair again.

"Who are you?" Goodnight blasted.

Berdie pursed her lips. "Constable Goodnight, I realize this is police business, but it's still my home and courtesy doesn't go amiss." She calmed herself. "This is one of my guests, Miss Devlin."

"Devlin." The constable pointed an index finger her way. "You related to the wheelchair fellow?"

Tillie's eyes flared. "Wheelchair fellow?"

"Tillie, this is our local constable, Albert Goodnight."

"Miss Devlin," Brice asked briskly, "you're former Chief Petty Officer Douglas Devlin's daughter?"

"Who are you?" she asked defiantly.

The young man stood and presented his police credentials. "Peter Brice." He then sat down again.

"Yes, I'm his daughter."

"Your father witnessed the explosion?"

"Yes."

"We need to speak to him. Where is he?"

Tillie pulled her shoulders back. The V-neck of her T-shirt revealed a red mark on her upper chest. The young woman's eyes seemed a bit puffed, weary, really. "I just gave him a light sedative. This wretched business has upset him terribly. Can't it wait?"

"We need to speak with him now."

"My father is an injured veteran of war, who has seen action in the Gulf, an honorable man. You've no idea how today's horror affected him."

"I'm sure that's very true, and we appreciate his

service, Miss Devlin." Kent's tone was respectful. "And we *do* need to speak with your father now."

Tillie's eyes narrowed. "I'll fetch him, but he'll not be good for more than a moment." She huffed from the room.

Goodnight folded his arms. "These young'uns."

Berdie felt rather sorry for the girl. "She's quite protective of her father."

"We understand there was someone, a man, who saw the whole affair along with Mr. Devlin." Kent looked round the table. "He pulled the commander from the fire?"

Berdie's eyes went to Carl Braunhoff, who nodded.

"It was I." Mr. Braunhoff's shirt had watery spots where Barbara had used a wet towel, attempting to wash out some of the bloodstains, only a few minutes earlier. "Although I didn't really cotton on to what was happening until the blast actually happened."

"It was Mr. Devlin saw it coming." Berdie rubbed her forehead. "He yelled out a warning at the commander and to me as well. I find that incredibly interesting, don't you?"

"A warning?" Brice and Jasper exchanged a quick glance.

"He told us to get down. I was tending the children, you see."

"Children?" Kent seemed surprised. "Were we aware there were children at the scene?"

Peter Brice shook his head.

"OK, who was actually around before, during, or after the incident happened?"

"Doug, Mr. Braunhoff. There was Mrs. Limb with the children, but she came and left before the actual crisis occurred."

"Why was she here?" Kent blew on his tea.

"She brought the children, Max and Emmy, here to catch a ride to Tea Time Club at St. Matthew's."

"I thought the children were to be collected from the school."

"Yes, but she said something about a previous dental appointment, and that the church was closer. They're her grandchildren, I believe."

"You believe?"

"I just met her at church last Sunday. I know nothing of her or the children, really." Berdie became conscious of how unreliable she must be sounding. "I can tell you she was in a rush to get somewhere."

The chief inspector pointed toward his colleague, who had the iPhone positioned to enter data. "Rushed, you say."

Berdie could tell by the tone of his voice that Kent considered the woman's actions suspect. Berdie was unabashed. "Inspector, surely a grandmother wouldn't place her grandchildren somewhere if she knew something horrific was about to happen."

Brice raised a suspicious brow. "You know for sure these kids are her grandchildren?"

"They called her 'Nanna.'" Berdie wasn't often caught up short, but she was now. "No, I'm not sure."

"How can we reach Mrs. Limb?"

Berdie felt a slight flush of pink creep into her cheeks. She looked at Barbara, who shrugged. "The school will have information on the children."

"Anyone else around?" Kent asked.

Berdie recalled her box of unsorted produce that still sat on her kitchen counter. "Oh, I wonder if any of it's gone off."

"What?" Kent eyed her.

"I'm sorry. Yes, Sundeep was here."

Brice's neck snapped up from his iPhone.

"Sundeep, you say." Kent leaned forward. "Who's he, then?"

"He's the nephew of our village greengrocer, Mr. Raheem," Goodnight interrupted. "Young Asian fellow." He tapped his finger on his arm. "So he was here, was he?"

"Age?" Brice now moved his finger briskly over the iPhone.

"Approaching twenty?" Goodnight raised a brow.

"He seems a nice lad," Berdie redirected.

"How well do you know him?" Kent asked Berdie.

"He arrived in the village about three months ago."

"From where?"

"London?" Brice asked.

Berdie wondered what information the techno-savvy inspector was accessing on his tool. She hesitated. "Yes."

"Why is he living with his uncle here?"

Berdie thought back to Sundeep's comment in the hall, when Hugh was on the phone, when the desperate caller was shouting. What did he say? He left all the crazy behind him in London. What crazy? Something in her felt uncomfortable about relaying that information now, especially with Goodnight's penchant of jumping to unjust suspicions. "Why is he living with Mr. Raheem? I expect because his business is growing. The Raheems are well respected in our village. Sundeep's been helping them."

"Why was he here at the vicarage?"

"He delivered my fruit-and-vegetable order."

Berdie paused. "He brought in the first box and was searching about the delivery vehicle for the second. He was there on the street in front of the vicarage when I began to walk Max and Emmy to the people carrier. That's the last I saw of him or the vehicle."

Brice jutted his jaw.

Berdie's head throbbed. "Why this interest in a delivery boy? He made his delivery here and moved on."

"We must consider every possibility," Kent reminded as the hum of the stairlift was heard.

Berdie sighed. "Yes, of course." She suddenly wondered if she was too close to all this to have a clear view. The fact her head felt as if it was splitting open didn't help either. But she could count on a thorough and fair job by Jasper Kent. "I'm glad you're on the case, Chief Inspector Kent. I know you'll do a good job."

He smiled and brought the teacup to his mouth, taking a generous swallow.

Berdie decided to approach him about the question uppermost in her mind. She spoke softly. "Do you think Hugh could have been the intended victim?"

Goodnight, still standing and apparently earwigging their conversation, grunted. "The Yard doesn't send their crack team to scratch around vicars when there's terrorism involved." He stuck his head close to Berdie's ear. "What do you s'pose the boy wonder with his fancy toy is specially trained to sniff out?"

Berdie looked at Brice, who continued to enter data while conversing with Carl. *Terrorism?*

"Yes, thank you, Albert." Kent tapped his hat against his leg.

Goodnight seemed smug. "It was a bomb, you know, terror right here in our little village."

"I said thank you, Albert," Kent snapped. "We needn't broadcast it." While Goodnight glared, Jasper Kent looked Berdie in the eye. "And to answer your question, yes, we entertained the thought of your husband being a possible target. But it doesn't fit. He's been out of the military for years. A small village churchman is not a high-profile target these types go after. And there are other mitigating factors concerning the commander, which I shan't discuss. You can rest easy on Hugh's part."

Berdie released a slow sigh, though it wasn't an entirely trouble-free one.

"This needs to be done as quickly as possible" sounded like a command from Tillie's lips as she wheeled her father into the room and placed him at the table.

"They're just doing their job, Tillie." Doug looked drawn, dark under his eyes, just able to keep upright in his chair. His T-shirt had perspiration at the neckline.

"Formerly in naval intelligence," Brice stated more than asked, cool eyes rising up from his iPhone.

"You want to know what happened," Doug said matter-of-factly. "Of course."

"We understand you yelled a warning to the commander." Inspector Brice sounded accusatory. "How did you know the vehicle was going to blow up?"

Doug reared. "Know it would blow up? Know? I suspected." He squinted. "Just what are you implying?" Then it was as if a single quiver rippled through his body. "Commander Royce was a colleague, my good and decent friend."

"You're treating my father as a suspect?" Tillie's face went pink, and her shoulders tensed.

"It's a perfectly reasonable question, Miss Devlin. We just need an answer."

Doug worked at keeping his broad shoulders straight. "It was the dog."

"Sparks?" Berdie couldn't hide her surprise.

Doug's voice quivered. "Sparks was a military-trained bomb-detection dog."

Berdie knew her jaw visibly dropped. Sparks, a military bomb-sniffing dog, here, living in the vicarage garden, running amuck throughout the village? And no one told her?

Kent leaned forward. "How do you know that?"

"Cedric told me. He rescued the old thing after Sparks was found unsuitable for further service." Doug made several rapid blinks as if working to stay aware.

"And?"

"The dog sat down." Doug put his head in his hands. "Unsuitable or not, he sat down, right there in front of the vehicle." His hands began to shake. "I tried…" A quiet sob was all Doug could utter.

"We're done," Tillie announced. She put her hand on Doug's arm. "It's OK, Dad. We're going upstairs now." She stood tall and gripped the wheelchair handles. With fire in her tired eyes, she addressed Brice. "Do you see what you've done?" She wheeled her father away from the table. "He needs rest."

"We'll want to see him again tomorrow," Inspector Kent affirmed.

If heat could rise from one's eyes, Tillie's would have smoked. "Would my father have warned Cedric of danger if he wanted him gone?"

A fizz bubbled in Berdie's tired mind. Of course.

The logic of warning didn't fit with intent. It was the dog. She worked to focus her thoughts away from her headache, but with little success.

"If you're so eager to point fingers," Tillie all but shouted, "it's Chadwick Meryl you should be questioning. Ask him about the threats he made against the commander just this afternoon."

"What threats?" Goodnight, still standing, had an edge of animation in his words.

Tillie was off, Doug still with head in hands. She paid no mind to the question, pushing the wheelchair as if it was the last ounce of determined strength she possessed.

"Chad." Berdie shot a look at Lillie, who squeezed her lips together. *His life in ruins, and my hand behind it.* The commander's earlier conversation with Hugh ran through Berdie's mind. "Excuse me momentarily, Chief Inspector. I must see to my guests. Lillie, would you like to refresh everyone's cup?" Berdie rose from the table and followed Tillie and Doug into the hall while Lillie set to with a will.

"Tillie, I know you're upset, but do you really believe Chad capable of something as heinous as this whole affair?"

"He threatened the commander—you heard him." Her anger still colored her words. "How dare they accuse my father." A tear made an appearance in the corner of her eye. "How dare they think he could do Cedric in."

Berdie put her hand on Tillie's shoulder. "Tillie, Cedric's not dead."

"What?"

"He's hanging on by the most slender of threads."

A tear slipped down Tillie's cheek. She released a

long sigh and dropped down to face her father in the wheelchair. "Daddy, Cedric's not gone."

Doug was slumped in the chair. He mumbled something, but Berdie couldn't make it out. The sedative was doing its job.

Tillie stood and ran a finger across the top of Doug's shoulder. "Finally, some good news."

Berdie decided it best to give Tillie the whole truth. "Cedric's not expected to make it through the night, Tillie. But we're praying."

"Oh." She made a hard swallow. "Poor Avril must be distraught."

"Avril?"

"Cedric's daughter." She paused. "She doesn't know?"

"Are you acquainted with her?"

"We were childhood friends through sixth form, although we've not seen each other or talked in a long while."

"Do you know how to reach her?"

"I have her mobile number. Mind you, I don't know if it's up to date." Tillie stepped back. Her eyes grew intense. "No." She shook her head vigorously. Two more tears made their watery descent. "No, I can't possibly tell her. No."

"It's OK, Tillie." Berdie wanted to just wrap the young woman in a soft duvet and send her to bed with a cup of hot cocoa. This whole affair was taking a tremendous toll on her. "If you'll give me the number, I'll ring her. Or Hugh can. Remember, he's a vicar. He's very good at this sort of thing."

"Poor Avril." Tillie closed her eyes. "I'm so tired." She opened them and ran her hand cross her cheek. "I must get Dad up to bed."

"You should go to bed yourself as well."

Tillie nodded. "I'll leave Avril's number on the side table in the upstairs hall."

"Thank you."

Berdie helped Tillie get the half-awake Doug onto the chairlift.

"I don't know when I'll retire upstairs." Berdie made sure the safety belt was tight round Doug. "But if you need anything."

Tillie pressed the stairlift into operation, collapsing the wheelchair and carrying it with her. "Good night then."

"Good night, Tillie."

Berdie wanted to ascend the stairs and go to bed as well. But instead, she ran her fingers in circles on her temples and took dogged steps toward the "police headquarters."

She wondered as she entered the dining room again how much longer the questioning would go on. Both inspectors were talking with Mr. Braunhoff when she dropped down in her chair.

Lillie scooted next Berdie. "While you were out, they asked us if anyone knew what this Chadwick Meryl threat was about." She kept her voice low. "I didn't say anything. Is that withholding evidence?"

Berdie grinned. "Not to worry, Lillie. They'll find out all about it, not to worry."

"Should I fetch some biscuits for the tea?" Lillie seemed somewhat keen to leave the table.

"Good idea." Berdie tried to smother a sizable yawn as Lillie departed.

Goodnight approached Berdie with a lifted chin. "You ask your husband, there on the phone, 'bout that 'help-me-come-now' call he got today?"

"What do you mean?"

"I did," Goodnight gloated. "Hoax. And wasn't it just? All that way to Old Barn Road to find nothing but sedge, hedgerow, and empty road. No such house, no such people."

"That's what he said? Poor Hugh."

"It seems our vicar was set up like so many china ducks in a shooting gallery. I told the big boys while you were out of the room." Goodnight rubbed one of his buttons as if it was a gold star. "No, someone wanted your Commander Royce gone."

"And we're going to find out who it is," Chief Inspector Kent stepped into the conversation. "I promise you, Berdie, there won't be an upright stone left in Aidan Kirkwood, or anywhere, until we catch the slime that's responsible for all this."

4

Was that a cry for help? Berdie's eyes refused to open as she lay upon her bed. The events of the day, her headache, and the questioning by the inspectors had made her hunger for sleep. Even now, the dark enticed her. But she worked to rouse her hearing enough to listen with intent to what seemed to come through the open bedroom window.

The air of the late-May night, still tainted with the scent of smoke, played upon her nose. *Perhaps I was dreaming.* She rolled over in the bed and stretched her arm to where Hugh usually lay, only to find it cool and empty. She wondered how long it would be before he returned to her side. Sunday, tomorrow, was his busiest day of the week, and she was sure he'd be done in.

Then she thought about Cedric. *Give him grace, Lord, to hold on, and if it is his appointed time, may he go in peace.* Berdie found herself drifting back to sleep. That is, until a muted bang and clipped steps on the stairs told her Hugh had come in. She focused to bring herself back into the moment.

The bedroom door opened. Berdie could feel the presence of the man she'd loved for nearly thirty years even before her eyes became little slits to see the night-light-etched outline of his body.

He moved through the motions of discarding his

day garments somewhat laboriously and slipped into his pajama bottoms.

Berdie pushed the pillow she slept on against the headboard and raised her upper body to lean her back against it. Her headache was dissipating. She rubbed an eye.

"Oh, sorry, love, did I wake you?" Hugh stepped to the bed.

"Not really." She yawned. "You must be absolutely shattered."

"The hospital staff urged me to go home and get a couple hours of sleep. Loren said he'd call if there was any change in Cedric's condition."

"Good."

"Did you locate the commander's daughter?"

"As it happens, she's a friend of Tillie. Yes, I rang her, only to get her voicemail." Berdie lifted the duvet. "I told her to call right away due to a family emergency. She could ring anytime."

Hugh eased himself into the bed and under the duvet. He winced.

"Done in, love?"

"I've certainly had better days, but then at least I'm here to tell you that."

"Indeed. As much as I care for Cedric, I'm so glad it wasn't you." Berdie ran her hand up and down Hugh's arm.

"Rollie's going to the hospital, in a couple hours actually, to stay with Cedric. All through tomorrow as well if needed, or is that all through today?"

Hugh eased his back against the headboard and released a slight moan.

"Lean forward, my mighty oarsman," Berdie commanded.

"What?"

She placed her hands on the back of his shoulders and began a circular movement. She could feel tension from an emotionally draining task mingled with stiff, over-exercised muscles all across his back.

Hugh let go a low sigh as he slumped forward.

Berdie tried to massage into his flesh with her palms as much as she could manage, being half awake in the wee small hours.

"I hope Goodnight didn't get up your nose too much," Hugh drawled. His drooping head moved up and down with each push of her palms.

"When does he not? He said your urgent call this afternoon was a hoax to catch you out."

"I don't know, Berdie. It sounded like real people with real problems."

Berdie moved her fingers down his arms in rhythmic pulses.

"All I got on the phone was the name of Bryant, and that they lived in the cottage just next the Cathcart Carlisle farm off Old Barn Road. I felt such a fool when I knocked at the door and found the Georgeson family on the other side of it watching TV. They had no idea what I was on about." He sighed. "I kept asking myself if I may have missed something in the directions, and then when I arrived at St. Matthew's…"

"The investigative team believes too that the call was a ruse to get you out and away."

"As much as I detest the whole idea of such a thing, it does smack of a planned deception."

Berdie paused her fingers. "If the commander was the target, how could they know he would volunteer to drive the people carrier in your place?"

"He accompanied me to the club for several days

on the trot, even drove the vehicle yesterday. It's a part of his leadership nature to take over. He enjoys being with the children." Hugh barely shook his limp head. "Unless they had a sighting, I really don't know."

"A sighting," Berdie said under her breath and returned her rotating grip to Hugh's shoulders. "Doug tried to warn the commander when Sparks sat down near the vehicle."

"The dog's nose must be half functioning." Hugh yawned. "I doubt Cedric trusted Sparks's damaged sniffer, but Doug was right to sound an alarm."

"It seems I'm the only one who didn't know the animal was in the military."

"You exaggerate." Hugh's head bobbed.

"Do you think there's any chance Chad could be a suspect in all this?"

"Chad?" Hugh paused. "I know it looks bad, Berdie, but I don't think Chad could...I mean, he wouldn't be the same man if...he's impulsive, yes, but premeditated..." Hugh's words trailed off until Berdie massaged an apparently tender spot between his shoulders and he flinched.

"Sorry, love." Berdie patted his now-warm back. "Time to sleep, I should think."

Hugh pulled his head up, turned, and placed a gentle kiss on her cheek. Then without a word, he slid down to place his head on the pillow.

Berdie lay down beside him and snuggled close. Glad her man was home and next to her, she could feel herself drifting off already, until she became aware of a cry, like the cry that first awoke her earlier. It became louder. She rustled. It came again, but louder, until it became obvious someone was calling out in need. She felt Hugh jerk into consciousness.

"Berdie?"

"Yes, I heard it too." Berdie decided to pursue the source. "You stay still, love. I'll see to it."

"Sure?" barely eked from Hugh's lips.

Berdie got out of bed, grabbed her robe, and put it on as she padded toward the bedroom door. When she flung open the aged oak wood, the plea she heard wasn't coming from outside at all. It seemed as if it came from the direction of the hall.

Doug's bedroom door was just slightly ajar. A beam of soft light spilled cross the dark hall's wooden floor.

"It's OK, Dad." Tillie's voice was just audible.

"Call in. We need fire power," Doug yelled.

Berdie rapped on the door with her knuckles. "What goes on?"

She heard movement, and Tillie slipped into the doorway. Doug, who was sitting up in his bed, was just barely visible. "I'm sorry, Mrs. Elliott, did we wake you?"

"What's happening, Tillie?"

"Don't worry. I can take care of him. He's just a bit overwrought."

Doug let go a chilling scream, leaned forward, and covered his head with his arms.

Tillie left the doorway, still just open, and hurried to the bed's edge, where she sat and put her hands on Doug's shoulders. "Dad, you're OK."

Berdie could see, when Doug glanced at his daughter, how his eyes flared, almost glazed. He swallowed hard. Beads of sweat made his forehead glisten. "Watch out," he barely whispered.

"Doug?" Berdie stepped into the room.

"No, no, get on," he screamed at the top of his

voice. "Go, go, go." He pushed Tillie's hand from his shoulder.

"Father, please." Tillie's plea was anguished as she stood.

Berdie moved to stand by the bed.

"Mrs. Elliott, what are you doing?" Tillie implored.

"This has happened before?"

Tillie didn't speak. She pursed her lips so tightly their soft pink went almost white.

Doug looked into Berdie's face. Fear, that's what she read in his tired blue eyes, fear and panic. Fear and panic from another time and place.

She bent down close to him and put her hand on his arm. "Doug, it's Berdie, Berdie Elliott."

An apparent light of faint recognition danced into his frightful stare as he slid his arms from his head.

"You're in our old vicarage, safe as houses."

"Is everything all right?" Hugh now stood at the fully opened door.

"No," Tillie snapped. "There's already too many in the room. It makes him uneasy."

"Captain Elliott." Doug gazed at Hugh and began a military salute, but stopped. He eyed Hugh up and down as if just recognizing there was no uniform, no epaulets, no shouted commands. Just Reverend Hugh Elliott, standing before him in his dressing gown.

He redirected his gaze to Berdie, and then flushed.

"Doug." Berdie clasped his hand.

He gave a quick nod, his blond hair moist upon his forehead, and dropped his chin.

Berdie let go his hand, stood, and Hugh came near. He placed a hand on Doug's shoulder. "You're a good man, Douglas Devlin. Now try to get some sleep."

Again, Doug nodded and slid down into the bed, lying on his side, facing away from them.

"I'll get you some more sedatives from the bathroom chest, Dad." Tillie pulled the duvet up round Doug's shoulders. She bent low to his ear. "Love you, Daddy."

Hugh took Berdie's hand and gently guided her back out into the hall. Tillie followed behind.

"He's terribly embarrassed, to the point of shame." Tillie blinked as wet gathered in her eyes.

"He needn't feel that way," Berdie assured. "Many of our bravest soldiers suffer in such a way."

"Well, it's a wretched pity. Life should never take this course." Tillie's words bit into the dark. Then she eyed them. "You needn't tell anyone about this?"

"Tillie, all who have served in wartime, to some degree or another, share in combat fatigue." Hugh's voice was certain, despite his sleep deprivation.

"Nonetheless, it's no business of anyone else. He's been doing quite well, actually, until all that happened today." Tillie lifted her chin as if struggling to rise above it all.

"Discretion is a churchman's promise," Hugh confirmed.

How could you simply pass by the situation at hand with a simple promise for discretion? Berdie wanted to know more about Doug's health, about Tillie's wellbeing. She glanced at Hugh and had the sense he saw the inquisitiveness in her eyes.

"Come along, Berdie." Hugh squeezed her hand. "Let Tillie get on with her care." He smiled gently at the young woman. "If you need any assistance, you know where we are. Otherwise, we'll see you in the morning then."

Hugh moved Berdie along with him to their bedroom entrance.

"Oh, Reverend Elliott, how's Cedric?" Tillie questioned.

"I'm afraid his condition hasn't changed." Hugh sighed. "I wish I had better news for you. I'll let you know the moment I hear anything, Tillie."

Once in the bedroom, Hugh closed the door.

Berdie couldn't help herself. "There's so much left unsaid about Doug's situation, Hugh."

"I understand." Hugh undid his dressing-robe belt. "And doubtless you will find out all about it." He took off the garment. "You and Tillie will have a confidential discussion, over a warming cup of tea, in the light of day, Berdie, when Tillie brings the matter into your conversation."

Hugh did have a point. Approaching 4 AM may not be the best time to discuss such things. After all, she and Tillie were under the same roof. They would have some time together. She would see to that.

"Let's try to make the best of the minutes we have left to sleep. Busy day tomorrow. Or rather, a busy day today." Hugh got into bed and patted the spot next to him.

Berdie removed her dressing robe and threw it on the end of the bed. She scrambled under the covers and nuzzled close to Hugh again.

In no time at all, Hugh was asleep.

Berdie had to work at getting past her curious nature that wanted answers to her questions right now. Had Doug received any treatment for what Berdie recognized as posttraumatic stress syndrome? How serious was it? How often was he sedated? Did his injury cloud his reasoning? And then there was Tillie. Had she received any support as his caregiver? Finally, of course, Berdie struggled to consider if there was really anything she could do to help. There was so much to sift through and consider in *all* the goings-on, but it just somehow seemed beyond her. In very little time, the warmth of Hugh's body captured her will to inquire, her brain waved the white flag, and slumber was a gracious victor.

****

The clear swell of the church bell beckoned Berdie on as she made way across the front garden to the edifice of faith, not more than a hundred yards from the vicarage.

Her most comfortable skirt required little to be fit for a Sunday morning, likewise her silk blouse that felt like cream on her skin. Just the thing after experiencing a frenzied day and distressing night. What wasn't just the thing was the headache that was back.

Berdie's nose picked up the scent of bacon, no doubt some nearby fortunate person's breakfast. And quite frankly, she would have loved to join them, not having had but a quick piece of toast. But she had another task at the moment, to nourish her needy soul.

She moved forward, and the ringing peals brought fresh thoughts, despite her brain still feeling painful and fuzzy.

For hundreds of years, when this bell sounded, fieldworkers dropped their tools, women busy in the kitchens of their meager homes interrupted their tasks, and the whole of the community answered the call to assemble. The gathering was to set aside uninterrupted moments for prayer and worship to the God who gave their lives meaning and hope. Though few could read back then, stained-glass windows told stories of miracles, sacrifice, judgment, and holy lives that lifted and inspired. It was a stolen moment of time to leave the world of everyday life behind. For a few blessed moments, they could enjoy the Divine promise of a better world to come, and restore their present strength.

Was it that much different now, today? After yesterday's events, if ever a community needed renewal and restoration, this would be the time.

"Good morning, Mrs. Elliott." Maggie Fairchild zipped the greeting and entered the church with four others unfamiliar to Berdie.

In the far corner of the church acreage with tape and tent, all the paraphernalia of a crime-scene investigation were in place. A few parishioners hung about near the spot, peering and peeking as if to satisfy some morbid curiosity. Tillie and Doug were among them, but Berdie had neither time nor inclination just now to be a part of it. Curiosity would probably mean a full house at church.

Hugh stood at the entrance of the twelfth-century building, whose windows had held up well despite the recent blast.

"You made it then," Hugh greeted. His usual vibrancy was tinged with lack of sleep.

"Just." A quick nod and Berdie eased past the young acolytes, lads dressed in choir gear.

"I'll bet you a candy bar I'll light my candle before you," one of them challenged the other.

Berdie hoped some of their energy might rub off on her, though it seemed unlikely.

Inside, there were few empty seats. She finally came to rest at a back pew on the far side of the nave. Only the uninterested or very late sat in this spot, because there was a large column that obstructed the view of the lectern and altar. Nonetheless, it was the vacant spot, so this was her place to roost for this morning.

On the far edge of the row at the central aisle, she spotted the white-haired Batty Natty and her caregiver niece, Sandra, who wore her lovely yellow gingham dress. It showed off Sandra's rich brown eyes and flattered her near-forty-year-old form.

When Mr. Castle, the church organist, began the voracious pounding out of notes announcing the processional, Berdie jumped, a reaction blamed on recent events and a broken night of rest.

"Mrs. Elliott." Mrs. Hall, who sat next her, was clad in a pink rolled-brim hat that drew attention to her rather large camel-like eyes. She offered to share an open hymnal with Berdie as the first notes of "Soldiers of Christ, Arise" sounded from the congregation.

"Thank you," Berdie offered rather sheepishly.

She joined in singing with the congregation. *"From strength to strength go on. Wrestle, and fight, and pray."* Berdie tried to sing as if she had energy and no headache, but it came out rather breathless. Still, the words buoyed her. *"Tread all the powers of darkness down, and win the well-fought day."*

Berdie caught movement out of the corner of her eye, only to see Tillie bring Doug in his wheelchair to a halt next to Sandra at the far end of the row. Tillie set the brake on his chair, and as quickly as she entered, departed, leaving Doug on his own.

Sandra, like Mrs. Hall, offered her open hymn

book to Doug, who took hold of it with her, giving a nod and a smile.

As the hymn ended and the service continued, Berdie found herself staring at the pillar, which she had already scrutinized in detail. She blinked rapidly, hoping the flutter may exercise her concentration into vitality.

"The Lord is my refuge," arose from beyond the pillar.

Who was doing the first Scripture reading? Berdie didn't recognize the voice that sounded flat as a board. She tried to move her head, craning her neck, to a place where she could see the reader. But then she got right in Mrs. Hall's way.

"Sorry." Berdie pulled her head, like a tortoise, back to its shell.

She looked down the row, as unobtrusively as possible, to see Doug and Sandra sharing a Bible, reading the lesson together.

Rarely had Berdie seen anyone following the lesson in a Bible, and certainly never sharing with someone. Doug caught Berdie's eye and gave her a rather large grin and returned to reading. *Well,* Berdie thought to herself. *Well, well.*

Back to her attempted listening. It wasn't but a few moments and several goes at repositioning her body that she peeked Doug's way again. A hint of grin still graced his mouth as he glanced at Sandra, who glanced back at him and smiled.

Now Berdie grinned. Despite an interrupted night of rest, it seemed Doug had his attention piqued, but it wasn't the service. *Apparently, warm fires glow in our cool stone church.*

Though it gave her a momentary distraction, she

knew she couldn't stare or watch for long.

Reluctantly, she moved her eyes to the ancient pillar before her, when patriotic music sounded forth and made her sit straight up and blink. It came from her bag. She flung the thing open and began digging through until she found her mobile, which she obviously had not turned off, but now did. *Lord have mercy.*

Mrs. Hall stared at her.

"Sorry," Berdie whispered.

Berdie eyed the caller ID. Avril Royce. She let go a gasp.

Whoever had not been staring at her when the mobile phone blared was looking her way now.

She flushed. The pillar in front of her almost seemed a gift. It would avert the glare she was sure Hugh could be sending her way right now. "Excuse me," she whispered to Mrs. Hall again. "Emergency."

Berdie, as discreetly as possible, scooted from the pew and out the main door, not even giving a glimpse in Hugh's direction. "Dear God, let her still be available," Berdie prayed at the bottom of her voice.

Outside and away from the church door, she checked her voicemail. Nothing.

"I so wish Hugh was available to do this," Berdie moaned. But she didn't want to risk not finding Avril available. She rang up the commander's daughter and took a deep breath.

"Yes." Avril's voice was anxious when she answered.

"Avril, this is Berdie Elliott. My husband is a former naval officer who served with your father."

"Yes, what's happened?"

Berdie swallowed. "Well, your father was

spending time with us here in Aidan Kirkwood when he was involved in"—Berdie paused—"a rather awful accident of sorts."

"Accident of sorts? What does that mean?" Avril almost sounded irritated.

Berdie pulled her shoulders back. "This may be difficult for you to comprehend, but I'll tell you straight. Your father was in a vehicle that burst into flames and..."

"Is he...?"

"Hanging on by a slender thread."

There was a labored pause. "Did this happen on the road?"

"No, the vehicle was parked. I'm afraid foul play is suspected."

"Foul play." Another uneasy pause ensued. "So what you're saying is that my father was the victim of a bomb blast?"

"It's still under investigation, but it does appear so."

Silence seemed a gulf between them.

"Avril?"

"I was expecting to get a call like this. Most my life, I've been dreading a call like this."

"I understand how difficult..."

"Do you?" Avril interrupted. "The kind of work he did, military intelligence, all the horrible things that took place under his command, how could it not come back on him?"

Berdie was prepared for tears and distress from the commander's daughter, but not this.

"It had to happen eventually, didn't it? How long can you secretly carry on ruining people's lives and not be found out?"

Berdie gripped the phone, working at keeping even-tempered. She had to put the young woman's acidic views behind her. "Avril, you need to come to your father's aid. Whatever you may think or feel about his vocation, he is still your father. He could die at any moment and he needs you."

"Does he? Perhaps you should tell him that."

Berdie tried to comprehend the moment. "He's not in a position to be told anything." What on earth had happened between the commander and his daughter?

Berdie heard a bleep sound that created a quick break in transmission, and her thoughts took a different course. "Where are you, Avril?"

"I'm not in the country, if you must know. Neither my boyfriend nor I have the readies for air travel."

Boyfriend. How did he suddenly come into the conversation? Readies? That could compound the issue, but not if Berdie could do anything about it. "Avril, we can work out any financial assistance you may need, and you're welcome to stay in our home, the vicarage, in Aidan Kirkwood."

There was no response.

"Avril, you can't just leave your father."

"I love him desperately, you know."

Berdie detected a slight tremor in Avril's words. "Of course you do. You are his daughter."

"No, no, that's not what I mean. You don't understand."

"I understand that if you don't come to your father's side, you may carry a world of regrets to your grave. You really must come."

"I'm sure you'll be very kind. He'll be in tender care with you. Tell Daddy"—her words were unsteady—"goodbye for me."

"But, Avril."

Click.

"Avril, Avril?" Berdie literally shook the mobile phone as if it would bring the young woman back. She hurriedly rang up Avril's number again. No response.

Berdie sighed. Now she was not just tired, she was second-guessing herself. Should she have left this call to Hugh, who, having had training in discussions of this sort, may have gotten a different response? A moot point now.

Having just made a hash of things was certainly not something Berdie fancied.

She heard a slight screech of brakes and looked to the road, where Doc Honeywell had brought his old car to a dead stop at the edge of the church garden. He opened the car door and stuck out his balding head, glasses halfway down his nose. "Mrs. Elliott, how fortuitous that you should be out here. I need to speak with you."

She walked toward his vehicle. "Yes, Dr. Honeywell, what is it?"

The man made a strained effort to rise.

Berdie knew the retired doctor, now in his eighties, would be more comfortable being seated. "Please stay seated, Doctor."

"Thank you." He smiled. "These old legs don't always do what I want them to."

Berdie was already at his car.

"I just wanted you to know that the dog will be put down this afternoon at Dr. Stoddard's animal surgery. I thought you should know."

"Dog? Sparks? Sparks is alive?"

"Is that his name? Bad shape, I'm afraid. Terrible shape, really. It's a sure thing his master can't look after him." He nodded. "Most humane thing, you know."

Berdie felt suddenly sorry for the creature that had invaded and disrupted her home. Sparks most surely saved lives yesterday. What an ignominious ending for a dog who served his country. To be put down with none in attendance to recognize his contribution to the welfare of countless troops seemed unthinkable. "What time?"

"Time?" Doc Honeywell squinted.

"What time is Sparks to be put down?"

"I'm sure I don't know."

"Could you ask Dr. Stoddard to delay until someone known to the dog can be present?"

The doctor grinned. "I think it unlikely that the animal would be affected by such a thing, but I'll ring the vet and make the request if you wish."

"Yes, please. I'll be at the animal surgery this afternoon then."

"As you think best, Mrs. Elliott."

"Thank you, Doctor."

The man kept his half-smile and closed the car door. Berdie watched him depart, knowing he thought her a bit silly. The old doctor, who probably had occasionally treated animals as well as people in his country practice, generally thought in terms of livestock rather than pets or companions.

Nonetheless, it was the honorable thing to do, to see Sparks off. She was sure the commander would have done the same if he was able. And so she would do it, by God's grace. She may even secretly shed a tear for the once-lively animal.

5

Hugh scooped up the roast-beef sandwich as he raced for the back door of the kitchen. "Thanks, Berdie." He struggled to keep his flask of tea and small bag of crisps firmly gripped.

Berdie marveled at how Hugh kept going: first church, then eat-on-the-run lunch back to the hospital. "Now I know eating while driving can be tricky, besides having had little sleep, so please do be careful." Berdie wiped her hands on her floral summer pinny. "Ring me if anything changes with Cedric."

"Of course. I'll see you at the hospital then when you're done at the animal surgery?"

Berdie nodded. "Lillie and Loren should be here at any time."

"Kind of them to take you."

"Kind indeed." Berdie threw open the back door for Hugh.

Hugh placed a rushed peck on Berdie's cheek. "I'll see you at the hospital."

As Hugh departed, Berdie picked up the stack of Saturday post she had put aside yesterday and rifled through. "Mostly adverts and bills, of course."

A postcard slipped out from amongst the envelopes. It was from Reverend Angela Rockledge, a woman with whom Berdie disagreed on almost any topic. They had met when Hugh attended seminary where Angela was a student as well. She and Berdie had engaged in many lively discussions, each taking the opposite end of the spectrum. Still, they had a certain regard for each other.

Berdie read the postcard. *You're invited to a lecture given by myself, to be held noon, Wednesday this week, at St. Paul's, Slough. Spiritual Gifts and the Modern Woman. Q and A after. Love to see you there. Angie.*

"Angie?" Berdie said out loud. "Go all the way to London to completely disagree? Nice of you to think of me, Angela, but I'm afraid this modern woman hasn't the time."

Berdie discarded the postcard in the kitchen rubbish bin, when she heard what sounded like a scramble on the stairway.

It reminded her that she must tell Doug and Tillie that roast-beef sandwiches, piled thick with fresh garden tomatoes on horseradish-slathered brown bread, awaited them along with a large bag of cheese-and-onion crisps, pickled onions, and Scotch eggs, if Tillie would permit.

She ran a critical eye over the tabletop where the sandwiches were plated up, ready. Not much of a Sunday lunch, but then she really was doing her exhausted best.

When Berdie opened the kitchen door and sprang into the hall, she nearly ran over Doug in his wheelchair being pushed by Tillie at full tilt.

"Oh." Berdie placed her hand over her heart. "You gave me quite a turn."

"Sorry, Mrs. Elliott," Doug apologized.

"No bother. In fact, this is good timing. I've laid the table for your lunch. Just roast-beef sandwiches, I'm afraid."

"We won't be having lunch," Tillie announced. "I just came to let you know we're leaving."

"Leaving? But you didn't say. Still, I can wrap the sandwiches for later."

"I appreciate your accommodation, but we won't be here later. You see, we'll be staying at Kirkwood Green B and B for the rest of our stay in the village."

Berdie's jaw went slack.

"I should have left altogether, but the authorities have asked we stay close."

"Aside from poor Cedric," Doug added.

"But why, why are you departing?"

Tillie already maneuvered the wheelchair back into the hall and began to scoot toward the front door.

Berdie followed. She spied the luggage stacked near the entryway. This must have been why Tillie hadn't stayed at church.

"I should think I deserve some kind of explanation." After the sharpish sentence flew from Berdie's mouth, she realized she could have worded it much better.

Tillie pulled the wheelchair up short to turn and face Berdie, lips pursed. "All right then. It's no longer good for my father to be in this place. Every moment is a reminder of that horrible explosion. The very site's only yards away. Police in and out. It's disturbing and it only aggravates everything he's working to put behind him."

Berdie could feel her own aggravation rising. "But changing a location doesn't take care of the heart of the problem."

Tillie's jaw set. Her long blonde hair looked almost white as her face went red. "Do you have any idea what the heart of the problem really is? You haven't even an inkling of what my father has endured." She squeezed her eyes shut and shook her head. "This whole situation is a dog's dinner." She reopened them and set them squarely on Berdie. "Putting it in easily understood terms, I should think you'd realize that once you've been scalded by the hot water, you don't stay in the bath."

Berdie could see this conversation had gone completely pear-shaped. Being sleep deprived didn't do any favors for either of them. "Tillie."

The vicarage doorbell cut into the exchange.

"That's our cab," Tillie spewed.

Berdie raced ahead and placed herself between the door and the wheelchair and took an entirely different tack. "I got hold of Avril."

Tillie stopped her forward progress. "When does she arrive?" she snapped.

"Avril's abroad." Berdie eked the words out. "I'm afraid I have no certainty she'll be coming."

Tillie shook her head. "Please move."

This was no way to end a visit, cab or not. "I'm sorry you feel this way." Berdie looked at the now-somber man, who had been so lively and engaged at church. "Doug?"

He returned her gaze. "We appreciate all you've done for us." He turned his eyes away. "But Tillie's got a point. For all our sakes, it's best to go."

Tillie gripped the wheelchair handles with such ferocity her knuckles went white. "Now, if you please, Mrs. Elliott, move out of the way. Our taxi's waiting."

Berdie still held her back against the door. "Can we talk about this?"

Tillie's red face hardened as she nudged the wheelchair forward, nearly flattening Berdie's toe.

Berdie's strength to pursue the issue took a knockout blow. In what felt a defenseless gesture, she moved aside from the door.

"Thank you," Doug offered. He took Berdie's hand and squeezed it. "Thank you."

Berdie was a sail that had lost all its wind.

Tillie thrust the door open.

"Cab," Granville Morrison announced with sunshine.

"Get the suitcases please," Tillie briskly commanded. "And mind how you go. Don't dawdle."

"As you say." Granville, large frame standing nearly at attention, stepped inside.

"Yes. Well, we'll be in touch then." Berdie, still rather stunned, watched Tillie push Doug through the doorway with noticeable displeasure.

"Hello, Mrs. Elliott." Granville tipped his head and eyed the bags. "This lot will take two trips, I daresay."

"Yes," Berdie said absently.

"You OK?" Granville clutched a couple bags.

Berdie took a breath. "Yes, thank you, Granville, just a bit sad to see our guests go."

"Well, that one seems eager to push off. No great loss from what I can see."

"She's momentarily out of sorts," Berdie breathed.

"Any word on the general?"

"General? Oh, the commander. Sadly, the commander's condition hasn't changed, but he is still with us."

"Sorry to hear his dog's going to get put down. The beast done well, he surely did."

Aidan Kirkwood's ability to transmit word about in record time never ceased to amaze Berdie. "Yes."

She nodded.

Granville left, struggling with the heavy bags.

Berdie hadn't yet considered what scuttlebutt could be churning at the Copper Kettle, Aidan Kirkwood's tiny tea shop that was gossip central. And she knew all recent vicarage events were the topic of conversation at the local pub, the Upland Arms, without stepping foot in the place.

Granville returned and took the rest of the bags. "Salute the old soldier for me and my missus, if you don't mind, when you send the dog off."

"Yes. And God go with you."

It was then Berdie realized that there would now be even more tittle-tattle over scones and clotted cream. Granville would surely tell his wife, Polly, about the rancorous departure of Doug and Tillie from the vicarage. And Polly would tell her best friend, Mary Rose, who in turn would tell Villette Horn, her sister and the owner of the tea shop. And there it was. Everything would be for public consumption along with steaming tea. "This village goes one better than e-mail." Berdie sank onto an oak-wood step of the stairs in the hallway.

"Hello, Dr. Meredith, Miss Foxworth."

Berdie heard Granville's greeting and looked out the still-open door to see Loren and Lillie approach the entry.

"The angels are departing?" Lillie's smile went limp when she eyed Berdie closely.

"You look as if you need a cup of stout tea," Dr. Loren Meredith said in his most gentle of ways. His shoulder-length hair, pulled back and banded at the nape of his neck, though black, was graying at the temples. And it called attention to his smoky brown eyes that seemed full of empathy at the moment.

"I should think I do, actually." She glanced at the clock. "But we really haven't the time."

"Are you sure seeing this dog off is necessary? I mean, you didn't really ever take to it." Dr. Meredith offered his hand to help Berdie rise from her position.

Berdie placed her fingers in his and stood. "It's important, Loren. Yesterday we had several guests. Today we have none. I'm all out today on the art of difficult conversation. Perhaps I can get it right with a silent tribute to a departing service dog."

"You sound absolutely maudlin." Lillie didn't mince words.

"Not maudlin so much as just letting tired get the better of me."

"Well, we'll have to put a stop to that, for a start."

Thank God for her dear friend. Berdie smiled. "Oh yes?" She stood a little straighter.

"Right. You're not yourself, so carry on this afternoon. Go to bed early this evening and sleep well. Tomorrow you can properly sort apples from pears."

Berdie now chuckled. "Say, speaking of apples, there's some roast-beef sandwiches on the kitchen table just ready to eat. Interested?"

"I'll get them," Loren offered.

"They need cling film."

"Any tea in the pot?" Loren asked.

Berdie nodded.

"Well, get that pinny off and let's go to the car. We've a dog to see off," Lillie charged.

While Berdie removed the apron, Lillie started to the door and stopped. "Hello," she said with familiarity. "I'm sorry. We were just leaving."

"I know," Milton Butz said.

Berdie looked out the door to see Milton and his twin sister, Martha, on the front step.

"Hello, Miss Foxworth," Martha greeted. "Mrs. Elliott. We're aware that you're going to say goodbye to the commander's dog." Martha's short brown curls surrounded the face that Berdie always felt looked middle-aged, even at fourteen. "If we may impose…"

"My sister and me want to go to see the dog off, like."

Martha wrinkled her nose in consternation. "Milty. My sister and I."

"I see." Berdie put the apron on the pub-mirror peg rail and stood by Lillie.

"Our father has given us permission to go if we're not imposing on you," Martha finished. "We'll be respectful, honestly."

"Da said we couldn't go if we're going to blub like babies, so don't worry. We won't blub."

"Everyone's entitled to be sad," Lillie interjected.

Milton shifted his weight. "Our cousin Steven is in the military. He's over there, you know." Milton jerked his head as if signaling a specific direction.

"Afghanistan," Martha amended.

"His guys have bomb-sniffing dogs. He's told us about them in letters. Pretty wicked."

"Wicked?" Berdie queried.

"He means he appreciates the brave heroics the dogs perform." Martha apparently was Milton's interpreter.

"Steven's birthday is the same day as our big sister, Lucy." Milton was, it seemed, making an effort at small talk in an attempt to win a favorable reaction to them coming along.

"That's interesting," Lillie responded with a grin.

Milton looked at his sister and back to Berdie. "So, can we go?"

Loren's steps clipped in the hall and he arrived with the bagged sandwiches plus a small flask of tea.

"Here's our driver." Berdie turned to Loren. "Milton and Martha would like to say goodbye to Sparks with us."

Loren eyed Berdie, who gave a quick wink.

"All aboard." Loren pulled the car keys from his pocket.

****

Berdie had not expected the emotional struggle that plagued her now.

Nor had she expected Milton and Martha on the drive over to the vet's to bang on, regaling everyone with stories of the amazing heroics performed by military service dogs, as described to them in letters from their cousin Steven.

Loren jumped into the conversation as well. "We had a patient in poor health at the hospital that made a real turn round when his Jack Russell terrier was allowed to visit him. Quite extraordinary."

And now, despite the strong tea she drank in the car, here they all stood, and she just, in the operating room of the surgery.

Sparks lay motionless on his side before all assembled, the hero of mighty deeds and now a lonely figure on the operating table: solemn, rib cage bound, leg casted, spotted burns, and innumerable facial cuts with butterfly bandages holding things together. Berdie was questioning if termination of the animal was truly the right thing to do, despite his condition.

"Now we can say our piece on Sparks's behalf. Then we'll leave to let the doctor do her job." Berdie labored to sound convincing.

"Is there internal bleeding?" Loren asked.

"No, surprisingly. Bruising, but no acute internal bleeding as such." Dr. Stoddard's massive gloved hands prepared the hypodermic, her white lab coat starchy white.

Should a bull charge Dr. Stoddard, Berdie was confident the big-boned woman would win the challenge, no contest. Small wonder she was well respected for her work with large farm animals as well as the small pets. And in minutes she would finish her work with Sparks.

"Is he in horrible pain? He looks in pain." Milton eyed the dog's leg.

The vet adjusted her black-framed glasses. "Medication helps relieve some of his suffering."

Berdie found her thoughts flying off her tongue. "Would it be cruel to keep him alive?"

Dr. Stoddard stopped her needle preparation. She stared at Berdie, and then glanced at the children and back to Berdie. "Do we have reservations?"

There was a light rap at the door and an assistant poked his head in. "Someone else here to see Sparks."

Berdie turned to see Mrs. Limb with Emmy and Max. "I hope you don't mind. We won't stay but a moment." Mrs. Limb clipped the words and tautly looked round at all gathered. "They just want to tell the dog goodbye. He may have saved their lives, you know."

The doctor nodded.

Max rushed to the table where Sparks lay.

The dog struggled to lift his head, as if in

welcome, and the young lad gently laid his hand on the top of it. "Thank you, Sparks," he whispered. He moved his hand in measured strokes down the animal's neck. "Don't worry. I'll never forget you."

Berdie felt salty wet gather in her eyes. This was just a bit too much.

Loren's mobile phone broke into the moment when it sang out without respect for the proceedings. "So sorry," he offered and stepped outside the door.

"He got off easy," Lillie quipped in Berdie's ear and offered Berdie a tissue from her bag.

Berdie took it and then glanced at Milton and Martha, who stood sharp as soldiers, completely stoic.

Emmy stepped to Max's side. She took her brother's hand and stood on tiptoe to touch Sparks's paw that protruded from the cast. "I'll miss you, Sparks."

"OK, children, we must go now." Mrs. Limb's voice cracked.

Emmy and Max walked hand in hand back to Mrs. Limb, their faces rather downcast.

"Thank you," Mrs. Limb addressed the doctor. "Sorry to have disturbed."

Berdie, so caught up in present events, was prodded past what was before her to a moment of realization that this was an opportune time to catch Mrs. Limb and speak with her. She turned. "Mrs. Limb, if I may…"

The woman and little ones were already gone.

"When she said just for a moment, she meant it almost literally," Lillie remarked.

Berdie half frowned. "I'll just have to make a point to find her. She always seems in such a rush."

Loren reentered the room. "Dr. Stoddard, may I

have a word with you?"

"What is it?"

"In private?"

The woman lifted her brow and moved from the table to enter the hall with Loren.

"What do you suppose that's all about?" Lillie's inquiry sounded completely rhetorical.

And good thing, because Berdie certainly hadn't a clue.

"Should we proceed?" Martha asked. "I have a poem I wrote for Sparks, you see."

Berdie wanted to cut Martha short and tell her that she'd had quite enough with this whole affair, but knew it would be completely unacceptable to do so. "Let's wait for Dr. Stoddard," Berdie delayed.

"It's a good poem," Milton amended.

It was then Berdie noticed that Martha held a miniature British flag on a stick, the kind children wave when celebrating a royal visit. She had a vision of Martha holding the flag high in the air and reading "Ode to the Departing Hero Dog" with great sentiment when Dr. Stoddard lumbered through the door and straight to the table. "Anyone here in a position to care for Sparks?"

"What?" This seemed to be the day for unexpected turns. For the second time today, Berdie's jaw dropped.

"He'll require near-constant care. Pain medication is expensive." Dr. Stoddard put a hand on her hip. "I'll throw some in for good measure, gratis, for a week only, mind you. Poor creature thought he'd finally rest after giving all for king and country, and now this." Dr. Stoddard patted Sparks. "There's absolutely no room going spare here at the surgery. And there's no guaranteed recovery. Having said all that, can anyone help?"

Berdie felt a knot in her stomach.

The twins exchanged glances. "We'll take him," Milton declared.

"Milty. We can't say that." Martha's eyes bounced to the veterinarian. "We have to talk to our father."

Milton whipped an iPhone from his pocket. "Lucy's," he declared. "I borrowed it for just this very reason."

"Does Lucy know you have it?" Martha frowned. "She'll hang you up by your toes."

"I'm ringing Da up right now."

"What's happened, Doctor?" Lillie looked as perplexed as Berdie felt.

Loren came next to Lillie.

"Ask him," the vet said, shuffling tools about on her tray, demonstrating a slight annoyance at the disruption in her procedure.

"If, and that's a big if, someone volunteers to care for the dog and pay for his treatment, the hospital has approved Sparks to visit the commander."

"How did that come about?" Berdie stuck the tissue in her skirt pocket.

"Ask your husband." Loren smiled. "He heard the story of the little Jack Russell terrier as well and took it to those in charge. Seeing as the daughter seems to be a no-show, there's a certain compassion with it."

Milton, whose phone conversation contained repeated "Please, Da?" and "We promise we'll take care of him," raised his left thumb upright, as in victory, his smile a half-moon.

"My assistant will have a printout for you of all the home care Sparks needs. And he'll require at least forty-eight hours' complete rest, mind you, before any hospital outings."

"Brilliant," Martha gushed.

Brilliant indeed, Berdie thought to herself and released a rather prolonged sigh, realizing she was off the hook.

****

Berdie relished the dappled sky and cool breeze that flirted with her cheek. "Lovely morning."

Lillie rubbed her arms covered by a jumper. "A cold edge in that wind, I'd say. Just because you've had a proper night's sleep, the commander keeps holding on, and the Butz family is seeing to Sparks doesn't now make the world a piece of apple pie."

"That's not what I said." Berdie stepped lively as she and Lillie walked the High Street, where busy shops opened their doors to welcome a new day. They were making way to the Copper Kettle where strong, hot tea awaited them. "It's just I've set on a plan."

"Really?" Lillie's hazel-green eyes sparked. "You're on to who's responsible for the explosion."

"Oh my, no. The pieces of this mysterious puzzle lie scattered about me yet. I'm afraid my detecting head is still reeling."

"Surely not."

"Well, I tried to order the events of the actual tragedy this morning, and even that was a bit hazy."

"Go on."

"Simply put, the dog sat, Doug shouted, the commander sent the children back to me, as a precaution, I expect…"

"What?" Lillie frowned. "Sparks gave the signal,

right? Why would the commander proceed at all?"

"I've given it some thought. First, Cedric knew Sparks's nose was damaged. He may have given little thought to his sitting, especially here in a sleepy rural village, let alone at a vicarage in a church vehicle. What were the chances something tragic would occur? He simply underestimated the possibilities, I reckon."

"We all know better now." Lillie increased the pace. "Rather frightening, all of this."

"Yes, well, Jasper Kent's on the job. Very capable. Not so sure about Brice. But I've decided to leave them alone to do their work."

Berdie switched her market bag to her other hand as some unidentifiable twinge wiggled in the back of her brain. "Mind you, Peter Brice is a bit brisk for my liking. But still, with Chief Inspector Kent, they'll sort the crime."

"I don't believe for a moment that you're not interested in the investigation."

"Of course I'm interested, Lillie. Does sausage sizzle? Should Kent ask, I'm available, though I shouldn't tell Hugh that. No, this plan I'm about is something altogether different. I hatched the scheme for it yesterday in church."

"Should you be hatching schemes in church?"

"That's not the point. Besides, I sat in the pew seat behind the column. It lends itself to creative thinking."

"Ah, yes. So what's this scheme then?"

The distant shop bell of Raheem's Greengrocer tickled Berdie's ears as Maggie Fairchild, a member of the church-garden committee, departed the store and called out. "Mrs. Elliott, Miss Foxworth, good morning."

Maggie held the hem of her dress close to her thin

body for modesty's sake against a breezy bluster and scurried cross the road to Berdie's side. "Have you a moment?"

"What is it, Maggie?"

"I just wanted to inquire how the commander's doing."

"I went to the hospital yesterday afternoon," Berdie informed. "He's not improved, but then he's not gotten worse either."

"Poor soul."

"Hugh says he's hanging on as if by sheer will."

"Well, he's waiting for his daughter to arrive, isn't he? Yes, he clings on for her sake."

Berdie started. "Do you know his daughter?"

Maggie slipped out a slight chuckle. "My heavens, no, Mrs. Elliott."

Berdie's inquisitive stare prompted Maggie to explain.

"It's just that I was at the Copper Kettle earlier this morning, and Villette happened to say that the commander and his daughter weren't getting on when last together."

Berdie threw a glance at Lillie. "Villette told you that."

Maggie nodded.

"What else did Villette happen to say?" Berdie made sure her tongue was quite civil.

"Well, frankly, I should think we'll all sleep better when that fellow is in Constable Goodnight's custody."

"What fellow?"

"The one, you know, that threatened the commander at a lakeside picnic. What did she say his name was? Chandler? Chadwick?"

Berdie stood ramrod-straight. "And did Villette

tell you who or what her source of information was?"

"Why, it was one of your"—Maggie glanced down, then back to Berdie—"former guests, as a matter of fact, the nice young lady with the long blonde hair that's now staying at the B and B. She and her father had tea at the Copper Kettle yesterday afternoon."

"Really? And what exactly did Villette say about this fellow, Chadwick?"

Maggie's eyes enlarged. "Well, he hurled monstrous threats at the gentleman." She lowered her voice. "Demise was apparently mentioned." Maggie rubbed her index finger against her market bag. "Oh, I do hope they catch him quickly. It's unnerving to think someone like that is about in our community."

Berdie put a hand on the woman's shoulder. "You needn't worry, Maggie. First of all, he's not staying in Aidan Kirkwood, so breathe easy. But more importantly, there is no clear evidence that Chadwick had anything to do with the commander's assault. Threats are not acts. Besides, that rather lies in the hands of the authorities to sort. Wouldn't you agree? And we have some very capable investigators at work as we speak, who, I'm sure, can bring a quick resolution to the whole affair."

Maggie's face lit with relief.

"I needn't remind you, Maggie, that Villette most likely earwigged the conversation. And oft-repeated words can escalate to a whole new height of misinformation."

"Oh yes." Maggie nodded. "Oh yes. I shan't say any more to anyone about all this."

"Wisest thing, really." Berdie could see the sincerity in Maggie's rather guileless face.

"No question," Lillie agreed.

Maggie eyed the market bag Berdie held. "May I ask, Mrs. Elliott, are you planning a stop at Mr. Raheem's shop?"

"Yes." Berdie hoped to retrieve the rest of her produce order that Sundeep had failed to deliver.

"After a cuppa." Lillie pointed toward the tea shop that was home to imprudent lips.

Maggie leaned a bit closer to Berdie and Lillie. "I must say, Mr. Raheem seems a bit distracted."

"That's odd," Lillie piped.

"Yes. That's why I noticed it so. I asked him for King Edward potatoes and he gave me goldens. And then when he weighed my cherries, he gave me two pounds instead of three like I asked."

"He may have something on his mind," Berdie suggested.

"Yes." Maggie sighed. "Well, I suppose none of us are ourselves with all this to-do happening in the church garden."

"Yes." Berdie knew that only too well.

"We will continue to pray for the commander and for restored family harmony." Maggie smiled. "Must get on. Thank you, Mrs. Elliott."

"God go with you." Berdie watched Maggie make way.

"My, how word gets round." Lillie wrapped her arms round her torso. "I'm ready for that cup of tea."

"Oh, I'm ready for that and more," Berdie thundered. "Frightening poor Maggie like that, to say nothing of trial and conviction of Leftenant Chad Meryl. I shouldn't wonder if Villette's ears are absolutely burning her madly. They're about to get a very large flea in them."

6

"Mrs. Villette Horn." Berdie's words were a shot across the ship's bow.

All eyes in the Copper Kettle turned upon Berdie, who stood fully armed for the skirmish. She was doing battle for what was right and honorable.

Lillie took Berdie's arm. "Berdie," she whispered, "please remember your place in the community."

"That's just why I'm going to speak to her," she whispered back, but with just a bit more fire.

"But is elevenses the best time? The place is full to overflowing, with the attentive ears of the village at the ready."

Berdie became suddenly aware that every table and chair in the place was occupied and several others stood waiting. An air of anticipation, like royal guests at a jousting match, sizzled round, every face focused on her.

Berdie took a deep breath. Lillie was right. Her confrontation was with Villette, not the village. Coming in ready for a verbal punch-up was not the best way to begin a conversation, and it would do nothing for Hugh's reputation to make a fuss, right or wrong, in public.

Villette hustled from the Copper Kettle's tiny kitchen. "Someone called?" She stood, hands on hips, with a scowl that wrinkled her horseshoe-shaped face.

There was absolute stillness.

"Do you have any fresh teacakes on offer?" Berdie fumbled.

Villette's tiny eyes flared. "As you can see, second from the top." She jabbed her finger toward the blackboard where the day's menu was listed. "Teacakes." She lifted her chin. "And my teacakes are always fresh, Mrs. Elliott."

Lillie smothered a giggle.

Villette squinted as she strained her neck forward, looked past Berdie, and stared out the front shop window.

Berdie turned to see Mr. Raheem, forehead pressed against the glass window, peering into the shop with hands cupped around his eyes. "How unlike him," she whispered.

Lillie's brows lifted.

"Shells, bells, and little fishes," Villette squeaked. "What does he think he's doing?" She stepped to the door.

Now all eyes turned to the front window, where Mr. Raheem pulled quickly back from his awkward scrutiny of the shop and made way to the entrance. He entered, the shop bell clattering wildly.

"Good morning" snapped from his lips as his eyes rested upon Villette, a nearby presence hard to avoid, then danced from face to face. His anxious gaze alighted on Berdie. "Mrs. Elliott, are you busy? It's just that I'd like to see you for a moment," he said in his slight Punjabi accent, an edge in his voice. He angled his head toward the road.

As if the ball had now landed in Berdie's court, heads turned back to her.

She welcomed the interruption, a perfect opportunity to gracefully depart. "Of course, Mr. Raheem. Miss Foxworth is accompanying me."

He gave a tentative nod.

"Excuse us please, Mrs. Horn. Can we fetch a dozen teacakes when we finish our business with Mr. Raheem?"

Villette crossed her arms and pursed her lips. "If you think they'll still be fresh enough by then, Mrs. Elliott."

"Thank you." Berdie, not rising to the bait, stepped gracefully to the door, Lillie following.

Mr. Raheem gathered Berdie and Lillie and ushered them hastily cross the road to his shop like a dutiful sheep dog collecting his strays.

"Mr. Raheem?" Berdie didn't recall having ever seen the shopkeeper this fretful. She put the Villette Horn dispute behind her, something to be sorted at a later opportunity. "Is everything all right?"

He opened the door, herded them inside the empty shop, and locked the door behind them. "I want none of the interruptions." He turned the *OPEN* sign to *CLOSED*.

Berdie and Lillie exchanged glances.

"I'm sorry for the inconvenience, Mrs. Elliott." A mixture of harried activity and nervous energy dampened Mr. Raheem's upper lip. He wiped his palm cross his white work apron. "Thank you for coming."

"No, Mr. Raheem, you did me a favor. But you are not yourself."

"Indeed, I am not. That's why I hoped to speak to you. I think you can help."

"I'm glad to be of service, but help how?"

Mr. Raheem took a large intake of air and slowly

blew it out his lips as if practicing some kind of breathing exercise. "I'll come straight with it. It's my nephew, well, my wife's nephew, Sundeep."

"Nice lad. Yes."

"He's gone missing."

"Gone missing?" Lillie didn't even try to contain her surprise.

"He's taken my work van and disappeared." He cupped his hands together. "The last I saw of him, he was loading boxes in the van, ready for his deliveries, happy as the beach boy."

"Sand boy," Lillie corrected.

"Was this Saturday, Mr. Raheem?" Berdie wanted to be sure.

He nodded.

Berdie recalled Sundeep's rummaging round in the delivery truck but hadn't seen his departure.

"And what makes it worse..." Air caught in his throat as if the words would not come out. "The police have called round asking for him. I was out, but my wife...So many questions, it makes her brain spin." He swallowed. "They think our Sundeep is an insurrectionary, that he's involved with something terrible."

"It's DI Brice, I presume, that questioned her."

"A young man, she said, who was very"—Mr. Raheem paused—"to the point." The greengrocer ran the fingers of his right hand along the edge of a display of fresh strawberries. "She told them Sundeep was visiting friends in London and would return soon."

"Do you think that's where he is?"

The man shrugged. "He doesn't answer his mobile." He sighed. "She lied to the police, Mrs. Elliott. She was frightened."

"Has he ever done anything like this before? Just disappearing?"

"No. Not that I know. What will happen to him?"

"I'm sure all of this can be sorted." Lillie smiled at him in her gentle way. "You've come to the right people. Berdie is very good at getting to the bottom of matters like this. And I am glad to help her."

The man brightened. "Yes, yes, indeed. That's what I was hoping."

Berdie's eyes bored into Lillie's, but her dearest friend turned away, resisting any unspoken messages.

"Normally, Mr. Raheem," Berdie began, "I would be glad to help, but…"

The man's face fell. "It's too much to ask."

Now Lillie's glare fell upon Berdie with a very clear message that said, "How can you possibly deny this kind gentleman your aid and still call yourself a human being?"

It gave Berdie pause, and Mr. Raheem apparently spotted it.

"Please, Mrs. Elliott, if you would be so kind." He held his palms together and raised them to his chest as if in holy prayer. "Please."

"Mr. Raheem, you needn't…" Berdie couldn't bear to see the tender parishioner in such humble posture. "I'll see what I can do."

The fellow lifted his hands heavenward. "Oh, thanks to you." His usual sunshine smile returned. "Thank you, Mrs. Elliott, thank you so much."

"Mind you, I can't promise I'll locate Sundeep. We're quite busy at church with the Whitsun regatta and all that's going on with the aftermath of a horrible situation. But I shall try my best."

"I understand."

Lillie grinned, a bit smugly, as Berdie read it.

"Mr. Raheem, this is going to seem just a bit odd, but may I take one of your delicious cherries?"

"A hundred of them, if you wish."

"No, just the one. But Miss Foxworth would like to buy two pounds of them."

"Would I?" Lillie wrinkled her nose.

"And can you put those in a carrier bag, if you please?"

The greengrocer gave the single cherry to Berdie and began shoveling cherries into a plastic bag.

Lillie didn't seem particularly pleased but went along with it all, paying for the purchase promptly.

Quite unexpectedly, Mrs. Raheem appeared from the back of the store, her colorful sari flowing with her graceful movement. Her raven hair was pulled back, black brows rising when she spotted Berdie. The woman put her hand to her heart.

"Sharday," Mr. Raheem nearly shouted and spoke some words in his first language.

The woman broke into a broad smile that instantly gave way to tears. "Praises to God." She burst toward Berdie and Lillie, grabbed both by the hands, and gave them a generous squeeze. "Thank you, Mrs. Elliott, thank you. And to your help, Miss Foxworth."

"As I told your husband, Mrs. Raheem, I'll see what I can do, but we must be patient."

"Patient, yes. Oh, thank you, Mrs. Elliott."

Mrs. Raheem released their hands, only to fall into her husband's arms.

"We must move on." Berdie took Lillie's elbow, foregoing the elusive grocery order, and escorted her from the store, allowing the Raheems their privacy.

Not a moment outside the shop, Berdie took Lillie

to task.

"'You've come to the right *people*, Mr. Raheem?'"

Lillie bristled. "'Miss Foxworth would like to buy *two pounds* of cherries?'"

"Lillie, we can't go flitting into the tea shop without a bag of something. It at least needs to appear to have been some sort of business transaction."

Lillie tipped her head. "Oh yes, of course." She stopped. "But why didn't you buy them?"

"I owed you." Berdie moved on. "Please hear me out, my dear. You know my nosing in, even when helpful, is not appreciated by my husband. Searching for a lost young person who, as it turns out, is being pursued by the police? Hugh won't wear it."

"You'll talk him round."

"Lillie, you can't go volunteering me for every little situation." Berdie realized her voice was louder than intended.

"This is Mr. Raheem's nephew, not every little situation." Lillie looked askance at Berdie. "Tell me you're not keen?"

"That's not the point." Berdie's words sounded like a stomped foot. "There's so much that needs looking after."

"Like?"

"The hospitalized commander, in case it slipped your mind."

"Which Hugh and his fellows are handling brilliantly, and rightly so."

Berdie took a breath to launch into some form of defense, not quite sure what it would be.

Lillie grabbed the moment. "The Butz family is caring for Sparks, plus, as you said, the Yard's doing a first-rate job on investigating the crime. And plainly put, all your guests have flown." Lillie lowered her chin. "And here's an opportunity to assist by doing what you do best."

"What *I* do best. What happened to the 'right *people*' part of this?"

"Oh, I'm in."

Berdie had to admit that a slight spark had ignited in her gray matter. Did Sundeep have something to do with the explosion? But how? Why did he do a bunk? Was he running from or to something in London, if that's where he was? He might possibly confide in her rather than the law. But getting Hugh to agree could be tricky at best. Then she cast her mind to the postcard she had discarded yesterday. Angela Rockledge. She took a deep breath, grinned, and looked Lillie straight in the eye. "Does Wednesday suit you for a trip to the London area?"

Lillie let go a loud yelp and nearly danced.

"S-h-h." Berdie looked cross the street to see half the patrons of the Copper Kettle staring out the window at them.

"Not a word to anyone about this. I'm sure tongues have already begun idle speculations."

"Right." Lillie lifted her fingers in her Girl Guide salute. "Not a word. Not even to Loren."

"Especially not Loren." Berdie rolled up her empty market bag and put it under her arm. "Now, bag of cherries in hand as we sally forth."

Lillie lifted the bulging carrier bag.

"I should think a not-so-quiet mention to Villette of a donation of fruit"—Berdie held up the single cherry, then dropped it in the bag Lillie held—"for a cherry crumble at the next altar-guild meeting, along with an unabashed purchase of teacakes, is in order.

Then away home. It seems now I've two plans to hatch."

"*We've* got to hatch," Lillie corrected.

"Come, Watson." Berdie locked elbows with Lillie and they marched cross the road, ready to resist the gales of hot air that flourished in the Copper Kettle.

****

"These teacakes are delightful." Lillie took another bite. "Has Villette added an extra dash of cinnamon?"

"Lillie, we were talking about my first plan." Berdie added a bit more tea to the cups that sat before her and Lillie on the small table of the vicarage kitchen.

"Yes, yes, the idea you developed in church. You want to have a dinner for Hugh's rowing team."

"It's much more than that. Other special guests shall be invited too." Berdie sipped her tea. "It will lift the mood a bit, which we can all use. And besides, it's really a means of getting Doug and Sandra together, although I shan't tell Hugh that."

"My dear Berdie, you're matchmaking. Doug and Sandra?"

"Did you see them in church yesterday?" Berdie smiled thinking about it.

"Two people sitting together at church are hardly something to see."

"No, there was more. There was definitely more than just sitting together. For both of them."

"Well then. Just let them get on with it themselves."

"But Sandra is always at her Aunt Natty's beck and call—she rarely has a free moment. And I'm not entirely sure Doug has the confidence to ask Sandra to go out with him. At least not yet." Berdie tapped her teacup. "So, will you help me put it all together? The dinner and all?"

"Serve me up another teacake and I'll dance a jig if you like."

Berdie laughed and lifted the tasty morsel from its box. She ran it under Lillie's nose.

Lillie almost purred.

Berdie plopped it on Lillie's plate.

"So, if you get Sandra and Doug together, what will happen to Tillie?"

"Oh," Berdie quipped, "I'll find someone for her too."

Both women laughed.

"Now plan number two..." Berdie began.

Hugh grinned as he entered the kitchen. "It's more than tea that's brewing in here with your heads together like that. I can tell." Though it was his day off, if clergymen really have a day off, he wore his clerical gear.

"We've a teacake going spare." Berdie redirected the conversation and pointed to the box.

"Put my name on it for later, please. Must get off to the hospital."

Berdie stood and put her arms round Hugh's shoulders. "Things are bound to take a turn for the better with Cedric."

"We bring in Sparks tomorrow. If he and the commander hang on. It's a long shot, but we must certainly give it a go."

"Now, I know we've got a lot on, Hugh, but I wanted to ask you something."

Hugh put his hands round Berdie's waist. "Oh yes."

"I was thinking of giving a dinner party here for the fellows on the rowing team, inviting a few other people in as well. What do you say?"

"Actually, as long as the commander stays aboard, so to speak, I think it's a grand idea. A pleasant evening together could be exactly what the doctor ordered."

Berdie ran her hands down Hugh's arms and he released her waist.

"Good." Berdie looked at her friend. "And Lillie's going to help."

Lillie nodded.

"So that's why you had your heads together." Hugh exhibited a satisfied air.

"Would Thursday do for the dinner?"

"Sounds wonderful to me."

"Oh good," Lillie said, "that's settled."

"Now I have something to ask you." Hugh took Berdie's hand. "Dave called. Chad's staying with him at his flat. The authorities want both men to stay close by for obvious reasons. Chad's not doing very well. We've all been so taken with Cedric, Chad's been rather neglected. I feel my duty is to be by the commander's side." Hugh's blue eyes held what Berdie called his "mercy-on-me" look. "Could you drop in on Chad?"

Though Berdie felt a sizzle of excitement, she didn't want to overplay her hand. "What about transport—how will I get there?"

"Edsel Butz has offered one of his work vans, temporarily, for church use. It's parked over by the church. You can take it."

Lillie, still nibbling her teacake, chuckled.

"What about our car?" Berdie couldn't see herself

driving *Butz and Sons Electrics* through Kingsford to Dave's flat where Chad was staying.

"The hospital parking pass is on the car."

"Oh yes." Berdie tilted her head. "Is a special permit in order to operate a work van?" Berdie had clearance to drive the people carrier, but a work van?

"Edsel's seen to everything with Goodnight. Unless you wish to drive something that weighs over seven tons, your current license is adequate."

"Oh, seven tons, my, no." Berdie knew in her heart that she'd drive a John Deere tractor if it meant she could talk with Chad.

Hugh put on his authoritative voice. "Now, I think Chad will welcome the company and conversation. But, mind you, nothing terribly intense."

"That's rather up to him."

Hugh raised his chin. "Berdie, this is an official *church* duty. Leave your spade at home."

"I'll depart for Kingsford within twenty minutes."

"Keys are on the peg rail at the front door." Hugh kissed Berdie on the forehead, and then turned. "And remember to leave one of those cakes for me if you will, Lillie," he jabbed.

"Perhaps," Lillie returned, taking another bite.

And he was out the door.

"What time do we set out? Fancy you driving a van." Lillie's eyes had a twinkle.

"It can't be that difficult." Berdie ran a finger cross her chin. "But I think it best you not come. Chad's more likely to share confidences if I'm on my own, Lillie. I have another job for you."

Lillie's twinkle went flat. "Not more cherries, I hope."

"No, but it does concern Mrs. Raheem." Berdie

took a damp dishcloth from the sink and began to wipe the table. "Ring her, or better yet, stop by the shop and find out all you can about Sundeep: parents, why he's in Aidan Kirkwood for starts, who he spends time with, those kinds of things."

"Oh, that's all right then." Lillie perked. "Yes, indeed, I can do that." Lillie took the last bite of cake, arose, and rinsed her empty plate at the sink. "I'm to the off—I want to be timely with my investigative responsibilities."

"Yes, you do." Berdie wore an interior smile.

Lillie pointed a finger at Berdie as she made way to the door. "Mind how you go. Edsel's no taste for bent bumpers."

Berdie threw her dishcloth at Lillie. "Oh, be on your way."

A bit of a rummage and Berdie found the keys to the van right where Hugh said she would. She no sooner slipped them in her bag than the phone rang. Berdie contemplated letting it ring itself out, but decided she must answer. "Vicarage."

"Mrs. Elliott, it's Tillie."

"Tillie, how are you keeping?"

"We're doing better, thank you."

"I'm sorry to be so short, but may I ring you back later? I was just leaving on a church errand."

"This won't take but a moment, if you will. First of all, I'm afraid I was quite sharpish when we left your home yesterday."

"And I wouldn't have won any commendations for conviviality either, Tillie. Never mind, we're all a bit wobbly after what happened. I wouldn't give it a second thought."

"Yes. Kind of you. It seems, in my rush to pack, I

left a couple things behind. May I come get them?"

Berdie wanted to invite Tillie and Doug to the dinner, but she hadn't time now. "What is it you're missing and I'll bring them to you."

"Are you sure?"

"Of course. I'd be glad to do it."

"Well, there's a library book and a pair of earrings. I think they're on a bedside chest."

"I'll bring them round tomorrow morning. Does after breakfast sound good?"

"Yes, that works. Thank you. See you then. Ta."

"Goodbye, Tillie."

Berdie hung up and flew out the door before another possible phone call could delay her.

She rushed to the van and opened the door. A wrapped laundry parcel, limp and tied with string, sat on the seat. Berdie poked at it and pulled back a corner of the paper. Blue coveralls, boiler suits by the look of it, peeked through. "I wonder if Edsel needs these," she muttered. Still, she was on a mercy dash, *dash* being the operative word. She tossed them behind the passenger seat when Chief Inspector Jasper Kent approached.

"Changing careers again, I see." He thrust a thumb toward the blue letters of *Butz and Sons Electrics* that stood out against the white work van.

Berdie tilted her head. "Rather shocking, wouldn't you say?"

"Very droll, Mrs. Elliott, very droll." The gentleman removed his hat. "I'd like to speak to you for a moment."

"I've always got a minute for you, Chief Inspector." She closed the vehicle door.

"You and your husband know this fellow,

Chadwick Meryl."

"My Hugh served with him in the Navy. He's been to our home several times during his service."

"Yes, naval intelligence. We questioned him last night." He tapped his hat against his lower thigh. "I remember you as being able to suss out a person with a fair degree of accuracy. So what do you make of the fellow?"

Berdie was pleased that Inspector Kent valued her input, and she wanted to give the most viable information. "My husband seems quite sure that Leftenant Meryl was not involved in this crime, if that's what you're asking. He certainly knows him better than I, and he's a good judge of character."

"Yes, but what do *you* think?"

Berdie paused. "Well, frankly, I'd say Chad is rather impulsive. Words fly out his mouth and he thinks about them afterwards. He can be quick-tempered, I'll give you that. But this particular crime seems to need deliberation and planning."

"So you're saying this Chad is more a crime-of-passion fellow."

"Yes, I believe I am."

The inspector nodded and lowered his voice. "Can I speak to you confidentially and off the record, Mrs. Elliott?"

Berdie raised her brows. "Have we ever had a conversation that wasn't confidential and off the record?"

Jasper Kent smiled. "Small villages can have quite the loud jungle drums."

Berdie straightened. "Chief Inspector, there are both personal and professional ethics that I hold dear. Drumming is certainly not one of them."

Kent gave an amused chuckle. "That's one of the things I've always appreciated most about you, Berdie Elliott. You're a woman of character, always have been, and, I should think, always will be."

Berdie felt pink rise in her cheeks.

The detective ran a finger over the edge of his hat, glanced at the crime scene, and back to her. "In confidence. It was C4 explosive material, not particularly well done, a smaller amount than needed to do a really good job of it. It lacks precision, which tells us, most likely, the perp is not a military sort." He paused. "Or…"

"Or the perp is quite clever in giving the appearance that they've no expertise in working with explosives, eliminating them as a suspect if they are a military sort." Berdie finished Chief Inspector Kent's sentence.

"Precisely."

"But it bothers me. Who would want to go after Cedric, who's retired from active service and well into pipe-and-slippers time? Why? And why here? It seems so odd."

"We're often less guarded when on holiday. But apart from that, you know, I've thought about eventual retirement from the Yard myself. But somehow, I can't see growing cucumbers and leeks on a small allotment as taking up the lion's share of my time and valuable experience. I'd need some other *activity* as well. Do you understand what I'm saying?"

Berdie thought for a moment. *Snap.* "The commander was doing consulting work. In intelligence."

The inspector didn't say a word. His mouth simply turned upward on the ends.

"Well, if there's some kind of a group responsible, the more people that are involved in the planning and execution of a crime, the more likelihood of a weak link, harder to keep things quiet. But a single person on their own, that's a tougher nut to crack."

"There's a group who's claimed responsibility," Kent said hesitantly.

"Really?"

"It doesn't come off as terribly likely. This bunch has been pretty much off the radar for a while now. It seems more probable that they need to make people take notice of them again, claiming the crime as a kind of attention seeking, if you will."

"Fancy feigning destruction of a life as a means to appear strong and gain attention."

"It's a sad old world, Mrs. Elliott, a sad old world."

"Yes, but we are at work, you and I, Inspector Kent." Berdie stood her full height. "In our respective careers, we work to bring justice where there's none. We bring the light to expose darkness, a light no darkness can quench."

"Well." Jasper Kent nodded. "I've not thought of it quite like that. And righteously delivered, I might add. Yes, indeed."

"Inspector Kent," a young policeman called out from the crime-scene area. "We have a question for you, sir."

"I'll be right there," Kent responded. "Well, thank you, Mrs. Elliott." The man put his hat on and brushed a finger over the brim. "I must get about my work and let you go about your spreading of light." He pointed again to the *Butz and Sons Electrics* insignia.

"Now it's your turn to be very droll, Chief

Inspector." Berdie let a hint of smile appear. "And you're welcome. Anything I can do to aid in any way is a pleasure."

He grinned and departed for the crime scene.

"God go with you," Berdie said and got in the van.

"C4," she breathed. "Oh, my dear Hugh. I'm afraid my spade is permanently attached." She started the vehicle and made way for Kingsford, and whatever it might hold.

7

Apart from the manager of the flats barking out to her that workmen must park *behind* the building, and then squeezing down a one-car lane to get there, Berdie found driving the work van not unpleasant.

But now, standing at the door of Dave's flat, Berdie wondered how pleasant things might be with Chad.

She knocked, breathed a simple "Lord have mercy," and knocked a second time.

Finally, the door cracked open. An unshaved Chad, dark hair tousled, in his dressing robe and smelling a bit of gin, peered around the door's edge.

Berdie rocked back at the sight of him, and the aroma offended her nose. Still, she put on a smile. But before she could extend a hello, Chad jumped in.

"So they sent you" was his less-than-sparkling greeting. He opened the door a bit more, but he did not smile.

"They?" Berdie still remained pleasant.

"My dear old colleagues." Chad placed a hand on the door's edge, his other hand holding a small, empty, telltale glass. "Hugh rung up and told me you were coming"—his words bumped into each other—"but I can't find my way to receive anyone at the moment. Now, you must excuse me. I think it best you go, Mrs. Elliott."

Actually, given the state Chad was in, it probably was best not to enter the flat or pursue any lengthy conversation. Still, she had to make an attempt to engage him. "I'm sorry you're not feeling well, Chad. I know the chaps are concerned."

"Are they?" He leaned against the door's frame. "Are they really?"

"And so am I. Perhaps if you were to go visit the commander…"

Chad frowned and began to close the door.

Berdie caught hold of it. "Whatever has happened between you and him, forgiveness is always a good choice."

"Forgiveness?" he bawled. "Save it for your parishioners."

Berdie's indignation mingled with compassion. "Chad, you must realize you're suspect in all this mess. You threatened Cedric just hours before his terrible ordeal. But if you paid him a visit…"

Chad opened the door more widely, leaned his head forward, and narrowed his eyes. "If I had done the commander, I wouldn't have let him go out a hero, saving children, as is said, and there would be no hospital visits. It would have been a clean and accurate shot, done and dusted."

Berdie didn't flinch. "Well, now that we know what *didn't* happen, how are you going to deal with what *did* happen?"

"Deal? Deal? Let me ask you something." The tone of the young man's voice was rough. "Let's say you had a bean"—he shook his head—"a dean, or some churchman supervisor with whom you worked and respected."

She wondered how many of Chad's words were

fermented in drink and how many were somewhat reasoned.

"They accuse you of immorality, imprudence, carrying on with deceptive intent, all the things that are worst in your line of work. Not that you're guilty of any of it, mind you. But someone else's honor is at stake and you can't grass." Chad tried to straighten his shoulders a bit. "You've put in years of faithful service, and you think surely that will win the day. But no, they tell you that you're a traitor to the country...church."

Berdie considered momentarily. *Grass*, meaning to rat to authorities about someone, wasn't a common term. He was speaking about his time in the intelligence unit and likely revealing things that shouldn't be spoken about in public. Though gin-generated, his intent could be decoded. Berdie listened rather more intently.

"Then they quietly push you out of your job."

"Why push me out quietly if they believe I've done horrible things? Why not expose me?"

"And embarrass the coun—" He paused. "And embarrass the church? Reveal its dirty laundry and put lives at risk?"

Lives at risk. Aha.

"They push you out and make sure you can't possibly work within your chosen field ever again." He brandished his empty glass like an exclamation mark to prove his point. "You've given them your best, and they send you home stripped of all but disgrace. Now, how would you *deal*?"

Berdie considered her answer. She looked Chad straight in the eye. "As long as I let the feelings of injustice, caused by that high-ranking individual, burn within me to the point of loathing down to my very soul, that person continues to have control over my life."

Chad cocked his head and blinked as if her words were a sobering cup of black coffee.

"For my own health, wellbeing, and vibrancy, as well as for that of the other person, really, I must move on. By God's grace, and purely by His grace, there is a way. As an act of the will. Forgiveness is the means to do that. Forgiveness is a bridge to freedom, Chad."

"Oh, so we're back to that."

"You asked how I would deal."

Chad leaned his body against the doorframe, his glass at his side. "I s'pose I did."

The fellow's posture began to slip.

"I won't keep you any longer, Chad. But do think about what I've said. Oh, and going in an entirely different direction, I'm having some guests to dinner Thursday night at the vicarage. I'd love to see you there. Will you come?"

Chad wore surprise and tapped his glass on his chest. "You're inviting *me*?"

"And the rest of the rowing team as well."

He simply stared at her.

She leaned her head closer and lowered her voice. "I should shave before you come."

He drew a hand over his stubble.

"Thank you for your time, Chad. Do feel better." Berdie turned to go.

"Mrs. Elliott." Chad's gentle response was quite humane. He looked at the floor. "Good of you to call."

Berdie nodded. "God go with you."

As she retreated down the hall, she heard the door close. She sent an arrow of prayer up on Chad's behalf with the sincere hope that he would think on her words and no longer seek empty solace in the bottle.

On her drive home, Berdie attempted to puzzle pieces together. The commander had dismissed Chad from service for what Chad considered some illegitimate reason, still unknown to her. Chad's words, "Someone's honor was at stake...I can't grass," stuck in her head. Someone close to him was guilty of something, and he knew about it, but no one else did. Who? And what did they do? Did any of this matter tie in with the commander's misfortune? Things seemed to bump and jumble a bit in her head. And *she* certainly hadn't been on the gin.

Berdie tucked the conversation with Chad into a corner of her brain. She had done her church duty as Hugh requested and garnered new information at the same time. Well done for now.

Once back in Aidan Kirkwood, she stopped at the White Window Box Garden and Gifts Shop to get a small gift to take to Tillie tomorrow morning, a kind of peace offering.

As Berdie got out of the work van in front of the shop, Ivy Butz hustled toward Raheem's Greengrocer on the other side of the road, giving two-and-a-half-year-old Dotty Butz a ride for her money in the pushchair.

Upon seeing Berdie, Ivy delivered a full-throttle wave of her large arm that seemed to emanate from her very toes. Berdie returned the gesture.

"How's the van working out for you then?"

"Thanks to you and your husband's generosity, wonderfully. Cheers, Ivy."

The full-moon cheeks that blossomed at the ends of Ivy's gracious smile always made the day seem a little brighter. Though she kept her ample body moving toward the grocer's, her boisterous call, a family trait amongst the Butz household, boomed with exuberance. "Sparks is doing well. My Martha and Milty are so taken with him; it's all I can do to get them to my dinner table."

"Vets in training, no doubt," Berdie returned.

Ivy enthusiastically nodded and continued her march onward.

Two villagers that stood near Berdie glared at Ivy, then at her.

"Mrs. Elliott," one snipped in greeting and gave a terse nod.

The other leaned close to her friend. "Yelling in the street like a pair of fishwives," she said just loud enough for Berdie to hear. "And her a vicar's wife."

Berdie had too much to do to invest negative energy in reacting to such a comment.

"God go with you," she called with some grace to the two and stepped into the White Window Box.

Berdie knew just what she wanted to give Tillie. She whisked past the floral counter and went straightway to the shabby chic cupboard that was filled with bath accessories. She chose three lavender bath balls. She took in the lovely scent, being sure Tillie would enjoy a relaxing soak. The young woman would inhale the fragrance while the ball melted with a fizzy action in the warm bath, inducing comfort. After all, lavender was stacked and burned in the wilds to appease restless lions. It would surely help lessen Tillie's stress.

"Hello, Mrs. Elliott." Cara Graystone Donovan's long blonde hair was bound up in a single braid that draped her left shoulder, making her gray eyes and lovely cheekbones even more prominent.

"Cara, hello." Berdie placed the bath balls in the woman's hands. "Just purchasing a gift. Could you wrap these, please?"

"Oh, we've some newly designed gift-wrap just in that will go quite well. And new ribbon. I'll just go round the back and take care of it for you."

"Lovely, Cara. Thank you."

The young mother bounced behind checkout and disappeared through an open door to a back room.

The jingle of the shop bell danced as someone entered. Berdie recognized the young man right away. He was Mrs. Hall's nephew, Stuart, and the dentist recently come to Aidan Kirkwood. He had spent boyhood August holidays in Aidan Kirkwood and so loved the place. He now served the village part-time since the bulk of his newly established primary practice was in Timsley.

"Mr. Hall, good afternoon."

"Hello, Mrs. Elliott. Although I must say it perhaps is not so good for my Aunty Dora." The rather short dentist ran his tongue on the inside of his lower teeth. "Her oral surgery was today."

"Yes, probably not a wonderful afternoon for her. My husband plans to call."

"Ah. Just going to order a small posy to wish her a speedy recovery." Stuart's broad smile was dazzling white.

"That's very kind. I'm sure it will bring comfort to your aunt."

"Yes." The fellow looked round.

"Cara should be right out to help you. She's wrapping a gift for me."

Mr. Hall nodded.

"Everyone is quite excited about your practice here. You must be amassing patients by the minute."

"A far greater amount than I anticipated." The doctor tapped a finger on the floral counter.

"Including the little Limb children?"

"Sorry, who?"

"Oh, perhaps their last name isn't Limb. Little Emmy and Max. Sweet children. About five and seven? They had an appointment with you late Saturday afternoon."

The fellow shook his head. "Saturday. No, Jeffry Lawler had two fillings early on, a couple from Mistcome Green had exams, and Mr. Gordon came in with toothache, but no children. In fact, I closed an hour after lunch."

Berdie tipped her head. "No small children then?"

"Not a one, Mrs. Elliott."

Cara reappeared. "Here you are, Mrs. Elliott. That's four pounds fifty." She handed the perfectly wrapped box to Berdie.

"Mr. Hall." Cara turned her attention to the young man. "What do you need then?"

Berdie pulled money from her bag and passed it to Cara, who continued her conversation with Stuart Hall while finishing Berdie's transaction.

Out the door, Berdie sat in the work van and pondered. Why should Mrs. Limb say the children went to the dentist when indeed they hadn't? It seemed so odd. Did they go to a dentist in Timsley? But that made no sense. She said the vicarage was closer. "Not a one." Berdie repeated the dentist's words. With this information, Mrs. Limb, Max, and Emmy became extremely interesting. Now she added another chore on her "must-do" list along with searching out Sundeep and preparing for Thursday's dinner: find Mrs. Limb and get to the bottom of this strange matter.

****

Berdie told Hugh over dinner that evening about her discussion with Chad.

"I really do need to call on him." Hugh put down his fork full of lamb cutlet on his dinner plate. "I've just had so much on. Rollie and Dave as well. Trying to juggle our moments so that there's someone with Cedric at all times has been an all-consuming undertaking."

"Cedric is critical; he's your first priority." Berdie placed her hand on Hugh's arm. "Your time with Chad will come."

"I know he's struggling. And can you blame him?"

"I'm sure you know much more about this Chad-Cedric situation than you let on, love, but it's Chad's problem to resolve."

Hugh nodded.

"Trust, Hugh, trust." Berdie removed her hand.

"Ah yes. Small word, massive effort."

Berdie took a bite of crispy roasted potato. "May I ask, at the picnic Chad gave a toast to someone, let's see, someone Fox, was it?"

"Wolf." Hugh leaned back in his chair. "Yes, Ennis Wolf."

"Was he one of your military chums?"

"In our unit, yes. Good man. Had a lovely wife and family." Hugh sighed. "He was captured and eventually died on one of our intelligence operations."

Berdie eyed Hugh, who had gone quite pensive.

"Ennis and Chad were like brothers. Horrible loss for all of us, but Chad took it quite hard. Extremely hard."

"Did he?"

Hugh took a deep breath as if to clear the air. "Shall we move on to more pleasant matters?"

Berdie could see that this discussion did not lend itself well to Hugh enjoying his dinner. And she had something important to ask of him.

"I saw Ivy Butz today, and she said Sparks is doing well."

"Ah, now there's some good news. Yes, I believe Sparks comes to the hospital tomorrow, if able. Can you be there?"

"Wouldn't miss."

"Good, very good."

"I'm calling on Tillie and Doug in the morning. Lillie's going with me."

"Grand idea."

"I was hoping to invite them to Thursday's little gathering."

"Excellent. I must say, I'm looking forward to Thursday."

"I'll serve apéritifs in the back garden, weather permitting. It will be a pleasant time. What you think?"

"Good, yes." Hugh lifted his forkful of lamb to his mouth and munched.

Good, Berdie thought. *We're moving on.*

She now considered her agreement with the Raheems: seeking out the whereabouts of Sundeep. She knew Hugh would not be keen on it. But she thought to present herself in an entirely different manner. Her postcard from Angela Rockledge, though she had discarded it yesterday, could make a good excuse to go to the London area.

"And I wanted to ask you, Hugh."

"Yes?"

"Angela Rockledge is giving a lecture at St. Paul's, Slough, on Wednesday, and Lillie and I should like to attend."

"Reverend Rockledge? But you two never see eye to eye. It's always fireworks between you both. Mind you, I've had to put out a few fires of my own with her."

"It's just that she's sent a personal invitation."

"That landed in the rubbish?" Hugh nodded toward the bin, and then took a drink of water.

Berdie raised her eyebrows. "Oh." She made a hasty stab at digging herself out of this metaphorical hole. "I've reconsidered."

"Listen, love, I know this mess has been hard on you as well. Actually, a day out for you and Lillie may be just the thing. It could be worth it simply to hear what dear Angela is on about this time."

"There's a Q and A after."

Hugh pointed his empty fork at Berdie. "No questions, nor answers, nor any discussion in the least between you and Angela. Your word sparring would lead only to the need of extending apologies to the good people of…"

"St. Paul's, Slough."

"Yes, Slough."

"On my word, Hugh, no word spars."

"Right. Well then, while you're there, you and Lillie must have lunch out as well."

Berdie ran a finger cross Hugh's chin. "Now that I can do with nary a thought of sparring at all."

****

Morning meditation, prayers, exercise, and breakfast behind her, Berdie swept into the guest bedroom Tillie had inhabited.

She had several church activities scheduled today, but visiting Tillie and Doug first thing was her special task.

Sure enough, on the bedside chest was a library book, and earrings, just as Tillie had said.

She stuffed them into her shopping bag that also held Tillie's wrapped gift and rushed down the stairs, out the front door, and hurried the entire length of the High Street to the village green where Kirkwood Green B and B stood in a stately manor just cross the grassy expanse.

Lillie had agreed to meet Berdie at the bed and breakfast at 9:15 AM. Berdie hoped she would be punctual. After the upheaval of Doug and Tillie's departure, Berdie wanted all to go well.

"I met with Sharday Raheem yesterday afternoon," Lillie informed when Berdie met her just inside the door of the B and B. "I've so much to tell you."

"And I want to hear it all, once we do what's at hand at the moment."

"Hello, Mrs. Elliott, Lillie," Cherry Lawler greeted. Her bright smile was just what you would expect from the young wife who, along with her husband, Jeffry, owned and operated the gracious country home-cum-bed and breakfast.

"Mr. Devlin's expecting you. I'll just let him know that you're here."

Cherry had the scent of grilled bacon about her, a

leftover from preparing breakfast for her guests, no doubt. The band she wore in her pixy-cut blonde hair contrasted with the colorful apron that covered her petite body.

"The sitting room's open. There's hot tea and coffee available on the tray at the sideboard." She pointed to the cozy room that had no fire in the inglenook but was warm with sunlight that streamed through glass double doors overlooking a terrace.

Berdie and Lillie stepped into the cheery room when the clatter of Doug wheeling his way into the reception hall sounded.

"Your guests are here, Mr. Devlin," Cherry chirped.

"Good morning," Doug offered as he entered the sitting room. He looked rather tired.

"Doug, I hope we find you well." Berdie's voice was summery as she and Lillie sat on the sofa. "Sleeping soundly, I should hope."

"As well as can be expected." He rolled to the double doors and rapped on one.

Berdie spied Tillie, in exercise gear, doing stretches on the terrace. Her hair pulled back, the body-hugging spandex she wore showed her figure well and had an open neckline that bared her upper chest. Berdie couldn't help but notice the large red line of thick horizontal scar tissue now made visible by that neckline.

Berdie heard Lillie lightly gasp.

Tillie looked at her father, who pointed to Berdie.

"Come in, love," he said in high volume.

The young woman, instinctively it seemed, put her hand over the unattractive area and grabbed a nearby fleece jumper, which she quickly put on, covering the mark.

Berdie glanced at Lillie, who returned the stare with eyebrows raised. It was obvious to Berdie that both she and Lillie wanted to know what had caused the unsightly blemish, yet it seemed rude to ask.

Tillie moved to the door, opened it, and stepped into the sitting room.

"Getting ready for a morning run," Tillie announced.

Yes, Berdie remembered her occasional morning runs when she was still a guest in her home.

"Your regular exercise?" Lillie asked with a smile.

"I shouldn't say regular, no. Only as often as I've time for," Tillie quipped.

"We won't be long." Berdie pulled the earrings and book from her shopping bag and set them on the coffee table. When she did, two photos fluttered from inside the book and landed on the polished wood floor.

Berdie picked them up. The first picture was a family portrait. Doug, pride written on his face, in naval uniform, stood next to a seated attractive woman who dressed in trendy clothes for the time. A young lad sat in her lap. Berdie assumed the woman to be Doug's wife and the boy, a son. Young Tillie wore a sweet smile, her golden hair in curls as she stood next her father. The portrait was obviously taken of the family before Doug's injuries.

"What a charming family portrait." Lillie cocked her head to see it. "You must be very proud of your children, Mr. Devlin."

"Child," Tillie corrected. "My brother isn't with us anymore."

"Oh, I'm sorry," Lillie apologized.

Tillie sighed. "Unfortunately, there was a

childhood accident."

"I've not heard you speak of your brother before," Berdie said with a slightly diffident tone while handing the photo to Tillie.

"No, you wouldn't," Doug mumbled and looked at Tillie.

"It benefits no one," she said. "Needless to say, he left us too early. We loved him dearly."

"Of course you did." Berdie worked to rescue this conversation that seemed to have taken a sad turn.

She reached down and retrieved the second photo from the floor. It was Doug and young Tillie. He had his arm round her shoulders, both wearing outdoor gear, both sporting huge smiles. And beyond rugged terrain about them, a dazzling blue sky set it off. "Well, the two of you look ready for a celebration in this picture."

"Oh, yes." Doug pulled forward, eying the snap. "That's when we reached the summit of Mt. Snowden."

Berdie passed the picture over to Doug.

"Quite an accomplishment," Lillie cheered.

"Just one of our many conquests." Tillie rather beamed. "Let's see, we hiked in Scotland…"

"And Ireland," Doug added.

"Yes, and the Pennines. All through the Lake District. Where didn't we go?"

"Sounds lovely," Berdie chirped.

"Dad was Sir Edmund Hillary and I was his Sherpa Tenzing." Tillie laughed.

Doug's smile widened as he drew a finger cross the photo. "Marvelous, that was. Mind you, young as she was, Tillie seemed to never tire, never complained anyway. She was half mountain goat."

"Only half? Who did you think made the cloven hoof marks in our back garden after that climb?"

Everyone grinned while Doug handed the photo to his daughter.

Lillie eyed the book. "*Cloak of Deception*," Lillie read the title out loud. "Sounds like a good mystery."

"Yes, it is," Tillie asserted. "Required reading for a class I'm taking."

"Is it?" Doug stared at Tillie.

Tillie took up the book and earrings. She held them to her chest. "It's an online class, Dad. Don't you remember? I told you."

"Did you?" Doug's gaze drifted to the coffee table. "I, I must have forgotten."

Something seemed painfully awkward. Was Doug's medication creating blanks in his memory?

"I must get on," Tillie announced.

"Oh." Berdie grabbed the gift from the bag and stood. "This is just something for you, Tillie. I thought you might enjoy it."

"How kind. Thank you, Mrs. Elliott." Tillie took the gift-wrapped box while Doug turned his wheelchair toward the sitting-room door.

"Before we go, I have an invitation I'd like to extend to you both. I'm having the rowing team for dinner Thursday, round seven, and I'd love for you both to come."

Tillie looked at her father, who had stopped at the doorway.

He put his gaze on Berdie. "Chad's coming?"

"Well, he has been invited. But I've invited others as well, including Natty Bell and her niece, Sandra." Berdie watched for Doug's reaction.

He perked, but not quite as much as Berdie had

hoped. "Sandra? Really? Well, yes, I'd say Tillie and I would love to come. Right, love?"

"If you like, Dad."

Doug smoothed his hair with a finger. "We'll be there. Thank you, Mrs. Elliott, Miss Foxworth. That's me off then."

When Doug left the room, Tillie watched after him. "Who's Sandra?" she asked Berdie.

"A woman he met Sunday at church. He sat next her."

"A very available woman," Lillie added as she stood.

Berdie glared at Lillie.

"Available?" Tillie sounded a bit alarmed.

"*Unattached* might be a better word," Berdie quickly corrected.

Lillie stammered. "Oh, yes, what I mean to say is that she's very kind, modest, thoughtful, and single," Lillie explained. "It seems your father may rather fancy her."

"Does he?" Tillie was less than joyful. "Does she have any interest in Dad?"

"It appeared so." Berdie's grin slowly faded as she watched Tillie shake her head.

"We're only here until this investigation moves on, you know. Then Daddy can get back to where he's comfortable."

"Well, yes, but I thought..."

"Thank you for bringing my things, Mrs. Elliott, and for the gift."

Berdie paused. "You're welcome of course, Tillie.

"Enjoy the rest of your day. Please excuse me."

"God go with you," Berdie called after the departing woman.

"I should have thought Tillie would love for her father to make a female acquaintance, even if it is just for an evening." Lillie frowned.

"I didn't consider how she would feel about this." Berdie took the handles of her shopping bag with both hands. "I should have thought. Tillie: the little protective mother. Had I considered, I would have approached things a bit differently."

"Does she think Sandra, whom he met at church, will ravish her father on an evening, and then throw him to the wolves?"

"Once she meets Sandra, she'll feel much more comfortable about it all."

"That was certainly quick." Cherry Lawler stuck her head around the corner. "Did anyone get any tea?"

"Sometimes it seems the rush of modern life is all jingling bells and whirling dervishes, Cherry." Berdie spun her finger in a circle. "No tea had by anyone, and Lillie and I must get on as well."

"Event planning," Lillie added. "London calling," she whispered Berdie's way.

As if on cue, Lillie's mobile sang out. "Hello?" she answered.

"You see, Cherry?" Berdie clipped. "Jingling bells."

"Oh my," Lillie squeaked. "Yes, I'm so sorry. I'll be right there." She dropped the mobile back into her bag. "Music lesson rescheduled. Mrs. Hazelgrove. I completely forgot. Must run." Lillie took aim for the door. "We'll speak tomorrow, Berdie, yes, tomorrow."

"See you then." Berdie looked after the friend who skittered out the front door.

"What was that you said, Mrs. Elliott, about whirling dervishes?" Cherry chuckled. "Well, I hope all the events you're planning go smoothly," she offered. "And prayers for the commander as well. I understand the dog visits him tomorrow. Let's hope it's a tonic for both."

Berdie took a deep breath. "From your mouth to God's ear, dear Cherry, to God's ear."

8

"Doesn't he look much healthier?" Milton asked Berdie.

"Actually, he's still very delicate. He's not regained consciousness as yet."

"Sorry, Mrs. Elliott, I don't mean the commander. I mean Sparks."

"Milty." Martha's tone was irritation let loose.

"Still. Doesn't Sparks look better than the last time you saw him, Mrs. Elliott? He's eating some, you know."

"Oh, Sparks. Of course that's who you mean. Yes, much improved. You and Martha have done wonderfully."

Berdie stood, flanked by Milton and Martha Butz, behind the protective glass that guarded Commander Cedric Royce's intensive-care room.

A policeman, Cedric's assigned protector, sat in a chair near the door. He glanced occasionally at Berdie and crew.

The early-morning sun filtered through the half-opened blinds of the single window that brightened the cubicle.

Mr. Hayling, the civil servant from the Department of Agriculture and Rural Affairs, was responsible to liaise with the hospital for animal therapy. He stood inside the room's entry, Sparks next him on a lead. The small man with a kindly smile gently led the barely mobile Sparks to Cedric's bedside. Despite his splinted leg, bandaged midsection, and stitched head, Sparks was certainly more alert than when Berdie last saw him at the vet's.

Hugh and Rollie stood at the end of the bed, watchfully scrutinizing Sparks.

"How's it going?" Loren, in his hospital garb, came behind Berdie and peered over her shoulder.

"Just starting," Berdie answered. "On duty, are you?"

"Indeed. But I had to come to cheer the process on."

"Mr. Hayling told us how Sparks came to belong to the commander," Milton quipped.

"How's that?" Berdie was all ears.

"To start, Sparks's smeller"—Milton touched his nose—"got ripped."

Martha sighed. "Damage occurred to his nasal area where smell receptors are located," she interrupted, keeping scrupulous watch of her canine patient.

"Yeah, well, anyway, the military couldn't have a wounded soldier go back in action, so they were going to put him down."

"Usual course of action for military service animals, I'm afraid." Loren moved to the other side of Martha.

"Well, the commander got wind of it. Commander Royce thought it would be nice to have Sparks honorably retire with him."

"Should do," Martha added.

"After an appeal, the commander got him. So, you

see, he actually rescued Sparks from death."

"Now things are coming full circle," Berdie breathed. "Let's see if Sparks can rescue the commander."

"Bear in mind, this is only the first visit. I shouldn't expect too much this first go," Loren warned.

"True." Martha spoke the word unconvincingly. She was utterly absorbed in watching the scene before her.

Mr. Hayling released Sparks from his lead.

The huge Labrador went to bed's edge and sniffed the air. Then he thrust his nuzzle upward and lightly pushed it against the commander's elbow.

"He knows it's the commander. Look." Milton pressed his forehead against the glass.

"The question is: does Commander Royce recognize Sparks?" Loren half whispered.

The Labrador made another attempt to nuzzle his master's arm. Even through the glass, Berdie could hear Sparks emit a whine.

There was no response from Cedric.

Sparks's tail gave a tender wag as he patiently stood at the bed. Then as if aware of his master's state, he simply lay down next to it.

Mr. Hayling stroked Sparks. All eyes now rested upon the silent creature that seemed determined to stay at his post.

"Did you see that?" Martha asked excitedly.

"See what?" Berdie scrutinized Cedric's room, and the guard arose and snapped to the window.

"The commander's little finger. It moved."

"No, I didn't see it. Even so"—Loren placed his hand on Martha's shoulder—"sometimes, Martha, comatose patients have involuntary movements."

"No," Martha snipped, "he knows Sparks is there. And he wants to pet him."

Loren caught Berdie's glance and smiled, and the policeman went back to his chair.

"I didn't see his finger move," Milton countered.

"You were looking at Sparks. I was watching the commander."

Just as she said it, Cedric's little finger made the slightest of movements.

"See, you see." Martha pointed.

Berdie raised her brows as she viewed Loren. He shook his head in the negative.

"Sparks is going to make him better. I just know it. We've been praying, and animals are instinctive when it comes to this sort of thing."

Mr. Hayling, and Hugh with him, exited Cedric's room to join Berdie.

"Sparks is having an impact, isn't he, Mr. Hayling?" Martha's tone was so optimistic.

"Early days, Martha."

"How long will Sparks stay here?" Milton asked.

"The greater part of the morning, perhaps into afternoon."

"Really?" An element of excitement filled Milton's voice. "No Composition class today. How sad."

"Oh, you needn't stay. I'll bring Sparks home. No, you mustn't miss all your classes. Reverend Elliott here is giving you both a lift."

"I promised your mother that I'd take you straight to school from here," Hugh added.

Milton looked disappointed.

"You will keep us informed," Martha stated more than asked.

"Of course," Mr. Hayling answered. "Fully

informed."

"Don't forget you're also taking me to meet Lillie at the train station as well," Berdie reminded Hugh.

"Oh yes," he said.

"A foray into the London area and a lecture." Loren turned to Berdie. "Hmm, now why do I have the sense that there's more to your little jaunt than just listening to someone rabbit on?"

"There is more," Berdie affirmed. "Lunch."

"You ladies must go to The Red Star. It's in Slough, a delicious Indian, operated by a friend of Mr. Raheem," Hugh interjected. "I went there for lunch following a church workshop in the area. The chicken tikka masala was excellent."

"A friend of Mr. Raheem." Berdie wondered if Hugh could see the tingle of excitement in her eyes. This played straight into her plans. "Sounds a treat."

"Look," Martha nearly gasped. "He lifted his index finger. The commander lifted his finger."

Everyone had been so involved in conversation, except Martha, who kept an eagle eye on him, that none noticed anything in Cedric's room. Now everyone was eying the patient.

Berdie stared at Cedric's hand, but saw no movement.

"Perhaps Rollie saw something," Hugh reasoned.

But when Berdie turned her gaze to Rollie, he was seated in a chair, head in a book, intrigued by a good plot by the look of it. "Or perhaps not."

"I'll apprise you of any changes," Mr. Hayling offered Martha. "I think you need to be on your way."

"We do." Hugh pulled car keys from his pocket.

Martha nodded. She spread her hands out on the glass and leaned slightly forward. "Good boy, Sparks," she said softly. "You're a tonic for him. I know you are."

****

Berdie tapped her fingers against her trousered legs and looked past the crowd in which she and Lillie stood to shoot a glance down the empty railway track. "And to think Hugh rushed me here from the hospital."

Lillie yawned.

"Late night?"

"A later-than-usual dinner out with Loren."

"That's not the only thing that appears to be late."

"The destination board said it's supposed to be on time," Lillie announced.

"And certain undergarments are supposed to never ride up, but we all know how that goes."

Lillie laughed. "You are a wag, Berdie."

In a flash, Lillie's joviality faded. "Look who's here." She glanced past Berdie's shoulder.

When Berdie turned, she saw Constable Goodnight, somewhat authoritative in his just-a-bit-too-small uniform, amongst the train-station crowd. And he was coming their way.

"Off to London then?" The constable raised his bushy brows. "You have permission, I presume."

"Certainly," Berdie retorted. "And what brings you this way?"

"Dropped a chappy off, headed to the Smoke as well," he whispered a bit smugly. "One of those working on the case."

"And how's the case coming along?" Berdie questioned with no care to secrecy.

Goodnight glanced about. He brought his index finger to his lips and presented a walls-have-ears frown.

"Just as well, we've a train to catch," Lillie pronounced and began a forward motion.

"If you can see your way clear to keep your voice down, I may have heard something."

"Oh yes?" Berdie whispered. "Your prime suspect, perhaps?"

"As a matter of fact, it's Raheem's nephew."

Lillie froze in place.

"Sundeep?" Berdie's whisper reversed volume.

"Will you keep your voice down," Goodnight all but shouted. He again glanced round. "The call your husband received Saturday was placed from the lad's mobile phone. He's our man." Goodnight lifted his chin with certain swagger.

Berdie shook her head. "Sundeep stood in our hall, holding my grocery order, at the very moment Hugh spoke to the caller."

The constable narrowed his eyes. "It's never just one with these insurgent types, is it? No, there's bound to be several others in on it."

"Is there evidence that it's more than one? Is Sundeep involved in some questionable alliances?"

Goodnight pursed his lips. "He's traveled outside the country." He pointed his index finger toward Berdie. "He's been questioned before."

"Surely not for murder?" Lillie's eyes went round.

Goodnight waved his hand toward Lillie as if to dismiss her question. "Does it matter what for? A bad apple is a bad apple." He rested his hand on his truncheon. "Find him, we find the mastermind."

"And I find that terribly hard to believe," Berdie

blurted.

Goodnight stood stick-straight and pulled on the hem of his uniform jacket as if to straighten the entire situation out. "We'll see about that," he grumped. "Waste my breath and all. Good day, ladies." He briskly moved along with a certain agitation etched on his visage.

"Sometimes, Lillie, I marvel how that man manages to keep his position in the law."

Lillie bit the inside of her bottom lip. "Perhaps, in this case, we should pay more attention to him."

"What?"

The rumble of the train's arrival signaled a crowded rush forward, Berdie and Lillie in the crush.

Berdie found side-by-side seats. She and Lillie snatched them quickly as people crowded about.

"Why should we pay Goodnight any mind?" Berdie asked.

Both Berdie's and Lillie's bodies lurched with the forward movement of the train.

"It's what Mrs. Raheem told me." Lillie's tone was serious.

"Does she think Sundeep is a criminal?"

Lillie shook her head.

"Then what is it?"

"I know this all started as a missing-person search on behalf of the Raheems, but I think it's more." Lillie pulled a small notepad from her bag and opened it. "I jotted the information down after speaking with Sharday. First, her sister, Sundeep's mother, brought great disgrace on the traditional Indian family when she married a gentleman from Pakistan."

"Oh, that could create some friction all right."

"Right. However, when Sundeep was young, just

a toddler if I recall correctly, his father died in some kind of military strike near the Pakistani border with Afghanistan. Now, Sharday didn't say it was coalition forces that carried out the deed, but it stands to reason, doesn't it?"

"Lillie, are you suggesting that Sundeep, motivated by revenge for the death of his father, went after the commander?"

"Wouldn't you?"

Berdie's body jerked slightly sideways as the train tugged and etched its way along the urban track.

"Lillie, we know nothing of hard facts surrounding his father's death. Sundeep was, by your own admission, a toddler, which means he had little or no recollection of events. And until the full story is known, it's purely speculation."

"Well, don't be too sure about that. There's more." Lillie eyed her notebook and sniffed. "I suppose you'll disregard this as well."

"I'm not disregarding, Lillie. I'm just being reasonable. I'm listening—go on."

"After some time, Sundeep's mother came to England, bringing him and his big sister with her. His mother met an English citizen of Indian descent, a fine man, by Mrs. Raheem's account, and they married. But Sundeep and the fellow had difficulties adjusting to one another. An uncle, Sharday's brother, tried to act as mediator, but to little avail. It's not been the happiest of relationships."

"Not entirely unusual, I'm afraid."

"Don't you s'pose he longed for his natural father, even became angry about it?" Lillie paused.

Berdie didn't respond.

"And then there was some kind of run-in with the

law. It was shortly after that Sundeep was sent to live with the Raheems."

"When you say 'run-in,' what does that mean?"

"Sharday didn't know what it was all about, except something illegal was suspected."

"But the authorities let him go, right? Had she noticed any odd or unusual behavior on Sundeep's part?"

Lillie shook her head.

"And his friends? How did he fare at school?"

"Mrs. Raheem didn't know much about friends. Well, she mentioned his best friend, Amol. He and Sundeep have known each other since childhood. Lives in the London area. And this uncle who tried to help Sundeep with his stepfather, Uncle Chander, he was close to the lad. Sundeep's mother and stepfather have heard no word, but both mentioned Amol. Apart from that, she knew little about his acquaintances. He completed his schooling successfully and was on a local sponsored football team."

"I see." Berdie paused. "So, that's it then?"

"Isn't it enough?"

"There's nothing there to suggest he's an architect of destruction. He's no more than a young man who perhaps needs a bit of growing up."

The train began to gain speed.

"Berdie, you've always said everyone's got a dark side. Yet you're not giving any consideration to Sundeep as a possible suspect."

"It's so unlikely. In the contact I had with him—it was limited, I admit—he impressed me as a good lad."

"Impressed. You see? How well do you really know him?"

Berdie felt a nibble of doubt in her brain.

Something felt out of sorts.

Lillie verbally placed her hands on hips. "Berdie, are you too close to the situation?"

There it was. It hit Berdie like a harpoon, and her stomach tightened.

"Am I too close, or too far?"

"What?"

Berdie took a deep breath. "Since the blast, it's been nibbling away at me. Is my investigative nose growing dull?" Berdie felt a sense of disorientation as the words tumbled. "I trust Chief Inspector Jasper Kent. Yet I still try to put the puzzle pieces in place. But when I do, I can't see clearly. It's almost as if the pieces are there, but they're colorless, shapeless, evasive. I've never had it before, this…loss."

Lillie looked Berdie straight in the eye. "And we know that's not at all like you, Berdie."

There was a dark edge on Berdie's thinking, and she could barely let the words escape. "Am I losing my ability to reason things out well, to connect the dots, to see past deceit?"

"Heavens, no." Lillie placed her hand on Berdie's arm and gave a squeeze. "Four days ago, you experienced a monstrous shock in your own back garden. And you've had demands on your time without a proper opportunity for some breathing space. You just need to stand back a bit, catch your breath, reenergize. You have a grand gift, Berdie. It's just taken a wobble."

Berdie appreciated Lillie's reassurance, but there was some kind of stirring, agitation, really, within her. What was going on? *Lord, You may be the only one who knows the answer to that question.* "A wobble," Berdie repeated and sighed.

"Now listen, Berdie, you're going to be right as rain. All I'm asking is that you open your thinking to the possibility that Sundeep could be less than 'a nice lad.' That's all. Fair enough?"

Berdie sighed. "OK, Lillie. As long as you'll be open to the fact he may not be guilty at all."

"That will do." Lillie put her notepad away and yawned. "Now we must move on to the next great question."

"Which is?"

"Where's the buffet car? I'm parched."

****

Berdie stared out the taxi's window, watching the crowded streets of Slough with its rushing pedestrians and harried drivers.

She was surprised to have found Angela's lecture, with the exception of a couple small issues, actually flat as a plank. No fiery statements, no pushing of her personal agenda, no controversial stands on issues.

"Uncharacteristically quiet lecture, Angela," Berdie told the woman when leaving the church after.

"And you would know." The forty-something single mother of two grown children threw her head back with a chuckle, sending her raven hair into a swirl. "But I'm not losing my verbal punch, you know," she said in a low voice. She threw a glance toward the stoic Reverend Rishi, who spoke quietly with some congregants. "I'm afraid I'm still his curate. And as such, I've had to turn down the rhetoric a notch," she confessed. "Still, I was hoping that if you came, we'd have a blazing good row after."

"Not this time, Angela. It seems we're both on best

behavior," Berdie countered. "Must push on."

Now, sitting in the taxi on the way to lunch, it wasn't just Angela's lecture that was flat. She began to question if she may have overstepped her bounds by giving the Raheems hope that she could locate Sundeep in such a place.

Lillie, who worked to stay awake for Angela's lecture, now dozed, seated next Berdie.

"You know, Lillie, if Sundeep is tied to the investigation, Chief Inspector Kent will find him. They've got everything at their disposal."

"Hum?" Lillie was barely audible, eyes closed, head leaning to the side.

"Not that it would be a pleasant thing if he did find him, but innocence could win out. At least I hope it would."

"A-hum." Lillie trailed off.

"But how can I disappoint the Raheems?" She sighed. "It's your fault I'm in this, you know."

"There you are, ladies," the cabdriver announced. "The Red Star Restaurant."

Berdie gave Lillie a nudge.

Lillie roused. "Sorry," she mumbled.

"I looked for him but couldn't find him," Berdie prodded.

Lillie perked and fluttered her eyelids. "Sundeep?"

"No, a handsome prince, to come kiss you awake."

"Very hard to come by these days, I should think," Lillie quipped as she stretched her arms.

"Hang about, it's closed." The cabdriver nodded toward the restaurant.

Lillie sat up straight.

Berdie eyed the shaded windows and *closed* sign. "Bang goes our connection to Sundeep," she moaned.

"Why would Mr. Raheem's friend close shop in the middle of the week?"

"There." The driver pointed to a small sign. "Closed for renovations."

"Bang goes lunch," Lillie spurted.

"We need to pull a divine rabbit from a cosmic hat to find Sundeep now. We should just go back to Aidan Kirkwood."

"Well, I'm famished. I'm not going anywhere until I've had a good Indian."

"If I can be of help," the cabby interjected, "I know a place with excellent Indian food and reasonable prices. Jewel of the Eastern Wind, not far from here."

"Good chicken tikka masala?" Berdie queried.

"Blazing good." The fellow chuckled.

"Then, dear sir, lead us on," Lillie commanded.

The Jewel of the Eastern Wind was chock-a-block with people. Still, they didn't wait long amongst the red-and-gold décor to be seated. Once at the table, Berdie began to scan the menu.

"Lillie, did you hear anything I said in the cab?"

Lillie ran a finger down the menu. "I think I'll get a vindaloo."

"Enjoy lunch. We're going home when we're done," Berdie pronounced. "I'll explain to Mr. and Mrs. Raheem I should never have agreed to try to find Sundeep."

"Berdie." Lillie lifted her chin. "You're in a hairshirt mood, aren't you?" She leaned forward over her menu. "It's that conversation we had this morning, isn't it? You think you're past it."

"Not past it," Berdie snapped quite sharply. "I never said I was past it."

"There's the spirit." Lillie smiled.

A waiter pushed by their table. "It's not enough we're packed in here"—he lifted his voice to another server—"but some fool's double-parked out in front. There's a jam." He glanced toward the kitchen door, where a young man had just entered the dining room. "Amol, where have you been? Take care of your table." He nodded toward Berdie and Lillie.

"Amol?" Lillie stared at Berdie. "That's the name of Sundeep's best friend. Do you suppose?"

"Lillie, this is Slough. How many Amols do you imagine there are?"

A young man Sundeep's age hurried to the table, pad and pencil at the ready. "Welcome to Jewel of the Eastern Wind," he said, a bit breathless. "My name is Amol, and I'll be serving you. What can I get you to drink?"

"Yes, Amol, hello," Lillie greeted. "Permit me to ask you a question, if you will. Are you a friend of Mr. Hardeep Raheem's nephew, Sundeep?"

The lad started. His widened eyes shifted and went into a squint. "No. Who wants to know?"

Berdie caught her breath. He didn't have long ears or a cotton tail, but she knew a divine rabbit when it stood before her very eyes.

"No, never heard of him." The fellow turned his gaze to the pad. "What to drink then?"

"Tell me, where I can find him? His aunt and uncle are beside themselves with worry." Berdie was firm.

"Who are you?" A horn outside blasted, and Amol's eyes darted to the large window at the front of the restaurant that faced the road. His cheeks took on a flush and he discharged a tiny gasp.

Berdie looked the direction in which he gazed.

Now *she* gasped. The white van double-parked in the road outside read *Raheem's Greengrocer* cross the side.

"Lillie," Berdie clamored, "get your bag."

On her feet, and disbelief thrown to the eastern wind, Berdie scrambled for the door. "Stand aside, please," she shouted as she pushed and elbowed her way to the entrance, Lillie trailing behind.

"He's done nothing wrong," Amol shouted after them. "Nothing."

Once out the door, Berdie allowed nothing to stand in her way as she rushed to the street. A car blasted its horn, making her jump, but she soldiered on until she was within arm's reach of the van. The vehicle engine roared, and it lunged forward. "Stop," Berdie screamed. "Sundeep, stop."

Berdie heard the squeal of brakes as Lillie stepped into the road. A cab came to an abrupt halt.

"You mad?" the cabby screamed at Lillie from his opened window.

"Get in," Berdie shouted at Lillie. "Get in the cab."

Berdie raced to join Lillie at the black vehicle.

Lillie tussled with the door and rammed herself in the backseat, leaving the door open.

Horns blared from several vehicles.

Berdie scooted onto the seat next to Lillie. "Follow that van," she commanded the driver.

"This isn't Hollywood," the lean cabby retorted.

Berdie watched the van screech to a halt as two people tried to cross the road in front of it.

"Follow that van and there's twenty quid in it for you," Berdie bribed.

"Thirty."

Berdie grimaced. "Get on then."

The cabby set his meter, and Berdie flew back

against the seat as the car launched forward to the chase.

"This is exciting," Lillie squealed, obviously past napping.

"You pay my fine if I get nicked." The dark-haired driver glanced in his rear-view.

Berdie huffed as the work van commenced forward again. "Just keep the van in sight and mind how you go."

"Truth be told, I've always wanted to do this," he barked while accelerating. "I just always imagined it would be with some hardened and famous DI."

9

"Hello, I'm not going to try that." The cabby stopped his vehicle and nodded toward the narrow alleyway between two small warehouses, where Raheem's greengrocer vehicle just barely eked through.

Berdie and company were in the heart of Slough's industrial area, littered with warehouses, outbuildings, and cargo-shipping containers the size of mobile homes.

The fellow spoke over his shoulder. "Besides, just three streets over and not over a week ago, a cabby was relieved of his cash at knifepoint."

"I see," Berdie retorted. "That's fine—we'll walk from here."

Lillie reared. "Walk?"

"You know: two legs, one foot in front of the other, that sort of thing."

The cabdriver laughed.

Lillie didn't. "Is that wise?"

Berdie got out of the cab, industrial odors assaulting her nose, and handed the driver his promised thirty pounds, plus the fare.

"Are you coming, Lillie?"

Lillie wore a face Berdie would only describe as vexed, but nonetheless, her dearest friend gave a quick glance about and exited the cab.

Berdie knew the untidy litter in the area, stained and broken objects on the verges, windblown papers, to say nothing of the nearby factory odors, wouldn't appeal to Lillie. But these things were a part of their tracking process. And so be it.

"Want me to send a copper round in a bit?" The cabby closed his window halfway.

"Yes," Lillie clipped.

"No, but thank you." Berdie began forward progress into the alleyway.

"It was a doddle, you know, not the chase I imagined," the fellow yelled from the window opening and rocketed off into traffic.

Lillie watched the retreating cab.

"Come along, Lillie. The more swift we are, the more likely to catch Sundeep up."

Lillie looked wistfully in the direction the cab had taken, and then stepped after Berdie. "You've had some half-witted ideas, my dear Sherlock, but this one takes the biscuit."

"Look. He can't be going far now. It looks as if the alley is blocked just beyond us. You see?"

Several yards past the opening where they now walked, a huge metal shipping container sat at a rather awkward angle. Berdie could see the work van pull to the side of it and stop.

"That was hardly an exciting chase," Lillie mumbled. "Sundeep drove like my granny."

"When a nineteen-year-old lad drives like that, it tells us he's into something dodgy. He didn't want to call attention to his movements because he's in some sort of trouble. Speeding would be too risky."

"Didn't he realize he was being followed?"

"I shouldn't think so. Our cabby was quite clever

about staying covert, and I daresay Sundeep would have put on a bit more speed if he noticed."

Berdie grabbed Lillie by the arm and pulled her flat against the nearby wall of the warehouse.

Sundeep emerged from the van with a carrier bag, the logo for the Jewel of the Eastern Wind printed on it. He strode to the door of the brown metal storage container and easily opened it, entering without showing any concern.

Lillie took a quick breath. "He's been living in a cargo box?"

"Give him a moment to settle."

Berdie deftly began her forward movement and noted that the tire tracks the van had made were the only ones in the area. There were clangs and bangs from nearby factories, but nothing especially close.

"Are we just going to knock at the door?" Lillie asked in a whisper as she followed.

"Oh yes, and to think we didn't bring a housewarming gift." Berdie half laughed under her breath. "Most of these containers have locks that can't be opened from the inside. Obviously, Sundeep comes and goes, so the lock must be disabled. That's what we'll assume."

"You're not suggesting we barge in."

"Lillie, would I do this if I thought we were in real danger?"

Lillie swallowed.

"We just want the element of surprise on our side. You pull the door open in one go, and I'll step inside. Oh, and let me do the talking."

Lillie paled. "What if he's armed?"

"Perhaps a plastic knife from his takeaway? Surprise, Lillie, is a one-up factor."

"Right." Lillie didn't sound convinced. She opened her bag and silently rummaged, producing a fingernail file that she slipped into her skirt pocket. "Right."

Berdie moved to the non-hinged side of the door. "Lord have mercy," she whispered, and motioned Lillie forward.

Lillie grabbed the handle with both hands.

Berdie nodded.

With pulling momentum that rivaled a plow horse, Lillie swung the metal door open, being carried backward with it.

Bag over her shoulder, Berdie thrust herself through the opening, anchored her feet, and stood her full five-foot-six height, plus two-inch wedge heels. "Hello, Sundeep."

The clatter of a plastic fork hit the metal floor and echoed round the container as the stunned teen jumped to his feet. Eyes wide, he gaped in astonished silence. Then he found his voice when recognition dawned. "You're the vicar's wife."

"Mrs. Elliott, yes."

With one swift glance about, Berdie took in the tatty metal lanterns that provided a pittance of light. It revealed several boxes, including one on which lunch balanced, and an open sleeping bag sitting atop a large wooden pallet. She returned her gaze to the young man. "It's OK, Lillie, you can come in," she called out.

Lillie appeared in the doorway, holding her shoulder bag against her chest like an ancient military shield, with one hand in her pocket. She frowned. "Did you try to do in the commander with that bomb blast?"

Sundeep jabbed his index finger toward her. "You see?" he yelled. "Do you see? That's exactly why I did a bunk, yeah? Profiling, that's what it is."

Berdie drove her palms forward. "It's OK, Sundeep. You needn't lose your rag. Stay calm," she soothed with an even, quiet tone. "I'm not here to accuse. Now, why don't you just continue eating your lunch, and let's have a chat."

"How did you find me?" His voice was ragged.

"We went to lunch at the Jewel of the Eastern Wind."

"We didn't actually eat lunch," Lillie murmured.

"We came upon Amol, and then we saw the van. We followed you."

Sundeep threw his head back, almost as if in disbelief, and slumped back into the folding garden chair from which he had stood. "Bloo—"

"Ah," Berdie cautioned. "Ladies present."

"Right, here in the Palm Hotel tearoom." His words dripped with sarcasm.

"If you're not guilty, why are you hiding here?" Lillie asked, still clinging to her designer shield.

"It's the ambiance, yeah?"

"OK," Berdie interjected. "Lillie." Berdie pointed to a large wooden crate, big enough to sit on, near the door. "If you please." Berdie then pulled another sturdy box closer to Sundeep and sat down on it.

Lillie edged her way to the crate Berdie had ordained and sat tentatively.

"Sundeep, I'm here because your aunt and uncle are worried sick about you." Berdie used her disgruntled-mother voice.

The lad dropped his head. "I'm sorry about that."

"And your parents don't know where you are."

He shook his tousled hair.

"Why did you leave the way you did?"

He gave a terse nod toward Lillie. "Did you hear

her accusation?"

Lillie lifted her chin.

"Tell *me*, Sundeep. I'm here to listen. Why did you run off?"

"Straight up?"

"Out with it."

"When I went to your home, it just felt weird: some nutter going ape on the phone…"

"Go on," Berdie urged.

"There were people in and out, everything seemed all go, and when I heard the blast, I panicked, yeah?" Sundeep took a deep breath. "My aunt and uncle are established in that village, but I was the new kid, an outsider. I knew the Old Bill would target me. I've had a slight tangle with them here before, yeah?" He looked down. "And I'm not a grass," he barely mumbled.

"What?" Lillie coaxed.

Ignoring Lillie, he gazed at Berdie. "The further away I got, the further I had to go."

Berdie looked into Sundeep's dark brown eyes. "Innocence usually stays and pleads its case."

Sundeep shifted his eyes downward. "Yeah, well, it didn't this time."

Berdie tilted slightly forward. "Is there something that you're not telling us?"

"And then there's your mobile," Lillie interrupted.

Sundeep sat up in the chair, looking almost relieved. "My mobile? You found it then?"

Berdie glared at Lillie and then directed her conversation to Sundeep. "No, we've not found it. You've lost it?"

The lad nodded.

"When did it go missing?"

"That day, I had it in my pocket when I left my uncle's shop." He jammed his hand into the pocket of the leather jacket he wore. "In here, yeah, but when I went to ring up my uncle, just before I got to your house, it wasn't there anymore. It must have fallen out. And I've searched every inch of the van. Nothing."

"You lost it doing your deliveries that day?"

Sundeep shrugged. "Must have done."

"A likely story," Lillie snapped. "You do realize the call that sent Reverend Elliott on a wild-goose chase was made from your mobile."

Sundeep knotted his brow. "I've never rung the vicar." He paused. "You mean the call at the vicarage? That crazy call? It was made from my mobile?"

Berdie nodded.

"But I was there, right there in the hall. You were there. You saw me."

"Yes, Sundeep, I know you didn't do it, but *someone* used your mobile to make that call."

Sundeep groaned and put his hands to his head. He looked at Berdie, his eyes pleading. "They're going to try to pin this on me somehow, aren't they? The golden boy from London."

Berdie wanted to say something comforting, but "Yes, you're the main suspect" wasn't exactly fitting. "Things can work out, Sundeep."

The young man leapt from his chair. He kicked the edge of an empty box, sending it through the air until it crashed against the side of the cargo container.

Berdie heard Lillie slightly gasp.

"I think we should go," Lillie squeaked.

Sundeep turned to face Berdie. "I didn't blow anyone up. I have nothing to do with any of it, I promise you."

Berdie silently nodded. "Try to calm yourself."

Sundeep closed his eyes, as if to block out all the dark injustices of the world, and gradually reopened them. He stuck his hand in his trouser pocket. "Please tell Aunt Sharday that I'm sorry about all this. And let Uncle Hardeep know I'll pay him back for the petrol."

He pulled a small, shiny object from his pocket and handed it toward Berdie. It was a key. "I know it's a cheek, but would you take the van back to my uncle, like?"

Berdie stood. "Why don't you drive it back and apologize yourself?"

Sundeep held the key forward in his palm.

Berdie took a deep breath.

The distressed lad pointed to a cardboard box. "That was part of your delivery order, Mrs. Elliott. I'm afraid I've eaten most of it. I'm short of readies, but I'll make it right."

"Sundeep, I'm not concerned about you paying me for what you've eaten of my order. You're welcome to it. But I really think you'd be better off going to the police. Tell them what you've told us."

He fumbled the key in his fingers. "Mind your driving. It accelerates a bit slow off the mark, yeah. The left rear light is dodgy, and the window on the passenger side sometimes sticks."

He extended his palm, the small, shiny object nestled in it.

Berdie pursed her lips. It would be far better if Sundeep were to return the van himself, which would be cake with icing on it. But on the other hand, if she returned with the van, the entire family would have a modicum of relief and they'd get their vehicle back. Better a cake without icing than no cake at all. She grasped onto the key tightly.

Lillie jumped up and was at the door. "Leaving is a splendid idea."

"She's going to grass me up?"

Berdie heard Lillie rummaging through her bag, and it prompted Berdie to open her own shoulder bag. She removed a St. Aidan of the Wood Parish Church business card and gave it to Sundeep. "If you remember where you might have lost your mobile, try to ring me. If there's anything I can do to help, you know where I can be found."

Lillie was already out the door when Berdie took her first steps toward it.

There, near the box on which Lillie had perched, a ten-pound note lay on the floor. Berdie half grinned and turned toward Sundeep. "And I shouldn't think Lillie will grass on you, tell the police where you are."

Sundeep didn't appear convinced, but he saw Berdie to the nearby door.

She noticed a wire-coat-hanger-DIY lock of sorts. "You made this?"

"Got a book at the library that explained how to do it. Not bad, yeah?"

Berdie didn't have the heart to say a gnat could break it open. "Very resourceful."

"You have to be when you live in the Ritz."

"Yes. Well, God go with you." Berdie offered it as a prayer as much as an admonition for the lad as she stepped outside and he closed the door behind her. She could hear him fiddle with the lock and push an object against the door. "Safely circle him, Lord," she prayed.

She and Lillie went to the van.

Lillie paused. "It's not going to blow up, is it?"

"Oh, Lillie," Berdie stormed. She got in and started

the engine.

Sheepishly, Lillie got into the passenger seat.

****

"I had my mouth set for a vindaloo. Fish and chips lack that curry wow factor." Lillie pushed a couple more chips in her mouth as Berdie drove the van amongst the vehicles about them on the motorway.

"The chippy was handy, Lillie, and I wanted to push on." Berdie glanced at the nearly empty takeaway container in Lillie's lap. "Yes, I can see it was a real struggle for you to eat the lot."

"You're doing rather well driving this beast." Lillie licked her fingers. "Our cabby wouldn't attempt that narrow passage back at Sundeep's, but you maneuvered it with skill."

"I'm practiced."

"Yes, I suppose you are."

Berdie sighed. "Lillie, you don't still think Sundeep planted that bomb now, do you?"

Lillie looked ahead out the front windscreen. "He's got guilt written all over him."

"Oh yes, I agree there. But for what?"

Lillie took a deep breath.

"I saw the money on the floor near your perch back there, the ten-pound note."

"Oh?" she said feebly and shifted in her seat.

Berdie laughed. "Lillie, how many mad bombers ask you to return their uncle's work van with apologies and promise of reimbursement? Do they offer to pay for the food they've eaten from your grocery order? He's not responsible for the blast."

Lillie sighed. "OK, I *doubt* he did it," she snapped.

"Lillie?"

"It's just that, well, I usually love the excitement of a good nose-about. But this situation is different. I hoped it would be all over, done and dusted, when we returned home. The commander's still critical, those starchy investigative fellows are still all over our village, and gossip and rumors swirl about like North Sea winds." She pursed her lips. "I had hoped we'd corner Sundeep, he'd confess, and then the village would be one step closer to life as normal. As it is, we've caused more questions than answers."

"Oh, Lillie, I'm sorry you feel that way." Berdie removed a hand from the steering wheel and gave Lillie's arm a quick squeeze. "I know it's not easy. There's no one in Aidan Kirkwood who doesn't want this to be resolved. And it will be, soon, I should think. Good people are working hard to crack it."

Lillie nodded.

"We've narrowed some things down. Think of it as forward progress."

"Berdie"—Lillie sounded cautious—"just how fast is our forward progress at the moment?" She pointed at the speed indicator.

Berdie glanced downward. "I'm just barely over."

Lillie nodded at the passenger-side mirror of the van.

Berdie glanced in the mirror on her own side.

Red and blue flashes of light whirled.

She could just make out the edge of a police vehicle directly behind. "Do you suppose they want to pass?" Berdie asked with little hope.

Lillie lifted her brows. "If wishes were fishes, we'd have a feast."

Berdie slowed. The police car slowed. Berdie felt a

grumble in her stomach. "This could be awkward," she breathed as she pulled to the verge of the motorway. She brought the vehicle to a stop.

The police car stopped behind and another pulled up in front of the van.

Berdie looked at Lillie, who looked at Berdie. "Oh dear" was all Berdie could think to say.

"Armed police. Turn the engine off, and get out of the vehicle," a loudspeaker blared. "Keep your hands in plain sight, in the air."

"Berdie, what's happening?" Lillie pushed her empty takeaway onto the floor and raised her hands above her shoulders.

Armed police? "I'm not sure, Lillie, but do *exactly* what they say and don't make any sudden moves. Lord have mercy," Berdie breathed.

****

The officer in charge gave a snappish nod with tightened lips toward Berdie and Lillie. "We're done with them."

The harsh glare of ceiling lights, combined with gray walls, made the reception room of the police station completely uninviting. The wood bench that Berdie and Lillie occupied could have been stone, for the comfort of it. Despite the flourishing potted plant by the lone window, nothing really appealed, and especially now.

"They're all yours, Chief Inspector," the officer said. "Must admit, we've not had a vicar's wife terrorist before." The uniformed policeman clucked as if scolding and left the area.

Chief Inspector Kent folded his arms. "Well, well,

well."

Berdie felt an odd mixture of relief and stomachache.

"Chief Inspector Kent, please accept our deepest apologies for this to-do," Berdie offered.

His jaw tightened slightly.

"Did you travel all this way"—Lillie cleared her throat—"just for our situation?"

"*Your situation*, as you call it, caused a national alert." Jasper Kent was prickly. "They thought they were onto an insurrectionary."

Berdie worked to calm the blush she felt rushing to her cheeks.

"And no, I was already here on other business. Just as well for your sakes."

"Why a national alert?" Berdie realized the answer as she said it. "It's the van. You've reported it as missing, driven by a dangerous suspect, approach with caution."

Kent lifted his chin.

"Has Mr. Raheem reported it missing?" Lillie asked.

The chief inspector uncrossed his arms. "He didn't have to." He looked at Berdie. "It doesn't take an Einstein to twig it when the Raheems are observed making shop deliveries in their family car, knowing their nephew is 'somewhere off visiting friends in London.'"

"No," Berdie admitted, "I shouldn't think it would take an Einstein."

The investigator's right eye went into a squint. "A lecture and lunch, you said when you left. Why didn't you tell me you were contacting Sundeep as well?"

"As well?" Berdie's shoulders tightened.

"We didn't know for certain that we would find him," Lillie blurted. "It was a stroke of divine intervention, really."

"Find him?" Jasper Kent wore a hint of a smile. "That implies intentional searching, doesn't it, Miss Foxworth?"

"Wait a moment," Berdie interrupted. "Let's go back a step. What do you mean by 'contacting him *as well*'? How do you know we indeed did attend the lecture or even saw Sundeep?"

"You had the van." Kent made a quick glance out the window and tapped a finger against his thigh.

"You followed me from the village, the whole time," Berdie exclaimed.

Lillie's jaw dropped.

"Not me personally, per se."

Snap! "The chum Goodnight deposited at the train. You *had* me followed then—what's the difference?"

"Us followed," Lillie corrected.

"You know any inspector worth their salt would have done the same. It's procedure," Kent said unapologetically.

As much as she wanted to carry on, Berdie reined in her displeasure. He was right. He was doing his job. Even though there was a certain professional friendship between them, and even if there was a sense of personal intrusion, he was right to do what he had done, and she, for whatever reason, had not considered the possibility of him doing it. "Point taken," she miffed.

"Now, permit me to ask," Kent said in a mannerly tone, "why the clandestine snooping?"

"Snooping, as you call it, is second nature to

Berdie." Lillie went on. "If you know her at all, you know she's rather gifted, rather good at it."

"It's OK, Lillie," Berdie calmed. "And it wasn't snooping," she defended, "and it wasn't so much clandestine as confidential. More related to church work actually."

The inspector appeared to be amused. "I can't say I've ever known anyone to use that line of reasoning before. Nosing round being church work."

"It's all a bit tricky." Berdie took a deep breath and came to her feet. "I was asked by a parishioner, who was aware of my past detection background, to see if I could locate Sundeep. I was not aware of his being a suspect in your investigation when I agreed to do it, and certainly not a primary one. And as a church representative, there's a certain confidentiality in these matters."

Kent put the matter in a non-confidential nutshell. "So the Raheems asked you to locate their nephew, and you didn't tell me what you were about." Jasper Kent glanced aside, as if in thought. "Well, as you say, church matters are in play. You would have told me on your return, I assume. Anyway, as it turns out, you led us right to him."

Berdie pursed her lips. Sundeep would no doubt think she and Lillie "grassed him up."

Kent looked Berdie in the eye. "I know you're a woman of character and above board on making sure there's no withholding of evidence?"

Berdie glowered. "I would not withhold anything I considered pertinent to your investigation, and you know that."

Now Lillie stood. "I can tell you absolutely that Berdie respects the law," she snapped. "And she trusts your skills. She's told me that more than once."

"Right." Inspector Kent paused. "You can take the woman out of investigating, but you can't take the investigating out of the woman. It takes a certain amount of guts, going off like that on your own to locate a suspect that had done a runner."

Berdie straightened. "Run he did, but he didn't plant any devices, Chief Inspector Kent."

"No? What makes you so sure?"

Berdie held her stance. "He told me he didn't."

Kent looked at Lillie. "There's a new one, hey?"

"And I believe him," Berdie finished with zest.

"Do you? Would you still say you believe him if I were to tell you he spent three months in northern Pakistan recently?"

Berdie tried to hide her surprise. She studied Kent. "All that really tells us is that he traveled outside this country."

"Perhaps." Kent tipped his head. "Or perhaps not."

"He's guilty of something," Lillie burst out. "We don't know what it is, but he's hiding something."

Berdie glared at Lillie.

"Now, that seems helpful," Inspector Kent crowed. "I'm sure we'll find out all about it. Local officers should have him in tow by now."

"You will give him a fair hearing?" Berdie admonished as much as asked.

"A fair hearing." Berdie heard an all-too-familiar voice say, only to turn and see Hugh, who had just entered the room.

Loren was with him, face like thunder.

"We have a bit of fair hearing of our own to do when we get home, don't we, Berdie?" Hugh's left eyebrow skyrocketed as a flushed pink danced at the edge of his white collar. "Chief Inspector Kent, I appreciate your time and trouble on this matter. With your permission, we'll take the remorseful parties home. Please accept my assurances that nothing like this will happen again. Ever."

Kent's face wore a doubtful expression. Still, he tipped his head to Hugh. "As it turns out, your wife and her friend have assisted our investigation."

Hugh's blue eyes steeled as he glowered at Berdie. "Have they now?"

"Hugh." Berdie knew her husband could hear the tension in her voice. "It's all perfectly simple. I can explain."

10

Berdie and Hugh went to the Raheems' straightway when they returned to the village, and Berdie explained all that had happened with Sundeep, the work van, and the police. To Hugh's chagrin and Berdie's delight, the Raheems expressed real gratitude to her and even thanked Hugh for letting Berdie exercise her extraordinary talent in detection work while in the midst of busy preparations for the Whitsun regatta. Hugh didn't appear completely won over.

While Hugh and Hardeep continued in deep conversation, Berdie entered the kitchen, where Sharday was in the midst of making tea for all gathered.

"Sharday, if I may," Berdie lightly prodded, "I understand Sundeep made a recent visit to Pakistan, yes?"

"Oh yes, to visit his dead father's parents. His grandfather has been very sick, very sick."

"I'm sorry to hear that."

"His grandmother called my sister for Sundeep to come to help her care for him. Sundeep stayed until his grandfather's better." She smiled and stirred the teapot. "He tells me he feels the fish in no water there."

"Fish in no...oh, like a fish out of water."

"That's how you say. Yes. He's happy to be home,

he said." Her smile slipped. "But now this."

"Pray, Sharday, that all goes well for Sundeep."

"Yes. Our Sundeep is a good boy. He just needs the good path."

"We all do, really."

Now, twenty-four hours past that conversation, and despite the slight frost toward her that still clung to Hugh's shoulder, Berdie was delighted that the dinner party was in full swing and had generated a warmth all its own.

And a great deal of that warmth was due to the fact that Hugh had promised that he would share an exciting surprise when all guests were present.

"It must be good news," Lillie prattled on whilst helping Berdie arrange another tray of canapés.

"Whatever it is, it seems to be lifting everyone's spirits, and that's good enough in itself. The weather is cooperating as well. It's lovely in the garden."

"Let's see, who's yet to arrive?" Lillie replenished little puffed cheesy bits in a circular pattern on the tray, being sure not to drop any crumbs on her melon-colored silk dress. "Tillie and Doug just arrived. Rollie and Joan are here, Sandra and Natty. And, by the way, doesn't Sandra look lovely?"

"Indeed," Berdie sparked. She placed fresh slices of a chicken-liver peppercorn terrine on a platter emblazoned with summery patterns. "Natty told me Sandra bought a new dress for the occasion."

"And it suits her." Lillie nodded. "It makes the best of her figure. She's had her hair done up as well."

"I do believe she's quite hoping to impress someone."

"And I shouldn't be at all surprised if indeed she does," Lillie agreed. "Doug cuts a fine figure this evening as well. Did you notice how his dark blue jacket shows off his broad shoulders and blond hair?"

"Oh yes." Berdie added thin slices of rye bread to her tray. "And with the moon's cooperation tonight, a romance can surely spark."

"Or inflame an already-existing one." Lillie raised a brow and glanced at Berdie.

"You noticed Hugh's coolness then?"

"Moonlight can be magic," Lillie purred. "Now, back to who's here."

"Carl and Barbara Braunhoff are present. And of course, your Loren."

"My handsome Loren." Lillie sighed. "That moon could do us some romantic favors as well. He was not pleased about all that happened yesterday."

"At least the Raheems are pleased." Berdie wiped her hands on a tea towel. "I assured them that Jasper Kent would give Sundeep fair treatment."

Lillie looked up from her chore. "May justice be served." She returned to her work and put the finishing touches. "Oh, I say, we haven't seen the other fellow from the rowing team yet, Dave, is it? Yes, Dave. He isn't here."

"Nor Chad," Berdie added, taking the filled tray from Lillie.

"Chad? He's coming?" Lillie sounded surprised.

"He is a member of the rowing team, Lillie, and currently staying under Dave's roof. His chums are very fond of him, even though he's sometimes a bit indelicate."

"Indelicate?" Lillie went to the sink and washed her hands. "Rude and horrible, I should think, and suspect besides."

Berdie removed one of the cheese puffs from the

tray and popped it in her mouth. "Yes, well, if Chad is brave enough to come, and that may say something about his innocence, we must remember the past is behind us. I shouldn't think we'll get an apology for his outburst at the picnic, but I expect he will be on his best behavior."

Lillie simply *humphed* as she dried her hands.

The familiar sound of the front-door chime sang out.

Berdie gave the laden canapé tray back to Lillie. "Speaking of. Do you mind taking both trays out to the garden? Offer them about and I'll get the door."

"Seeing as it's very likely to be Chad who has arrived, I'd be delighted to go to the garden."

"Be kind, Lillie," Berdie reminded.

Berdie's shimmery, gathered-at-the-waist taffeta skirt rustled as she walked the hall to the entrance. Something about the sound of it made her feel exceptionally feminine. She graciously opened the door.

"Dave, Chad, so pleased you've come," she greeted as the two stepped inside. "I'll just take you through to join the others in the back garden."

"Grand." Dave smiled, but Chad's square jawline looked rather taut, with the hint of a scowl creeping onto his brow. While Dave walked on, Berdie gently wrapped her arm round Chad's elbow. "I'm glad to see you've become friends with your razor again," she ribbed, noting the lack of any gin scent.

The smartly dressed Chad allowed the corners of his mouth to rise slightly. *A good sign*, Berdie thought.

"Look who's joined us," Berdie announced, still linked in Chad's arm. Dave stepped onto the stone-flagged terrace of the back garden, Berdie and Chad just behind.

"Hello, Dave," several greeted.

Tillie edged closer to Doug, Carl and Barbara nudged each other, while Lillie watched intently.

There was a brief tense moment that seemed to go forever.

"Good to see you again, Chad." Rollie extended his hand.

Chad graciously withdrew his arm from Berdie's clasp and shook Rollie's hand.

"Glad you've come," Hugh added.

"Yes, thank you," Chad stammered when he released Rollie's hand. The dark-haired fellow glanced about and took a deep breath. "I can understand how you may be surprised to see me here. Mrs. Elliott offered her gracious invitation and I accepted."

Everyone had stopped their chatter.

"And as many of you are aware, relations between the commander and I have been strained. It would be insincere to pretend otherwise."

Berdie clasped her hands together, working at appearing calm. What was this impulsive young man going to say?

Everyone was listening.

"But, going through all he has at this time, and still clinging to life, it would appear Providence has dealt the man a winning hand, at least so far, and who am I to dispute Providence?" Chad paused. "Well, that's it, really."

"Well said, old friend," Dave commended Chad. "And I, for one, want to celebrate that winning hand of Providence with a Pimm's and some of that delicious terrine."

"Oh, yes," Berdie urged, "everyone tuck in,

please."

The group returned to their casual chitchat and Berdie gave a silent *thank you* to the One who always hears.

"Can I interest you in some canapés?" Lillie asked Chad, extending the tray. She also offered a generous smile.

Kindness in action, Berdie thought.

He took an appetizer. "They look quite good," he offered politely.

"Pimm's on the table, just there." Lillie pointed.

Berdie took in the back garden prepared for this evening by her and her helpful crew: Lillie, Barbara, and Carl Braunhoff. Fairy lights looked like miniature stars caught in the branches of several smaller trees. Lanterns edged the garden walk as the scent of climbing roses and the blooming hawthorn splashed their fragrance into the evening air. The soft tones of a crooner, from memorable days gone past, lilted cross the garden from a portable speaker. The filled Pimm's glasses, laden with bits of floating fruit, sat atop a draped garden table. They caught the flickering light of hurricane candles in their sparkling bubbles. Dinner waited warmly, ready to be served at the gracious dining table inside.

And then there was that lovely moon, just taking on a glow that seemed to say all was well. It was almost unimaginable to think that, only days ago, a most horrific event occurred so near this spot.

Berdie watched Hugh as he finished a conversation with Barbara. For a rare moment, he stood alone.

In her university days, when she met Hugh, it was as if wild horses pulled her to him the moment he came in view. It wasn't just his height, golden hair, or even his dazzling blue eyes that she found unavoidably attractive. It was his confidence and his palpable faithful character. She could still hear those distant hooves pounding away madly, drawing her to him.

She walked toward the man she loved as the wild neighs of the thundering herd became louder. She stopped unusually close to him. "Are you enjoying your evening?" she asked. She leaned in, almost touching him, to be sure he caught the scent of his favorite perfume that she wore. Berdie dipped her chin and looked up into his intent gaze. She took his hand. "Are you enjoying yourself?"

It was almost as if she could see the frost that coated his shoulder evaporate into the moonlit air.

"Berdie, if you think you can tempt me and work your tender charms to get round me…"

"Yes?"

"Well"—Hugh gave her an easy grin—"you're probably right."

Berdie smiled.

Hugh squeezed her hand. "As a matter of fact, you look stunning this evening, love."

Berdie squeezed his hand back.

"And this dinner-party idea of yours was just what we needed to get past the events of recent days. It gives us time to catch our breath. I appreciate all the work you've put into it."

"Thank you, Hugh." Berdie's words were butter.

"And, truth be told, I'm pleased that you helped the Raheems, but I'm not pleased with your, umm, creative way of doing it."

"All behind us now," Berdie purred.

"You're a marvel, you know, a brilliant hostess" — he touched a finger to her cheek — "and a beautiful wife."

"Reverend Elliott," a small voice cracked, "I have a question to ask you."

Hugh, caught slightly off-guard, released Berdie's hand and turned to face the interrupter.

Natty Bell, known in the village as Batty Natty and looking slightly younger than her seventy-something years, stood by Hugh. Her hair was somewhat flighty, a bit like her mind, but she was well turned out in a lovely dress. She begged Hugh's attention.

Berdie half winked at Hugh. "Hold that thought. I'll just excuse myself."

She stepped aside and made her way to Rollie and Joan.

"Did Lillie offer you some canapés?" she asked.

"Oh yes. They're so good." Joan's pink-colored lips made her short white-blonde hair seem to glow.

Though Rollie was tall, his wife, a devoted homemaker, was of average height and build for her middle age. Though rather ordinary in appearance, she possessed a far-above-average appetite for books and reading.

"You know, I just finished reading *Entertaining in the British Home*. It had the history of canapés and wonderful recipes. I think these little cheese things were in it." She nibbled a bite from one. "I must copy that recipe out before returning the book to the library."

"Um, tasty," Rollie agreed, brushing a pastry flake from his lip, "only do remember to take my book back when you go as well."

"I noticed you reading at the hospital the other

day, Rollie," Berdie commented.

"That's the one." Rollie took a sip of Pimm's. "*Cloak of Deception* by one S. N. Flow. Nom de plume, no doubt."

"*Cloak of Deception*," Berdie repeated, thinking. "Oh yes, somewhat popular then. Tillie's reading that book as well."

"Tillie?" Rollie only just swallowed his sip of drink down. "Why would Tillie read something like that?"

"I started it," Joan said, "but just a few pages into it, and that was enough to put me off it."

"I told her she wouldn't like it," Rollie said with vigor. "Still, she had to give it a go. Too technical and too much blood, you said. I could have told you."

"Oh, I have no interest in wartime exposés and such."

"Wartime exposés, too much blood?" Berdie thought Tillie had said the book was a mystery.

Joan waggled her finger. "I've read other exposés that I quite liked. But this one, no. Give me a good historic romance or I'll even go a decent suspense, if you please, but not that gore."

"Now, had you said Doug was reading it, I could have understood it," Rollie countered. "Right up our street."

"Tillie said something about it being required reading for an online class she's taking," Berdie recalled out loud.

"What kind of class is that then?" Joan asked. "How to Wreck and Ruin in Five Easy Steps?"

"So it's a class on parliamentary goings-on," Rollie wagged.

Berdie found Rollie amusing, but she also had to wonder why Tillie told her it was a mystery.

Hugh tapped his Pimm's glass with a spoon. "May I have your attention, please? I believe we're all gathered now. I have something special to tell you."

Expectation danced around the garden as everyone became still.

Hugh's tone was light. "As most of you know, Sparks, the commander's dog who was trained in explosives detection, was spared a second time. He was brought to the commander's bedside in a rather farfetched chance, an attempt, if you like, to help Cedric along in his battle for life."

Berdie caught the stare Tillie riveted upon Chad, who exchanged his empty Pimm's glass for a filled one.

Hugh took a deep breath. "Well, in addition to an entire congregation praying for our friend, it would seem the arrival of Sparks has worked a sort of miracle. Cedric's vital signs have stabilized, and the prognosis has become more hopeful."

Grateful cheers sounded like celebratory bubbles popping throughout the group.

"Now, he's not out of the woods yet. There needs to be far more improvement before they can remove him from the critical list, but there's something positive to report at last. Since most my day has been spent in catching up on my church work, I wasn't at the hospital at the time. But Loren, Dr. Meredith, can tell us more about it."

"It's quite remarkable," Loren responded. "Had I not seen it myself, I'm not at all sure I would have believed it, but there it is."

"What happened?" Joan asked on behalf of all.

Loren snapped to. "I got word that the commander appeared to be losing ground. Sparks had arrived, and although he was to go home after a few hours, he refused to leave his master's side."

"Faithful old thing," Barbara whispered, just audible.

"Mr. Hayling, who works in animal therapy treatment, had Sparks stand up. With one leg in a cast, old Sparks had to really work at it, but with help, the dog was up. The therapist thought to put Sparks actually on the bed, so between the two of us, we lifted the creature and laid him next Cedric."

"He's a large dog. That couldn't have been easy," Carl noted.

"Sparks, for all the ferocious behavior he's shown, was like a spring lamb. He let us handle him with not so much as a growl."

"Amazing." Rollie said aloud what Berdie thought.

Loren placed his straightened hand against the glass he held. "Sparks lay right next the commander, close against his body, and put his chin on the old fellow's thigh." Loren moved his hand on top of the glass. "Mr. Hayling placed Cedric's hand on Sparks's head. The dog lay quite still, as if aware of his duty to help."

Loren paused and looked at the lush grass beneath his feet as if a vision of the event played across the blades, then raised his eyes to the group.

"Just a bit after, I noticed that the commander's breathing had become less labored. I asked Mr. Hayling if he had noticed it too. 'Yes,' he said with confidence. I could scarcely believe it. Then we both realized that his vital signs became less irregular, more consistent, his stats, numbers, reflecting an improvement."

Loren stopped again and shook his head.

"It was as if some kind of unconscious awareness stirred within him. Astonishing. Anyway, it appears he's making progress."

"Thank God," Barbara praised.

"And much is to be said for the thinking outside the box by the hospital staff that allowed Sparks to be brought in," Loren finished.

Hugh lifted his glass. "To God's creation and the wonders He performs."

All raised their glasses in a salute.

"Large dogs and small miracles," Rollie reiterated. "I must admit, I wouldn't have ever described that animal as a spring lamb in even the loosest of terms."

Laughter bounced, along with a few not-so-amused raised brows.

"All in all, the news couldn't be better," Tillie chimed. Her long blonde strands danced in loose curls that stood in rich contrast to the tasteful little black summer dress that adorned her svelte figure.

The young woman made her way toward Berdie as conversations ensued amongst the guests.

"It sets you at ease, doesn't it, good news?" Tillie observed.

"How blessed are the feet of those who bring good news," Berdie affirmed.

"Feet?" Tillie eyed Hugh's shoes. "Really?"

Berdie chuckled. "Yes. Really."

Tillie rubbed her finger round the rim of the glass she held. "I understand you found that young man, the suspect in the bombing, who's related to the greengrocer."

"A gift of divine timing was at work, but yes, Lillie and I found him."

"You're good at that kind of thing?"

"Some would say." Berdie smiled.

"Not to take the polish off the glow, but I've been thinking that there's something no one seems to have considered in this whole mess with the commander's mishap, and I was wondering if it may have crossed your mind."

Chad, who stood nearby, took in Tillie's pensive air.

"What is it?" Berdie asked.

"Well, my father said that Sparks sat down in front of the vehicle on that fateful afternoon."

"Yes, I saw him," Berdie confirmed.

"That means the dog was aware of explosive material—he must have smelled it. When a trained canine smells that kind of material about, they sit down as a signal."

"Yes."

"The commander knew that was the signal of danger. I mean, he had been in the military. So, why did he proceed to drive the vehicle?"

"I have thought about that, and I think it can be explained." Berdie wondered just where Tillie was going with this train of thought.

"Excuse me, I couldn't help but overhear, Tillie," Chad interjected. "I think I know what you're suggesting."

"Yes," Tillie went on. "Why send the children away from the vehicle, but carry on himself?"

"Right. Dave wondered the same thing"—Chad nodded—"and it pulled me up short when I realized what he was pointing out."

"I heard my name. Should my ears be burning?" Dave said.

"Sparks signaling the commander about the explosives," Chad said to his friend. "Tillie's asking the same question you did about what could be a possible motive for him to carry on."

"Oh." Dave's smile faded.

"Motive? What are you talking about?" Berdie knitted her brows.

"Was he aware that explosives were there?" Tillie asked with intent.

"Sparks had sustained a war injury to the smell sensors in his nose," Berdie informed them. "He was going to be put down because of it. I can only imagine the commander thought Sparks's detection sense was off, not functioning properly, but nevertheless sent the children away from the van as a safe measure. Why should he suspect dangerous materials in a church people carrier in a small village?"

"Possibly, but I think what Tillie's asking is, did the commander, well, had he given up?" Dave clarified.

"Given up?" Berdie felt warmth rush to her cheeks when she realized what the three were trying to say. "No."

"To be fair, Mrs. Elliott," Tillie went on, "his wife had died, he no longer had a proper job, and then there was his estrangement from Avril, his only child. By any standards, he was in a pretty dark place."

"Even if that's true, there's dozens of ways someone could do themselves in that would be a far easier and more effective means than explosives."

"What's this about explosives?" Rollie joined into the conversation.

"Cedric was in deep water," Berdie agreed as she widened her eyes, "but he wasn't the type of man to cash in his own chips."

"What?" Rollie all but roared.

Berdie could see this conversation gaining momentum, and she didn't want to give it any more life than it already had. "I can see how you may consider things from that dark perspective, but I truly believe the commander didn't have that self-destructive nature. In fact, I'll go out on a limb and say it's simply not the case."

Tillie, Dave, and Chad made skeptical eye contact with one another that Berdie tried hard to ignore while Rollie frowned.

"Perhaps this isn't the time or place to discuss this," Dave offered.

"Yes, I think you're right, Dave." Rollie looked a bit piqued.

Berdie extended her hand toward the back door. "Besides, it's time for our dinner."

"Well, I, for one, am hungry," Rollie answered.

"Let's make way into the dining room," Berdie urged.

"I'm not one to say no to food that smells delicious," Dave piped.

Within minutes, Hugh had offered grace and food and drink were being consumed with relish by all round the dining-room table.

Berdie enjoyed all the compliments on the food, which she redirected to Lillie and Loren, who had actually done most the cooking. Lamb cutlets with fresh mint sauce were the star of the main course, and dessert waited. In fact, Loren was in the midst of disclosing his secret mint-sauce recipe when the front doorbell rang.

Berdie caught Hugh's eye. "Well, we've made it

through the lion's share of the meal," she said discreetly to Hugh, who laid his napkin aside.

He stood. "Excuse me, I shouldn't be a moment."

Loren went on with his conversation, and general chitchat ensued. Berdie finally wondered, after a little while, if perhaps she should join Hugh. Though she was very aware of his absence, it seemed others paid it no mind.

But they noticed his arrival back to the dining room.

Hugh brought with him two people unknown to Berdie.

The couple reminded her of some sort of Bedouins, in from the desert. The handsome young man with dark features seemed a bit distant, even while standing just feet from the table, and not just because he appeared to be foreign. His dark eyes flitted about the room with a cool calculation. The slender young woman wore denims and a loosely fitted top. Sandy brown hair peeked out at the forehead from under her head-covering shawl that reached her elbows. Her pale eyes were somehow familiar.

"We have guests," Hugh announced.

Everyone took the couple in.

"Avril?" Tillie gawked.

"Tillie, I didn't know you were here," the young woman spurted.

Berdie, when she finally gathered her lips from their agape position, struggled for words. "Avril, welcome to our home. We're so pleased you've come." Berdie found her feet.

"And this is Mr. Aydin. Kabil Aydin," Hugh introduced.

"Mr. Aydin, welcome." Berdie smiled.

The young man's natural downward draw at the corner of his lips gave him an ominous appearance. His eyes skirted her stare. He nodded.

"Can we see to your bags?" Berdie asked.

"No, no. We're staying at the B and B on the square." Avril rubbed her hand on her trouser leg.

"That's where Dad and I are staying." Tillie rose and went to her friend as all watched what was unfolding.

The two women exchanged a brief hug.

"I'm glad you're here, Avril, but I'm so sorry for the reason you've come."

Avril's eyes revealed little sympathy.

"When did you arrive?"

"Just. We dropped our bags at the inn and came here. You remember Kabil, Tillie."

"Yes," Tillie said. Had the word been spoken any cooler, it could have iced the Pimm's.

Kabil dipped his chin but lifted his eyes to stare, motionless. "Tillie," he said with a foreign accent Berdie didn't clearly recognize.

"It was Kabil who prompted me to come." Avril wrapped her arm around the young man's.

Tillie raised her brows and Kabil glanced at the floor.

"Please, Avril, will you and Kabil join us for some dinner?" Berdie prompted. "You must be hungry after your travel."

"Turkish Airlines doesn't have outstanding food, but we ate on the flight. So, thank you, no."

"Turkish Airlines?" Joan repeated with distinct surprise.

Avril's eyes danced from Joan to Hugh. "Actually, we had hoped to go to the hospital straightaway."

"Of course," Hugh obliged. "I'll be glad to take you there immediately." He glanced at Loren, who nodded affirmatively and pushed his chair out from the table.

"I'll go as well," Dave said. "Chad, are you OK to come?"

Chad sighed. "You're driving, chum."

Tillie looked at her father. "Can you manage your own way to the B and B, Dad?"

"We'll see to it," Berdie assured.

"I'm coming with you, Avril." Tillie swept past Kabil. "I'll just get my handbag."

"Really, you needn't all come." Avril glanced about.

"Nonsense. Rollie and I said we were going to go visit the commander this evening anyway," Joan added, placing her napkin on the table. "Didn't we, love?"

Rollie stuffed one more bite of lamb in his mouth. "As you say, Joan."

With the speed of a springhare caught in alarming fright, half the party departed and the other half found it difficult to absorb what had just happened.

"Avril," Berdie said half to herself as she and Lillie took partially empty plates to the kitchen. "I wonder what made her change her mind about coming."

"And Kabil," Lillie added. "What's he doing here anyway? He seems ill at ease at best."

Plates clanked as Berdie placed them in the sink. "You're right, Lillie. Something's off. It just doesn't smell right."

"You and Sparks," Lillie barbed. "When has your nose for trouble ever been wrong?"

11

"Seconds, anyone, more strawberry mousse?" Berdie queried.

"I got it, I did," Batty Natty squealed and placed the two-dotted domino flush against the two-dotted domino on the games table. "I'm on a winner," she giggled.

"Indeed," Carl Braunhoff said, "you are."

"No thank you, Mrs. Elliott"—Barbara held up her hand—"the mousse was excellent, but I'm full to bursting."

"There are no more dominoes," Natty interrupted and moved her hands over the table space nearest her. "Oh dear."

"That's right, Natty." Carl pointed to the dominoes in play. "You played the last one. You've won the game."

Natty gasped. "Oh, I say," she offered with a very large grin, "isn't that a treat? I've won."

Carl half smirked and drew the dominoes into a heap.

"Again, again," Natty sputtered while clapping her aging hands in soft pats.

"You should buy a ticket for the pools, Natty, love," Berdie cheered and put the empty dessert dishes on her tray.

"Another game then," Barbara announced with

less than enthusiasm.

"I'll just finish tidying up," Berdie excused.

She entered the lowly lit kitchen, where the sound of the dishwasher sloshed its happy way through its evening-with-guests workout.

She carefully placed the crystal dessert dishes in a sink laden with suds and wiped the tray.

Events have certainly taken an unexpected turn this evening, Berdie thought. Half the crowd gone, there were just a few that stayed on to enjoy afters and one another's company. Even Lillie scurried home early, only after agreeing to meet Berdie at the Copper Kettle in the morning.

Feeling in need of a quiet moment, Berdie poured herself a cup of tea, added a splash of milk plus a teaspoon of sugar, and sat at the small kitchen table by the window. The cool of evening air filtered through the open window and soothed her busy-hostess warmth. She was just able to make out a familiar voice coming from the back terrace.

"I noticed you put that CD in the player. It's the newest Annaclare. Is it yours?" Sandra asked.

"You're familiar with Annaclare?" Doug sounded unusually relaxed.

"She's just my absolute favorite."

"Oh. Mine as well."

Sandra began to sing in clear tone what sounded to be a Scottish air with a contemporary edge, *"In the ebb and flow of love that lies from you to me."* She paused.

"We dance in the waves," Doug added in a strangled voice.

"For the sea will always be the sea," they sang in unison, then laughed together unapologetically.

Berdie thought it rather sweet. There was a

momentary hesitation, and she wondered if this was the point where Doug would nonchalantly slip his arm onto the back of Sandra's chair.

"I love late-spring evenings. Isn't it a lovely night?" Sandra's voice was as light as whipped butter.

"Truthfully?" Doug asked. "Give me the bright light of day anytime."

"Even on a beautiful moonlit night like tonight?"

"Even on a beautiful moonlit night like tonight. The dark is an unwelcomed companion."

Berdie could hear Doug stir a bit.

"Sometimes it feels like morning will never arrive." His voice was hushed.

Berdie remembered his torment the night of the explosion.

"I discovered an antidote to wrestling with the dark, well, sleeplessness," Sandra said.

"And what is that?"

"I sneak out to the garden and gaze at the stars. Their diamond sparkle trumps the dark," she lilted. "The Creator Himself is visible in the twinkling skies, you know. It's very calming."

"I've never thought of it that way."

"Oh yes, nights can be glorious," Sandra buzzed. "Did you know that God calls the stars by name?"

"Is that so?"

"Yes." Sandra had a playful edge to her words. "Now, take that little one, just there near the horizon. Perhaps that one's Shirley."

Doug chuckled and Sandra joined him.

Berdie leaned toward the window.

"Shirley, you say. Well then, I fancy that one over there could be Bob."

The two now gently laughed, and there was a

pause.

"I can tell you this," Doug said. "This grand, bright one, right overhead, do you see it?"

"Oh yes."

"It *must* be called Sandra."

Berdie shook her head and grinned at Doug's gallant attempt to be romantic. But it mattered little what she thought. Would Sandra find it off-putting, or perhaps charming? Berdie heard Sandra give a slight titter.

"I made you blush." Doug went on. "Did you know Annaclare is in concert this Sunday evening in Timsley?"

"Is she?"

"I have tickets. *Two* tickets," Doug declared. "I thought for Tillie to come, but she's not a fan and cried off. So…"

"Yes, I'd love to," Sandra jumped in.

"Sunday night then."

Without warning, footsteps lumbered in from the hall and the full dazzle of white kitchen light flicked on.

"Natty's begun to doze between turns at dominoes, and I'm seeing little white dots before my eyes. I think it's time we all went home," Barbara Braunhoff said with voluble zip.

Berdie drew up from the table, half wanting to shush Barbara so she could continue listening to the love story developing out her window and half agreeing with Barbara's suggestion.

"I've some hot tea ready if you'd care for a cuppa before you go," Berdie responded.

"I shouldn't think so." Barbara smiled. "It's really quite time for us to move along."

Doug and Sandra entered the kitchen by the back door.

"Is Aunt Natty tiring?" Sandra asked Barbara.

"Her dominoes victory has left her knackered, I'd say."

"I'm sure she's enjoyed your company, both you and Carl. Let me thank you on her behalf." Sandra hurried through the kitchen, Doug trailing behind her.

"We treasure Natty." Barbara opened the kitchen door to the hallway for the two stargazers.

"Thank you for entertaining us," Sandra directed to Berdie.

Berdie sighed, wishing for their sakes that Sandra and Doug could have had just a bit more time alone together, but they had Sunday evening. "So very pleased you came."

"It's been wonderful." Doug had a special sparkle in his eye.

"I'm glad to take Doug, Mr. Devlin, to his lodgings," Sandra volunteered. "And I'll tuck Aunt Natty in as soon as I get her home, of course."

"Yes, very good. Thank you, Sandra. I'm sorry things were cut short at dinner," Berdie apologized.

"Oh, not at all. As it turns out, it was all quite wonderful." Sandra grinned.

Berdie saw her guests to the door. Doug, Sandra, and Natty were gone when Carl paused before stepping out into the moonlit night.

"Thank you, Mrs. Elliott. And well done. Good memories were made in the back garden tonight to replace tarnished ones from recent events."

"Thank you for saying so, Carl." Berdie truly appreciated this shy, gentle giant. "God go with you."

As she watched Carl and Barbara launch out on

Church Road to begin their walk home, Berdie looked back on the evening. It created a fine memory, yes, but full of surprises at every turn. Chad's pluck, that ominous book *Cloak of Deception*, Tillie's fresh take on the commander with a "doing-himself-in" suggestion, Doug and Sandra finding their way to one another, and then there was the interrupted meal with Avril's arrival and her man in tow.

"Indeed," Berdie breathed, "God go with us all, wherever the road may now be heading."

****

Berdie held the closed umbrella against her spring-blue cardigan that chased away the morning chill and eyed the sky while making her way down the High Street. Last night had been so clear, but the light of day brought sagging gray clouds and a distinct scent that spoke of coming rain.

"Mrs. Elliott." A fellow villager nodded to Berdie, wearing a slight smirk as he passed her. She wondered if that smirk was significant.

Hugh's plans for the day meant Berdie could get on with her own activities, apart from visiting the commander in hospital this afternoon.

Hugh mentioned he would call at the home of Mrs. Hall by way of going to hospital. Village accounts had her in dreadful pain that needed further oral surgery, a discouraging development that Hugh hoped to ease. Berdie wondered if Mrs. Hall's nephew, Mr. Stuart Hall, would buy his Aunt Dora another posy of flowers to ease the news as well. The rest of Hugh's day would be divided between time with Cedric and another rowing practice.

At the moment, not only Lillie, but also steaming tea and fresh morning rolls awaited at the Copper Kettle. It was a relished opportunity to process information with her dear Watson. Berdie's investigative mind was gaining momentum.

Boyish laughter pulled her attention across the road where Milton Butz and Kevin McDermott had heads together. Whispers ensued.

What on earth are those two rogues about? Berdie wondered.

When the two saw her, they took steps to cross the road in Berdie's direction.

"Hello, Mrs. Elliott," Milton greeted. His sunshine stood in stark contrast to the gray sky.

"Hello, lads." Berdie smiled. She halted. "Isn't it time you were in school?"

"We are," Kevin offered. "That is to say, we're running an errand for Mr. Dud Head." Kevin wrapped his hand over his mouth.

"He means Mr. Dudham, our science teacher," Milton explained. "We were using isopropyl alcohol as part of a before-school lab experiment, and Cassie Lewis spilled the lot."

"It went everywhere." Kevin spread his arms out. "The entire room will be ashes if there's even a hint of flame anywhere."

"So, Mr. Dudham sent us to Joe's DIY to get some powder to soak it up and more alcohol so everyone can try the experiment again."

"I see." Berdie glanced in the direction of the shop to which they were going and then at the two boys. Stillness followed—odd for these two.

"Go on, Milty," Kevin urged. He nodded toward Berdie.

Milton wrinkled his nose at Kevin. "OK. Hold your horses."

Berdie lifted her brows in anticipation.

"Kevin was wondering," Milton began and hesitated. "It's just that, well..."

"Well, what?" Berdie encouraged.

"Did you have to slop out?" Kevin spurted.

"Slop out?" Berdie reared.

"When you were in the prison cell," Milton finished. "You know, did they make you dispose of your own..."

"Yes, I know what *slop out* means," Berdie said with a touch of impatience. "But I've never been to prison. Why should you think...?"

"You haven't?" Kevin's eyes grew large. "But the other day, near London, they said."

Berdie became aware of just why they had asked such an unusually personal, and thick, question. Word of her excursion to the police station on Wednesday must have hit the village jungle drums and it had spiraled out beyond all recognition. The vicar's wife had been imprisoned.

She wanted to yell, "You've the wrong end of the stick entirely. How do things get so out of hand, and why on earth would you even believe such a thing? And as far as the supposed prison practice of slopping out, the practice was discontinued in 1993. Plus, I must say, what impertinence."

But she gathered herself to give a statement of simple facts. "I'm not sure who *they* are, lads, those who misunderstood and mistakenly said I was locked up, but I can assure you, nothing of the kind happened. I simply answered a few questions for a respectable policeman concerning a case of mistaken identity. And it all took place at the police station in a very well-kept office that was clean and tidy."

"See," Milton nearly bellowed at Kevin, "I told you it wasn't likely."

"Well, thank you, Milton," Berdie said, hoping neither boy would spot the slight clench of her jaw.

Kevin was red faced and dragging his toe back and forth.

"Now you both know the truth." Berdie said it generally, but she directed the comment to Kevin. "No more silly talk."

Milton and Kevin nodded rather sheepishly.

"I should think Mr. Dudham is waiting for those supplies."

"Come along, Kevin," Milton commanded.

The two scurried toward Joe's shop.

Berdie tried to refocus, making a forward motion toward the tea shop. Setting the record straight on this rumor could take a bit of work, but she was already rolling up her metaphorical shirtsleeves to take on the task.

Chief Inspector Kent exited the Copper Kettle, sipping from a Styrofoam cup, with a bulging white bag in the other hand. His weathered coat bore the signs of constant wear along with a sprinkling of pastry crumbs. "Ah, Mrs. Elliott, good morning."

"Good morning, Chief Inspector."

"You're quite the topic of conversation in there." A slight smirk appeared while he nodded in the shop's direction.

"I can only imagine." Berdie took a deep breath and slowly blew air through her pursed lips.

"Just to let you know, I did put in a good word to the gossip-in-chief, Mrs. Horn, is it? I told her that you're quite an investigator and you've been nothing but helpful to the police."

Berdie held her shoulders straight and sighed.

"Speaking of helpful," Jasper Kent went on, "Sundeep scarpered off just after you left him in Slough, but we quickly caught up with him. The lad's in police custody. He's still saying he's innocent, though he admitted that his last delivery route included Old Barn Road, you know, the supposed address of the place your husband tried to find."

"Old Barn Road?" Berdie had a brain buzz. "Have you found his mobile?"

"Probably in some rubbish bin, but Constable Goodnight was keen on the mobile bit, so we assigned that search to him."

Berdie gaped.

"We felt it was a good match with his skill set."

"Skill set? You mean you wanted him out of your hair."

"Brice has assigned one of his trainees to the task as well, just keeping it low on Goodnight's radar."

"Well, I hope it's found, for Sundeep's sake. It could be the evidence to prove his innocence."

"You still believe he's not guilty."

"I do."

He tipped his head. "I'm beginning to wonder. His profile doesn't fit the crime, but is he telling us everything? I must admit, though, it feels we're chasing smoke."

"I should imagine," Berdie agreed.

Kent took a sip of what smelled to be fresh coffee. "Truthfully, things in this case aren't nearly cut and dry enough."

"How's that?"

"My head's bruised and aching from all the brick walls I've hit against."

Berdie felt a sense of disappointment. This was not the news she hoped for.

"We're missing something." Kent pressed his lips together. "My teammate and his techno toys, ready to save the world, and yet we're still missing something."

Berdie decided to speculate, though she could hardly let go the words. "Have you considered that perhaps the commander's misfortune was self-inflicted?"

"Odd you should say that," Kent mumbled. "With two and two making up three, we've begun questioning in that general area as well. Stupid way for the old fellow to go about things though."

"Practically, it just doesn't make much sense," Berdie concurred.

"What made you think of it?"

"Someone brought it up to me. They pointed out that Cedric was quite low, had a dismal family life, wife gone, retirement bringing a sense of loss, that kind of thing."

"And?"

"Well, it's so out of character for him. He's a soldier, a fighter, a man of integrity. I daresay, and most convincingly, should he consider that kind of act, he would jolly well do it quickly and cleanly so as to be sure the job was done properly."

"Yes, would do." Chief Inspector Kent took a large gulp from his cup and looked squarely at Berdie. "Our experts have good interview and analytical skills, probing techniques, and remarkable resources. But you have something we need: local knowledge."

Berdie felt a drop of rain on her cheek, then

another. "You are aware that the commander's estranged daughter arrived last evening? Her boyfriend, Turkish, I believe, has accompanied her from their apparent residence in that country."

Kent tapped a finger on his cup. "Your husband informed us last night. Intelligence operatives, even former ones that are now vicars, never lose the scent for something that smells fishy."

"And?"

"We're following it up." Kent didn't seem eager to expose any information on this drops-beginning-to-fall morning. "Well, time I got along."

Berdie glanced at the white bag that had the telltale scent of a blueberry muffin. "With the investigation or breakfast?"

"Both," Kent chirped. He paused. "You, if you don't mind me using the term, sit at the epicenter of this village. And I have the sense it's there, somehow, that the key to this whole thing may lie. So, keep your nose in, Berdie."

"Chief Inspector, I'm me. I live with my nose in."

Kent smiled. "We'll be in touch."

He stepped into the road and began a forward motion, little spats of rain decorating the landscape.

"God go with you," Berdie called to Kent.

He lifted his coffee as if in a toast to her blessing.

A sense of fresh and vital energy surged within her, despite the cool rain now splashing the ground. Chief Inspector Kent esteemed her a valuable resource. She knew that—he had said it many times—but at this moment, the truth of it took on real meaning. She felt the vigor of her discerning gifts pulse. She had a new vivacity of standing planted on her own investigative feet and kicked the idea that "my gift is faltering" to the curb. "Be prepared, Chief Inspector Kent," she said under her breath. "I'm going to solve this case!"

Berdie gathered her poise and entered the Copper Kettle. The entire tearoom became a din of low murmurs upon sight of her, with only the clatter of dishes in the back kitchen disturbing the tittle-tattle.

Berdie made sure her shoulders were straight, her stride confident, her chin properly poised, and her smile pleasant as she made way cross the shop to the tiny table where Lillie and a steam-spewing teapot awaited.

"You don't look to have prison pallor," Lillie teased softly when Berdie reached the table.

"And good morning to you as well." Berdie placed her umbrella against her chair with a thud and sat down.

Lillie poured milk from a floral-designed pitcher into the cup set for Berdie. "I see you in all-over institutional gray."

"What?"

She added a teaspoon of sugar. "With those little reformatory-issue shoes." She ran a finger up her arm. "And a grand tattoo: 'Don't mess with Mama.'"

"Ha, ha," Berdie said in a witty snap.

Lillie poured the hot tea into Berdie's cup. "Oh, come now, Berdie. What else can you do but laugh?"

"It's all very well for you." Berdie stirred her tea and took a quick sip. She glanced at a nearby table where she spied Mrs. Dora Hall, the oral-surgery sufferer. "I'll show you, Lillie, what else I can do. Two breakfast rolls and a very *public* private conversation."

Berdie stood and made way for the cash register. The clipping of her nicely polished shoes on the wooden floor was steady and solid until she stopped at the table where Mrs. Hall and a friend sat.

"Mrs. Hall, good morning. I'm glad to see you're enjoying a nice cuppa." She nodded to the guest seated with her and addressed Mrs. Hall. "Your nephew, Stuart, told me about your oral surgery while he was buying some flowers for you at the White Window Box."

Berdie could feel everyone's stares.

"Yes," Mrs. Hall acknowledged with a grand smile.

"Excuse me, but you don't seem to be in agony. It's just that my husband understood that you were really suffering and perhaps further surgery was in order. He's planning to call in later this morning."

"Oh my, no," Mrs. Hall said with some alarm. The woman, who was the chair of the local literary society, sent her camel-like eyes into a flutter and threw her brows heavenward. "He needn't come. Day of surgery was a bit rough, but I shouldn't say agony. There was never more surgical doings planned, never that."

Whispers from onlookers floated about the small room.

"Mind you, I have the odd twinge of pain now and again." Mrs. Hall rubbed her lower jaw. "But he needn't come. I'm much better, nearly all well."

"There you are." Berdie made every effort for her words to be clearly heard. "You're recovering just fine. Silly the way a simple event takes on a head of steam all its own, when in truth, it's nothing more than empty air. Some things do get exaggerated." Berdie shook her head. "You know, my simple interview with police near London was whipped up into my going to prison, if you can imagine."

Mrs. Hall went a bit pink. "Well, I never."

"No, I should think not." Berdie smiled. "Now, I'll tell Hugh that you're right as rain. And I'm genuinely pleased that you're better, Mrs. Hall."

"Thank you, Mrs. Elliott, I'm sure." Mrs. Hall grinned, the results of her oral surgery clearly on view.

Berdie wasn't sure there was such a thing as a group blush, but if there was, it happened that moment in the Copper Kettle.

And Villette Horn, at the cash register, was redder than most by the time Berdie stood before her.

"May we have two morning rolls, Mrs. Horn?" Berdie asked politely. "I know Lillie didn't ask for them when she placed her order, but I'm feeling quite peckish."

"I'll bring them straightway." Villette slipped meekly into the kitchen.

Berdie triumphantly returned to the table and all those present returned to speaking on other matters.

"You think you're so clever," Lillie cajoled as Berdie sat down.

"To quote the proverb, 'two birds, one stone.' And all done calmly and cordially."

"Hugh would be proud."

"I'd like to think so."

Villette bustled out the kitchen door, holding two pink plates, each filled with a large morning roll. At the same time, the shop bell jingled and the door opened. Natty and Sandra entered.

"Shells, bells, and little fishes." Villette smacked the rolls down before Berdie and Lillie.

"There's a problem?" Lillie ventured.

"Our Batty Natty is going to fuss and carry on. You just watch."

"How do you know that?" Berdie noticed Natty,

who looked round, then frowned.

"I can't keep the table she always sits at empty of customers on the off chance she'll come in," Villette huffed.

Sandra took Natty's hand, but the old woman was having none of it. Her eyes stayed on the man and woman who sat at *her* table. She shuffled her feet and fingered the edge of her damp raincoat.

"Look at her—she's a frightened lamb lost in the storm." Villette crossed her arms.

"There's an empty table, right near," Lillie pointed out.

"Oh yes, but she won't sit at it."

Berdie watched Sandra try to coax her aunt to the vacant spot. Natty refused to move, her bottom lip protruding like a perch on a birdhouse.

"How can she possibly expect the table to be empty anytime she chooses?" Villette was piqued. "Does she consult Madame Baltazar before she leaves home?"

"Mrs. Horn," Berdie quipped. "Madame Baltazar? Such foolishness."

"But you must admit, Berdie, it is an unfair expectation," Lillie countered.

Berdie felt a bolt of lightning strike her brain, a sizzle of fresh realization, and it wasn't from the storm outside.

She grabbed the edge of the table. "What did you say, Lillie?"

"I said that Natty can't expect the table to be available every—"

"That's it," Berdie almost yelled. "Lillie, you're a genius."

"Am I?"

"Is she?" Villette echoed.

"Something missing, Old Barn Road, smoke: If it walks like a duck. And that's the truth."

Lillie and Villette stared at Berdie.

"My dear Lillie, you've hit the nail on the head."

"What are you on about?" Villette asked.

"Lillie, we've *got* to find Sundeep's mobile."

"What? How?"

"Mrs. Horn, please bag the rolls." Berdie grabbed her umbrella.

"But I've only just brought them."

"Berdie?" Now Lillie looked like a lost sheep. "What on earth?"

"Old Barn Road," Berdie zipped, "we're going to Old Barn Road."

Villette took the roll-laden plates up. "And I thought Batty Natty was barmy." She hustled off.

"Why are we going to Old Barn Road? It's raining, and besides, I'm hungry."

"Eat on the way, Lillie. We'll take care of some business, walk to the church, and take the Edsel and Sons work van from there." Berdie jumped from her seat. "Quickly."

"Are you sure we can use the work van for something that isn't church related?" Lillie stood and buttoned her coat.

"Oh, but it is church related, my dear Lillie. It most certainly is."

12

Outside the Copper Kettle, Berdie and Lillie ran headlong into the crowd gathered at the Meat Mobile, an invention created by Mr. Raheem in conjunction with Cathcart Carlisle farm. An old ice-cream van had been converted into a mobile butcher's shop that parked in front of Raheem's grocery store twice weekly. It was a win-win for both the businessmen and the community. They sold high-quality food at knockdown prices. And despite the rain, plus bumping umbrellas, the road was full of customers.

"Lillie"—Berdie quickstepped her way through the crowd with Lillie behind—"go ask Mr. Raheem just what stops Sundeep was to make on his delivery run last Saturday. Get as much detail as you can."

"Right. OK. I'm sure he's extremely busy, but I'll do my best. And what are you doing?"

"Jumping the queue."

While Lillie pushed through to the grocer's shop, Berdie planted herself at the side of the villager currently getting her order at the Meat Mobile service window.

"There you are, Mrs. LaGrange." Bill Carlisle handed the woman a full-to-bursting carrier bag.

"Thanks, Mr. Carlisle."

The middle-aged man, who wore upon his skin the endless hours of working his stock outdoors, gazed upon Berdie.

"Mrs. Elliott, and how are things at the vicarage?"

"Better, thank you, Bill."

Bill shifted his eyes to the gentleman who was next in the queue. He held an umbrella with one hand and read the folded *Kirkwood Gazette* in the other. The fellow nodded his head.

"So what you be needin'?" Bill asked Berdie.

"Kind of you," Berdie thanked the customer behind as she squeezed to the service window. "I'll be quick, as I'm on a mercy dash," she explained. "Actually, I need some information. Can you tell me who lives next your farm on Old Barn Road?"

"Arthur Georgeson and his family. Why?"

"No one named Bryant?"

"The Georgesons have been on that land for years."

"There's nothing between your farm and his farm?"

"No. Constable Goodnight asked the same thing, and some young Yard detective as well, just a couple days back. I told them just what I've told you." Bill Carlisle wiped his hands on his bloodstained work apron.

Berdie heard a woman's muffled voice come from somewhere inside the vehicle.

"What?" Bill bellowed.

Mrs. Carlisle stuck her head round her husband's shoulder. Her straight hair framed the sun-kissed face that sported just a blush of lipstick. "Arthur Georgeson's cousin has that summer cottage, sits down the field in the wood," she touted.

"His cousin sold that place years back. Been abandoned. None but hedgehogs living in that hovel, and that's if they're not picky," Bill grumbled.

His wife bristled. "Farley Moss said he saw someone working on it a few months ago, and they were doing it up for a holiday let."

"Well, I didn't see anyone," Bill argued. "And Farley always has his gob in, doesn't know what he's talking about half the time. Besides, you get to that spot off Littlewoods Lane."

The buxom woman came from behind her husband. "There's that track, goes back there from Old Barn."

"No, there isn't."

Mrs. Carlisle's lips tightened. "You tellin' me I'm blind and thick?"

"Now, I didn't say that, Stella."

The woman tipped her head out the window toward Berdie. "There's a winding track goes back from the hedgerow on Old Barn Road, overgrown, but it's there. A gatepost and gate right there. Hard to see, yes, and seldom used, but there you go." The woman pulled back to face her husband. "And don't you say otherwise, Bill Carlisle."

The man behind Berdie cleared his throat and someone farther down the queue shouted, "What's taking so long?"

"Both of you have been tremendously helpful," Berdie said, hoping to restore peace. "And I'll take two pounds of your fresh beef mince, please," she requested almost apologetically.

"Right you are, Mrs. Elliott." Bill got right to it.

Berdie smiled at the fellow behind her. "Thank you again."

The man lowered his paper and simply offered a pasted smile that may have just as well been a bee sting in return.

Bill handed Berdie the packaged mince while his wife disappeared again. "It's added to the slate," he quipped.

"Good. Thank you," Berdie rushed. "God go with you."

She trudged toward the greengrocers and found Lillie just outside.

"I've spoken with Mr. Raheem. Let's get out of this mob," Lillie insisted.

"The sooner the better," Berdie agreed. "We're on a mission."

****

"This is Old Barn Road, and the Cathcart Carlisle farm is over there." Berdie tried to point while driving the work van on the narrow, single carriageway country lane.

"Yes, we've established that," Lillie said with an edge in her voice. "Slow down some—the rain makes it difficult to see."

"If I go any slower, we won't be moving at all." Berdie glanced out her window. "Now, the Georgesons are at the very bottom of this road."

"Berdie, this is at least the fourth time we've had this conversation." Lillie took the last bite of her morning roll. "There are no gaps or gates in the hedgerow."

"There has to be. Mrs. Carlisle said."

"OK. Let's go over this again from the top. Mr. Raheem said the delivery request Saturday was for the full grocery box to be left on Old Barn Road, next to the Carlisle property, at the gatepost that had a long white ribbon tied to it."

"Yes. That's the gatepost Mrs. Carlisle referred to, I'm sure."

"No white ribbon. Do you see one? It's not there." Lillie took a breath. "Mr. Raheem stated that the request for the itemized list of food came by post, prepaid cash, no return address, with those specific instructions: a white ribbon."

"Well, perhaps they only have the ribbon attached for special situations. Does that look like a possible gap?" Berdie opened her window and pointed to a spot she hoped might be a break in the tight scramble of bush that constituted the hedgerow.

Lillie didn't even glance toward the indicated direction. "Mrs. Carlisle said it was a holiday let, right? If this building even exists, the people who wanted the food could have come and gone by now."

"Rather coy, secretive even, and a white ribbon? That does *not* sound like holidaymakers." Berdie stomped on the brakes, lurching Lillie forward.

"What are you doing, Berdie?"

"There's a lay-by here." Berdie swung the van onto the small patch of dirt at the side of the road. "Sundeep had to walk the hedgerow to find the post, and that's when he lost his phone, I'm sure of it. We've got to walk it too. Let's set to, Lillie."

"It's raining."

"Well spotted, Watson."

"My trousers are dry-clean only. I don't want to ruin them in the rain, and I haven't boots. My shoes aren't made to scramble about in wet weeds."

Berdie eyed Lillie's clothing. "That's a poor choice for being out on a rainy day."

"If you remember," Lillie whipped, "I dressed this

morning to meet you at the Copper Kettle for tea. I hadn't any idea we'd be foraging in the wilds."

"Yes, you're right. Sorry." Berdie sighed. She decided she'd have to trek on her own when a thought came to her. She brightened. "Laundry."

"Laundry?"

"I found a laundry parcel in the truck when I used it to go to visit Chad. It's right here." Berdie reached behind Lillie's seat and pulled the desired object to her lap. She tore the paper to expose the uniforms. "I know we've not a proper changing room, but we can give it a go."

Lillie observed the blue work overalls. "You're serious?"

"You've always fancied blue." Berdie gave an overall to Lillie, who shook it open from its folded state.

"They're huge." Lillie held it against her slender body. "If I don't drown from the rain, I'll drown for the overall."

"Think of the size as a bonus." Berdie measured a uniform sleeve along her arm. "The bottoms will cover your shoes. Besides, you can't be a fashion plate one hundred percent of the time, you know."

Lillie's disgruntle was swept away with one giggle. "Oh, why not? This could turn into a real lark."

"Come on then," Berdie goaded.

Between laughter and struggles to get the silly things on over their clothes, Berdie and Lillie at last alighted from the van, covered in blue button-up work overalls, with *Butz and Sons Electrics* written on their front top pocket and across their backs in large letters.

"No umbrellas?" Lillie's hair was already losing its shape.

"They'll just be in the way." Berdie scanned the top of the hedgerow. There was a long stretch between the two farms, a good half-mile, Berdie reckoned, but a straight line of sight. "Lord have mercy," she whispered.

"I'll go this way." Lillie pointed toward the bottom of the road. "You go the other direction."

"We'll wave with both hands and yell, if we see anything," Berdie agreed.

She laughed to herself, watching the trudging Lillie, who nearly tripped over the long end of the uniform legs, hands hidden by the sleeves. Berdie knew she too must present quite a sight. But then, who would see them all the way out here?

Whilst staying close to the hedgerow, Berdie moved along in the opposite direction to Lillie, taking in every detail.

Apart from their task, Berdie enjoyed the hedgerows that were abundantly foliaged and profusely decorated by flowers and undergrowth this time of year. Some of the hedges were hundreds of years old. Bushes and trees had been set in place long ago, nourished, and clipped, to create natural, sturdy boundaries between fields. Hedgerows actually had their own distinct habitat, even today. When woodlands were cut down, many creatures that inhabited them took up living in the hedgerows.

Berdie trudged on, stopping now and again to look for a track. If it was overgrown, as Mrs. Carlisle said, it would take a keen eye to spot it.

Right now, Berdie didn't have a keen eye at all. She used her finger to wipe raindrops off her glasses. She decided to take them off and clean them with the overall sleeve that hung over her hand.

"Berdie." Lillie's distant call sounded an alert. "Look."

Startled, Berdie fumbled her glasses, which caught on a button at the sleeve's edge and then spun into wet vegetation.

"Oh, really." Berdie's poor sight hampered her chance of spotting the glasses amidst the undergrowth. "My dear Lord…" She bent over and used her hands to sieve the sedge and grass at her feet.

"Berdie," Lillie yelled again. "What are you doing? Look!"

Berdie rose up from her treasure hunt. "You've found the gate?"

"Berdie, can't you see? There's something coming our way across the field."

Berdie felt a kick of panic. "I've lost my glasses, Lillie," she yelled at the top of her voice.

"You've what?"

Berdie wasn't sure, but she thought she heard laughter spring from her best friend's lips.

"How does one lose their glasses whilst walking a hedgerow?"

"Easily, actually, when others yell out with alarm. Can you make out what it is that's coming?" Berdie could see the shape of Lillie down the lane "as a tree walking" of sorts, but when she looked across the field, she saw only a mobile black dot, and she only saw that by squinting. And it was well downfield from them.

Lillie walked toward Berdie. "Some kind of motorbike perhaps?"

"Motorbike?" Berdie said to herself. She felt her pulse pick up. "This could be a divine juncture. Lord, where are my glasses?" She bent back down and continued her search.

"Have you found them?" Lillie's words were salted with chuckles as she made way toward Berdie.

Just then, Berdie's ears heard the distant roar of the motorbike's engine. She looked up. The black dot was advancing toward the lane like a wild hare. "Lillie, stay on the motorbike."

"What do you mean, stay on the bike?" Lillie was only yards away.

"Stop. Go back, Lillie. A motorcycle means a driver, a driver who might have information we need. You've got to chase the bike, Lillie."

"Me?"

"They have to stop and open the gate." Berdie was on her hands and knees now. Rain pelted her back as she felt along the ground. "Ask for directions, stall them." She lifted her head to see Lillie motionless. "Don't just stand there, go, run. I'll catch you up."

"But my shoes…"

"Now," Berdie yelled.

Lillie grabbed the baggy trouser legs and lifted them, gripping them in her raised hands, nearly knee high. Had a gust of wind come along, she may have become a large blue Butz and Sons Electrics kite. But instead, she began a dash that looked to Berdie more a trot, like someone entered in the sack race at a Sunday afternoon fete. She would have rolled over in the wet with laughter if this wasn't a critical moment that could easily slip through their fingers.

"You owe me a new pair of shoes," Lillie called as she hastily waddled off.

Berdie, still on hands and knees, made her way along the hedgerow by moving her knees one at a time.

The sound of the motorbike grew louder, but it wasn't too loud to drown out the cruel crunch Berdie heard from below her knee. She froze. "Oh no." She backed up and ran her hand through the vegetation by her left knee. There they were, but her tortoiseshell glasses were definitely rearranged. The ear stems looked as if they had done battle with a great horde and lost. Berdie tried to gently bend one stem back to the proper shape while her wet hair dripped onto the unaffected lenses. The ear stem wasn't having it. "Blast."

The howl of the approaching engine screamed *lost opportunity* in Berdie's ear. She couldn't let that happen.

She stood and planted her feet, then rammed the glasses on, as they were. She felt one ear stem riding far above her left ear against her head, skewing the frames cockeyed, while the other stem felt to lie flattened across the middle of her other ear. She struggled to put the eyeglasses in their proper place, but they didn't yield.

"You won't get away," she yelled with gusto as her instincts told her to forego any concern for decent appearance and simply run like a madwoman.

Even though the rain was beginning now to ease, Berdie felt the resistance of the wet overall as she sprinted in the middle of the lane toward Lillie and the approaching rider. She held the damaged glasses with one hand and pumped her free arm in time with her feet to help her speed along. She could only imagine that if there were hedgerow rodents creeping about, they would shut themselves away at the sight of her.

The motorcycle slowed when it neared the hedgerow. Lillie raced toward the rider.

Berdie, as best she could see through the skewed glasses, watched the rider, clad in a dark leather jacket, helmet, and gloves, come to an abrupt halt at the spot that had to be the gate. The person glanced toward "the blue kite" that flew closer and appeared completely taken aback, staring in paralyzed wonder.

"Hello," Berdie could hear Lillie call in cheerful voice as she continued her flight forward.

The rider kept the transport running whilst dismounting and approaching the well-hidden gate. Vine-covered was putting it mildly. It was a mobile thicket. The rider kicked at it, then, feet braced, pushed with both hands, finally heaving the thing open.

"Hello there," Lillie called again.

Berdie continued her sprint while rain continued to ease.

The motorist remounted the engine and pulled forward to the road, alighted, and worked to swiftly close the gate.

"Come on, Lillie. Get there," Berdie prompted.

"I say, can I have a word?" Lille shouted with panted voice.

The rider sat on the bike and raised the helmet's visor. "Blimey, you electrics people are keen to service."

Berdie could just make out the rather-mumbled words.

"Service?" Lillie halted just a couple yards from the idling motorcycle. She dropped her "wings," the trouser legs rumpling downward. "Oh, yes, service." She ran a hand through her dripping hair. "The best electrics service indeed," she breathed between gulps of air.

Berdie gathered her own breath. "Hey there," she trumpeted. "We need your help."

The motorcyclist threw the visor down, revved the

engine, and thrust the thing in motion, springing onto the lane.

"No," Berdie yelled, hands flailing, and threw herself into the path of the transport.

The motorbike nearly spun out of control when the rider slammed on the brakes and stopped just short of crashing into Berdie.

"Are you daft, you silly woman?" the motorist raged and flipped the visor up.

Berdie stared into flared, angry, blue-shadowed eyes, mascara laden, and somehow familiar.

"You've already had one accident"—she thrust an arm in the direction of the van—"and now you're creating another?"

An accident? Berdie suddenly realized her skewed glasses, drenched hair, being wet through and on foot, plus a stopped vehicle up the road read as trouble to the young woman.

"We need your help," Berdie puffed.

The damp leather saddlebags that hung at the rear of the motorcycle stood in contrast to the tight, upright way the slim female sat on the motorcycle.

"I've got to push on," the woman yelled above the engine noise.

"Please, can you tell us how to get to the summer cottage, the one in the wood? I daresay, the one you just came from?"

The woman's eyes went into a squint as she tightened her grip on the handlebars. "You're calling to service electrics there?" She lifted her chin. "No, I've no idea of any summer cottage."

"Yes, you do," Berdie challenged her. "You do know. In fact, you live there."

"I've got to get to work." The woman revved the

motorbike and thrust her upper body forward.

Berdie kept her feet firmly planted on the road in front of the motorcycle. She braced her back and refused to move from in front of the vehicle, hands on hips. "Answer my question."

"Look," Lillie shouted and threw her index finger toward the road, where a small, well-worn car squeezed round the distant van on the lay-by.

"Mother," the rider declared.

The car, though the rain was now light, splashed its way on down the lane toward them. And it picked up speed, not the best for tiny, waterlogged country roads, Berdie reasoned, even more so when she spotted two youngsters in the backseat.

She glanced back at the bike rider, who bit her scarlet lip.

"Your mother, you say." Berdie looked the biker in the eye, as best she could with her cockeyed glasses. "Does she live with you as well?"

"No." The word dripped with venom.

"So, you *do* live there."

"Please, get out of my way," the rider bawled.

The car was upon them now and stopped dead in the center of the road. The driver door flew open, a woman sprang out, leaving the little ones behind, and didn't bother to close the door.

"What's going on, Jenny?" The older woman, gray hair in a knot, stood ramrod-straight, taking the situation in, despite the light rain that fell upon her.

"These electrical workers are looking for the summer cottage."

"There's no need. The electrics are fine," the woman told Berdie, her mouth almost motionless as she spoke.

"Mrs. Limb," Berdie spouted with recognition.

"Yes, who wants to know?" The woman eyed Berdie's dripping-wet hair that lay flat on the scalp, glasses at an angle, the too-big overalls, and despite it all, recall dawned on her face. "The vicar's wife?"

"Vicar's wife?" the young woman now known as Jenny questioned with disbelief. She ran her eye over Lillie. "And who are you? The Lord Mayor?"

"Choirmaster, actually," Lillie answered through wet lips.

"This requires an explanation." Mrs. Limb pressed her thin lips together.

"Yes, it does," Berdie fired back. "It's a simple misunderstanding never intended as a masquerade." She threw her shoulders back. "And I require an explanation from you as well, you who live secreted away in the wood and tell lies in front of your little ones about visiting the dentist," Berdie parried.

Mrs. Limb swallowed, and then stared at the ground. She took a deep breath, putting her hand to her chest as if pain raced through the very heart of her. "Oh, my dearest heaven," she said with a tremor, "we've been found out."

"Mother, you don't need to say anything," Jenny warned.

"Get on to work, love. You'll be late." Mrs. Limb's eyes grew moist. "Don't worry. I'll take care of this."

"I'm going nowhere until I know what these women are about." Jenny turned the bike engine off.

"I think you know what we're doing here," Berdie retorted. "What is it you're hiding, or perhaps what are you hiding from?"

"Nanna"—Max leaned forward from the backseat of the car as he yelled out the open door—"how long will we be in the road? When will we see Daddy?"

"Not long. We're just talking a moment," Mrs. Limb called back.

"And Daddy lives at the cottage house too." Berdie was becoming impatient. She felt heat rise to her face as the question that plagued her could no longer be held back and flew off her tongue. "Why did you call my husband last Saturday afternoon, Mrs. Limb?"

"She didn't." Jenny's words were landed punches. "I did." Her face took on the red of anger-tinged humiliation. "Mum was delivering Max and Emmy to the safest possible place she could think of, or so she thought! We needed her back here, or she would have never left them with you. Who could have ever imagined that something as horrible as a blast could happen at a vicarage?"

Berdie realized she was told two conclusive things in that blistering statement. First, for some reason, at that moment on Saturday, Max and Emmy needed to be in a safe place, and second, Mrs. Limb and her daughter were in no way connected to the blast.

"I'm sorry they experienced that chaos."

Jenny frowned, as if to fight back the tears that gathered in the corner of her eyes. "My little ones are resilient."

Mrs. Limb choked and brought a rigid finger to her nose. "Bless them. They've been through so much."

Lillie broke in. "Even though something monstrous happened, your grandchildren were in caring hands that afternoon. You both need to know that."

Berdie's severe attitude began to take on the quality of mercy. She stepped just to one side of the motorbike. "Why was the children's safety jeopardized?"

Mrs. Limb's gaze caught her daughter's eyes, and then looked to Berdie. "Why must you know?"

"Innocent people are in harm's way. We need the truth, Mrs. Limb."

"Can we trust you?"

"Of course," Berdie answered.

Mrs. Limb nodded toward her daughter, who began to speak.

"My husband suffers bouts," Jenny said. "He's a good man, a loving husband and father that came home from overseas military action carrying the scars of war. He deals with depression, PTSD, if you like."

"I have a small basement flat just outside Aidan Kirkwood," Mrs. Limb explained. "When necessary, Max and Emmy stay with me there, and my husband stays here with Jenny and Alec."

"My father, as well as Mum, know how to calm Alec."

"But why all the secrecy?" Lillie asked.

"Our home was near Birmingham," Mrs. Limb informed, "but our son-in-law had"—she paused—"some difficulties, let's say, that involved the law. One overnight stay, but no arrests. It was best for all that we leave."

"My husband needs a safe, peaceful place to recover," Jenny finished.

"So you rented the cottage, came here," Berdie surmised, "stayed cloistered under the radar. But when your Jenny's husband had one of his turns, instead of asking for police or medical help, you sought out the vicar."

"That was Mum's idea." Jenny rubbed her gloved

hands cross the handlebars. "She found out at church that your husband used to be in the military. She felt he would understand the situation and be discreet." Jenny pursed her lips. "But he never came. Mum said she saw him leave that day for somewhere, but it wasn't here."

"It was," Berdie defended. "He came to Old Barn Road, but he couldn't find your place. He had no return phone number. And look round you"—she thrust her hand out toward the hedgerow—"it's a one-in-ten chance that he'd have spotted this gate. You can't put the blame entirely at his door."

"Water under the bridge, really," Lillie spouted. "Misunderstandings that belong in the past."

"Where did you find the mobile phone?" Berdie delved.

"It was among the sedge grass near the gate." Jenny nodded at the hedge. "I found it when I picked up the groceries that were delivered that morning."

"Why didn't you return it to the greengrocer? You had to know it must have been his."

"The intent was there," Mrs. Limb jumped in. "We're not thieves, but after Jenny used it in the emergency, I told her, for Alec's sake, to throw it in the rubbish."

"Never," Lillie declared.

Jenny thrust the bike's kickstand down and got off. She opened one of the saddlebags and pulled out a mobile phone. "Here."

She shoved it toward Berdie, who took it.

Mrs. Limb gaped.

"I know, Mum, but what if Alec, what if it should happen again, another especially bad episode? I didn't want to be caught out."

Berdie stuck the mobile in a pocket of her overalls. "Thank you, Jenny, very noble of you." She lifted her wet chin. "And if I may say, there is help available for your Alec, and absolutely no shame in it."

Mrs. Limb and Jenny exchanged glances.

"At least let my husband call on you, now that we know how to find you. There's many who suffer the same problem as your Alec. My husband can help."

"He's very circumspect?" Jenny questioned.

"I know of few more so," Berdie assured.

"Yes, all right," Mrs. Limb agreed.

"Good," Lillie interjected, "you've made a wise decision. And I believe we all need to move on now so we don't catch a chill."

Jenny mounted her bike and started the engine.

"Aside from your husband knowing, our situation won't be put about the village, will it," Mrs. Limb reinforced.

"No," Berdie reassured. "My husband will come to call at your summer cottage. Now, we'll see you Sunday, you and the kiddies?"

The woman nodded.

"To the off then." Lillie took Berdie by the excess fabric of her overall sleeve and pulled her in the direction of the van.

"God go with you," Berdie called to Mrs. Limb, who worked to open the gate while Jenny blasted up the lane.

"Job well done," Lillie pattered. "We found all we were looking for and more."

"Yes, we did," Berdie mumbled and her heart gave a brief flutter.

"You don't seem very pleased."

"There's a much larger concern now. We've just

sharpened a double-edged sword, Lillie."

"And how's that?"

"Don't you see? We've discovered this rainy morning that there was no hoax call. It was all legitimate. There was no plot to get the commander in the vehicle." Berdie had difficulty letting the words slip through her wet lips. "I believe my Hugh was the intended victim after all."

13

"Mrs. Elliott?" Chief Inspector Kent, standing at the crime scene, tipped his head as he beheld Berdie. "Are you all right?"

"Oh, Chief Inspector, I'm so glad you're here. I just dropped Lillie at her home and got over here as quickly as possible." Berdie took a very deep breath. "That local knowledge you spoke of. I had to tell you straightway that I've found what's been missing."

Kent cocked his head to the side. "Proper-fitting eyeglasses, presumably."

"Oh." Berdie's concern for Hugh and getting pertinent facts to Chief Inspector Kent had entirely trumped her dreadful appearance. And the fact that the rain had stopped added a bizarre quality to the situation. "I do apologize. A mishap amidst curious circumstances." She ran a finger through wet hair and tried, unsuccessfully, to straighten her glasses. "It's just that I've discovered something that will turn your entire investigation on its head."

"Is that a fact?" Kent ran an inquisitive eye over her soaked blue uniform and half smirked. "Working undercover, are we? Is it electrics or plumbing?"

Berdie realized that her critical information would be better received without the distraction of her ghastly appearance. "Can you come to the vicarage in twenty minutes for a quick cuppa?" Berdie requested with the hope she could tidy herself up in that amount of time.

"Quick cuppa? I can see my way clear to do that." Kent smiled.

"Make it twenty-five minutes," Berdie corrected and turned from the crime scene to trudge her soaked body to the vicarage.

Getting herself in proper order again took some doing, but she was soon ready. She wasn't especially fond of her old black-framed spare eyeglasses, but they would get the job done until her other ones could be repaired. The floral-print wrap dress she wore was a deliberate attempt to regain some dignity in her dealings with the chief inspector. And in a timely manner, Berdie put the kettle on and toasted up some scones.

A strong rap came at the back door of the kitchen, and Berdie, who held two teaspoons, glanced at the clock. "Spot on," she quipped and pulled the door open.

"I hope you have a moment, because it's important I see you right now." Tillie, hair loose and denims tight, entered the kitchen before Berdie had a chance to respond. "I've been trying to get hold of you all morning."

"I've been out. What is it?" Berdie moved to the nearby kitchen table and put the spoons down among the other preparations for elevenses.

"Are you encouraging my father to make an absolute fool of himself?"

"What?"

"Are you?"

"Tillie, I'm sure I haven't any idea what you're on about. Come, sit down."

"You know very well what I mean. My father and

that Sandra woman."

"Ah." Berdie pulled out the chair. "That Sandra woman happens to be a very loving soul. Some tea?"

Tillie remained standing. "They've just met, and he's mooning over her like a schoolboy."

Berdie smiled.

"I found him out in the back garden of the B and B in the wee hours of this morning, and in his pajamas. Stargazing. Apparently, Sandra told him it was good for his soul. It's madness." Her volume rose with her anger. "And that's not all. He's been practicing with his prosthetic leg again, all to impress her."

"Is that so bad, Tillie?"

"It's not a proper fit. It gives him terrible sores." She knit her brow. "Isn't that just like you? Seeing things through rose-tinted glasses."

Berdie adjusted her black frames. Hardly rosy.

Tillie verbally stomped her foot. "What do you know about his past with women? When Mum left, his life was a shambles." Tillie's voice trembled. "It's just not fair."

"Tillie, take a breath."

"And now look at poor Avril. Why she ever took up with that man, I can't imagine." The young woman cocked her eyebrow. "I'm glad he's gone, frankly."

"Gone?"

"You've not heard? Kabil's done a bunk. Gone."

Berdie took a moment to let the news settle in. She knew Kabil had been ill at ease and distant. Somehow, she wasn't all that surprised.

"Cedric tried to tell Avril from the start that man was mixed up with a bad crowd. He warned her that she'd never be first consideration in Kabil's life as long as his cause held his soul."

"Cause? What cause?"

"Not only does she have to cope with her father's misfortune, now she's been abandoned. This whole thing is a complete dog's dinner."

"Tillie, perhaps you should sit down."

"Now Dad's going the same way."

"Tillie, you're overwrought." Berdie used her most soothing tone. "Your father is not Avril. His simple attraction to Sandra is different entirely. And who's to say she's not good for him?" She patted the chair. "Please, sit down."

Tillie's face went red, and her fist came down upon the table with such force it made the teacups rattle in their saucers. "I don't want to sit down. I want my father to see sense."

Berdie looked Tillie straight in the eye, and what she saw there was genuine anger. "Tillie, your father is a grown man. He's responsible and aware of what he's doing. He and Sandra are just enjoying time together. That's all."

"What does he see in her? What can he offer her? He's disabled."

Berdie expanded her eyes and balked. "Tillie, did you hear what you just said? Your father is missing a leg, not a heart."

Tillie clenched her jaw. She put her hand to her forehead and closed her eyes. "I didn't mean that. I don't know why I said it."

"You're upset."

Tillie straightened. "Yes, I do know why I said it. Because he's not financially capable. He can't support her or her scatty aunt."

"Hang about, Tillie." Berdie's tone was not so soothing now. "You're jumping way ahead of the game."

The young woman huffed. She looked askance at the table set for two. "Oh, you're expecting someone?"

"Chief Inspector Kent should be along any moment."

"I didn't know..." Tillie looked toward the half-open door and took a deep, calming breath. "I won't take up any more of your time."

"We can discuss this later. Come by or ring me."

"Just don't encourage my father in this silly business, Mrs. Elliott. That's all." Tillie turned and made for the door, wasting no time on pleasantries.

"God go with you," Berdie called to the disappearing woman and set about getting the clotted cream from the fridge for the scones.

Poor Avril. She must encourage the young woman to come stay with her and Hugh at the vicarage. And as far as Tillie's outrage, she couldn't help but wonder if the caregiver was a bit jealous of her father's good fortune. But that was all secondary to the thing that mattered most to her right now: Hugh's wellbeing.

Berdie heard a rapid knock at the door and hoped it was her anticipated guest.

"Come in, Chief Inspector."

Jasper Kent entered the kitchen and closed the door. "Blimey, she wasn't by half in a hurry."

"Tillie? Yes, she's in a bit of a spin." Berdie put the cream on the table. "Do you remember what life was like when you were in your twenties?"

"Before or after marriage?"

Berdie chuckled. "Please, sit down."

Jasper Kent took his hat off and hung it at the coat hook near the door, exposing his close-cut brown hair. He sat at the table.

Berdie removed the tea towel covering a basket of warm scones.

"This is quite nice. Scones and all."

Berdie sat in the chair opposite. "It is elevenses, more or less."

"Thank you. Certainly beats cold coffee and a digestive back at the station."

"Yes, well, God bless this table and our bringing of light to troubled situations," Berdie said in somewhat of a rush, half to Jasper Kent and half to the great Provider. "Tuck in. I'll pour."

He took a scone from the basket whilst Berdie splashed some milk in his cup.

"You were right about the young lad from London being guilty of something. Though Brice isn't sure, I've determined it's not setting the blast."

Berdie nodded and tried not to appear smug. "What's he done then?"

Kent glanced round the table. "Strawberry jam?"

Berdie lifted the lid on a ceramic dish shaped like a giant red strawberry, revealing the luscious fruit preserves.

Kent stuck a teaspoon in and ladled it onto his scone.

"It's his Uncle Chander, been importing illegal foodstuffs into the country, dodgy meat and vegetables without health certificates or import licenses. We cottoned onto it without the lad even implicating him."

"He's very fond of his uncle. Not a grass."

Kent filled his spoon a second time, and third, piling it on the scone. "Yes. Well, it seems Sundeep's been his delivery boy to certain buyers."

"I had no idea. He's in trouble then?" Berdie poured tea into Kent's cup.

"I should say, but he'll probably receive nothing more than a caution and community service since he's young, with no previous record, and he's been so forthcoming concerning the whole affair."

"That's good." Berdie splashed milk in her cup, and then added a teaspoon of sugar. "I think he's learned his lesson. He'll stay clear of trouble now."

Kent grabbed the spoon next the clotted cream. "Ah, lovely. My wife doesn't let me eat this at home, says it's bad for me."

Berdie watched him ladle five teaspoons of the almost-thick-as-butter cream atop his jam.

The chief inspector's mobile sounded from a trouser pocket. He puffed. "Excuse me, must get this."

Berdie was well-acquainted with interrupted conversations. After all, she was the vicar's wife in a small village. She smiled, poured her tea, and prepared her scone.

"Kent," he spoke into the mobile. "Yes." He paused. "Right." He made a clucking sound. "Please keep me informed then." He returned the mobile to his pocket. "Sorry, no rest for the wicked."

"Are you wicked, Chief Inspector?"

"It depends on if you're talking to the good guys or bad guys. Anyway, we have a new lead." Kent returned to his overflowing scone, took a deep bite, and chewed. "Um, nothing compares with scones and cream." He munched with satisfaction.

"New lead, you say?" Berdie probed.

"When we track him down," he said between chews. He dabbed a napkin at the cream on the corners of his mouth. "He's done a runner."

"Kabil?"

"There's no flies on you, Mrs. Elliott."

"Then you won't mind me saying that you're probably on a hiding to nothing on that one."

"Oh yes? He's got motive: the commander was dead set against him and his daughter getting cozy. And that's beside the fact that he's linked to some questionable organizations. And you never heard it from me." He took another bite of scone.

"What would be his motive for"—Berdie took a breath—"killing my husband?"

"Your husband? Why would you say that?" Inspector Kent slowed his munching and stared at the somber Berdie.

"The missing piece." She wondered if he could read the apprehension that surely played cross her face.

Jasper Kent set the scone down and continued to study her eyes. "You've found something out."

Berdie stood, walked to the kitchen dresser, and opened a drawer that held odds and ends. She pulled out a mobile phone.

Kent watched every move.

She returned to her chair and set the mobile next him on the table. "It's Sundeep's. A bit wet, but there it is."

The chief inspector leaned forward, eyes cautious. "Where'd you find it?"

"I didn't. It was discovered on Old Barn Road, near the grocery box that Sundeep delivered the morning of the blast. It was given me this morning."

DCI Kent leaned back in the chair and stretched his arms forward on the table, his fingers spread out. "I hope I'm going to get a straight answer on this." He paused. "Who gave it to you?"

Berdie took a sip of tea, avoiding his eyes, and

then lifted her chin. "The call made to Hugh that afternoon was legitimate."

Berdie watched Kent's jaw tighten as he drew his hands back to the edge of the table.

"So this comes under the heading of professional confidence, does it? The investigative reporter doesn't reveal her confidential sources?" He tapped a finger on the table. "The churchwoman's obligation to privacy?"

"Something like that. Yes."

Berdie observed a red tinge develop on the tip of the lawman's ears.

"You're going to have to trust me, Chief Inspector." She looked him in the eye. "Jasper. I *can* tell you this—"

"Berdie, please." The words yelled *extremely perturbed*.

"I can tell you this," she went on, her confidence building as she did so. "There was a family in great need, they used Sundeep's mobile phone to call Hugh, and their home is next to impossible to find from Old Barn Road." She folded her hands on the table. "I know this is extremely frustrating for you. I understand. I'm giving you as much information as I can at the moment. You'll get more later, directly from the source, if you step lightly. But please hear me out on this. Just consider: we've not found anyone who spied out the crime scene at the time of the blast. Your primary suspect, Sundeep, has, for all intents and purposes, been exonerated. In terms of motive, with Hugh as the target, your new lead, Kabil, is left at the back of the pack."

Kent shifted in the chair.

"And don't undermine your gut instinct. Just this morning, you told me you had a sense of trying to grasp smoke, that local knowledge could be critical. You're right. The commander was not the intended victim."

The inspector heaved an enormous sigh. "Berdie Elliott, if ever there was a woman so capable and at the same time so aggravating…"

Berdie leaned forward. "Be that as it may, Chief Inspector Kent, the real issue now is who wanted, or wants, to kill my Hugh, and why?"

****

Berdie, elevenses with Jasper Kent behind her, arrived at the hospital in good time. Now she could see clearly through the large window that opened from the hall to the commander's hospital room.

Dave stood near the end of the bed. Avril, in a chair, sat near the head of the bed, Sparks at her side. But all Berdie could really see was her Hugh. It looked that he was about ready to leave, so Berdie waited for him outside the door.

"Hello, love," he greeted when he entered the hall, Dave behind. "You're wearing your old spare glasses."

"Oh, Hugh." Berdie wrapped her arms around him and gave a tight squeeze. She couldn't help herself. She was so grateful he was still here to hug.

He returned the embrace, a slight red flush above his clerical collar. "Not that I mind, but why the special greeting?"

Dave, wearing a sheltered grin, moved a discreet distance away and looked out the hospital window.

"Hugh, you could be in danger."

He wrinkled his brow and smiled. "It's only a rowing practice, Berdie."

"No, I mean real danger. Someone may want to do you in."

Hugh chuckled. "The only ones who'll do me in are Rollie and Chad if I don't get to rowing practice."

"But, Hugh."

He took Berdie's hands. "I have the best news possible." He gave her fingers a squeeze. "Cedric's regained consciousness."

Berdie blinked. "Hugh, that's wonderful, wonderful, but—"

"Sparks ignited a spark, pardon the pun, and Avril lit the fire." Hugh's face beamed. "Thank God! In a week's time we've gone from despair to hope. We're so blessed."

"Indeed we are, Hugh, and not by half, but—"

"Now, although we have joy in the camp, Avril is still struggling. It's Kabil."

"Yes, I know, I heard."

"Raise her spirits, Berdie. You're good at that."

"Am I?"

"I think she should come stay with us at the vicarage for a while."

"I agree. But—"

"Good."

Dave cleared his throat.

Hugh planted a kiss on Berdie's cheek. "Who's a lucky boy then? See you tonight."

With that he released her hands and, happy as a sand boy, strode off, Dave beside him.

"But, Hugh." Berdie could see his determined steps and realized it was useless to try and dissuade him. She sighed. *Well, Lord,* she directed heavenward while watching her man vanish down the corridor, *You've faithfully kept watch over him these fifty-something years, and in some frightening circumstances at that. Please circle him with Your protection in the minutes and hours to come.*

She glanced back through the window at Avril, Sparks, and Cedric.

A nurse entered the room. Avril nodded her head and started for the door while the nurse closed the blind on the window.

Avril entered the hall and looked at Berdie.

"Oh, Mrs. Elliott. Good news." She barely managed the words. "It seems Daddy is going to pull through."

Daddy, Berdie thought. "Amazing."

Avril's eyes were red. Her drooping eyelids spoke of little sleep and deep heartache. She had no headscarf. With her tousled hair and messy clothes, standing alone, she looked to be twelve years old: a sheep looking for its shepherd.

"Avril." Berdie put her hand on the young woman's shoulder and gave it a gentle squeeze.

Tears welled up as Avril spoke. "Thank you for calling me, Mrs. —"

"Berdie, call me Berdie."

"Seeing my father again..." A tear fell on a now-pink cheek and the words stopped.

Berdie could see a dam about to burst. She moved her arm around Avril's shoulder and hugged her. The young woman covered her face with her hands, and her shoulders commenced heaving up and down as the pain of the last difficult hours rolled down her face.

"The wet salt of healing," Berdie breathed. "It stings but washes clean."

Avril clung on until finally able to calm and regain her composure. Berdie pulled a tissue from her pocket and placed it in the trembling woman's hand.

"You're so kind, Berdie," she choked, dabbing her face. "You must think horribly of me."

"Nonsense. Now, you must come and stay with Hugh and me at the vicarage."

She lifted her watery eyes. "Do you mean it? You'd do that for me?" She sniffed.

"Yes. And when your father's ready, he'll come home with us to recover. What say?"

Avril nodded her head.

"Good as done then."

Avril fingered the tissue. "You've heard about Kabil?"

"Yes."

"He said nothing—he didn't even leave a note. I tried ringing his mobile and the service has been discontinued."

Berdie could see the writing on the wall. Was this just an impulsive decision, or did Kabil plan this in advance? Was there more to this than met the eye? "And your flight was a one-way."

Avril swallowed.

"I should imagine you've little money to spare." Berdie tried to frame it gently.

"I've learned a very hard lesson through all this." She brought the tissue to her red nose. "Well, bittersweet, really." Avril looked at Berdie straight on. "The only person on this earth who truly loves me"— she fumbled her words—"*truly* loves me, is my father. And I've made such a hash of things."

"Avril, hear this clearly." Berdie kept the eye contact steady. "Your presence here has brought strength to your father and uplifted his will to survive."

"Do you really think so?"

"The bond that exists between a father and his daughter, since the dawn of time, defies all that's worst in this world. It's forever."

Avril wiped her eyes and straightened her shoulders.

The nurse opened the door to the room and put her head out. "You can come back now."

"Good." Berdie smiled at the nurse and then addressed Avril. "Now, you go wash your face and we'll return to the room much more refreshed."

Avril worked at a smile. "I won't be a minute."

Avril made way to the water closet and Berdie sighed. "Whoever said there are no more miracles in today's world needs to spend twenty-four hours in Aidan Kirkwood."

****

Hugh took a sip of his sherry, an apéritif before dinner. The moment he arrived home from rowing practice, showered, and got into his comfortable night robe, Berdie prepared his favorite chair in the library. And now they were in the midst of *the* discussion.

"You're sure?" he asked. "The call was legitimate then?"

"Yes, Hugh, it was." Berdie sat forward on the leather couch opposite him.

"Blow me down." He stared out the large library window. "They needed my help. And it was right of them to ring up. But I had no idea how to get to them." Hugh ran a finger up and down the glass stem. "If the main entrance to their cottage is on Littlewoods Lane, why tell me to enter from Old Barn Road where you can't see the place, and with an overgrown track at that?"

"The family is trying to live under the radar. They don't use the main entry because it draws too much attention to them."

"Sad, isn't it? Someone fights for their country; then they're secreted away simply because they're making a difficult life adjustment."

"Mrs. Limb actually seemed embarrassed about it all."

"Hopefully, I can help change that."

Berdie put her hand on Hugh's knee. "Yes. But, Hugh, there's a bigger issue in the whole affair." She braced herself. "You were the target for the blast."

Hugh downed the rest of his apéritif in one mouthful and plunked the empty glass on the side table next him. "As much as I hate the thought, it seems things point in that direction now."

"It's difficult to take it all in."

"I survived a war," he flared, "and someone wants to do me in at my small country vicarage?"

"Can you think of anyone who would want to hurt you?"

"It's absolute nonsense." Hugh ran a finger cross his lips. "Madness."

"I have to ask, Hugh. Is there something, someone, who may want to do you harm from your military past?"

"Do you mean revenge for something that happened when I was in the forces?" He frowned. "It's a bit late for that."

"No, I don't mean the enemy." Berdie framed her words carefully. "Isn't it notable that it happens when your old military chums are gathered here together?"

Hugh stared at her, taking in her meaning. "Rubbish, absolute rubbish." Hugh's voice blazed along with his cheeks. His left eyebrow arched dramatically. "You have no idea, Berdie. You weren't there. You wouldn't ask such a thing if you understood."

"Understood what?"

"We were—are—a brotherhood, family. We were ready to die for one another. That forges an irreversible bond."

"There had to be trouble, obstacles, disagreements, arguments of some sort."

"Fighting a war's hardly going to be all sweetness and light." Hugh rubbed his hand over the bathrobe that draped his leg. His irresistible blue eyes took on a distant stare. "We all had our crosses to bear."

"Hugh?" She could see memories of a faraway time steal cross his vision and tighten his shoulders. "And what was your cross to bear?"

"We needn't talk about this."

"Hugh, there's something that's getting to you. I see it. Tell me, please."

He dropped his chin, as though letting memories tumble forward. "We had an operation involving surveillance of insurgents. We prepared for a strike ambush." Hugh rubbed his hands together, as if trying to wash the event away. "I can only speak in broad strokes, Berdie. You understand that."

"Of course, Hugh."

Berdie felt the need to be closer. She positioned herself on the arm of the chair Hugh sat in.

"Using surveillance to determine what's going to happen is often simply making your best guess." Hugh took a deep breath. "Cedric was involved with another situation, and I was the officer in charge. I made the call to go in. I went with my men." Hugh's voice was strained. He paused.

"I'm listening, Hugh," Berdie whispered.

"I can still feel the desperately hot air, sweat trickling into my eyes. Somehow…" He shook his head. "They were waiting for us." Hugh leaned forward, pressed his fingertips together, and dug them into his chin. "We walked into a trap." His eyes squeezed shut, and then popped open. A deep furrow plowed his brow. "I can't describe the horror, nor do I want to. It's not for your ears."

Berdie put her arm around Hugh's shoulder. "No." She rubbed the back of his neck. "You survived, and I'm ever so grateful."

Hugh leaned back into the chair. "A miracle from God, we all did, but one. Rollie was the first one wounded. Even so, he tried to help when Doug went down. Dave took a heroic stand against sustained enemy fire, and Chad with him. I don't know if we'd be here today if it wasn't for their shooting skills and gut fortitude." Hugh's upper lip moistened. "By the time backup and medics arrived, Doug's leg had to go to save his life. Ennis was captured. He was found dead several months later in an enemy camp." He sighed. "There was some talk of a mole after that disaster, an informant. Cedric put a stop to that in a hurry." Hugh tapped a finger on his knee. "What a dog's breakfast it was, and all down to me."

Berdie grasped Hugh's chin and turned his gaze to meet her eyes. "I know you, Hugh Elliott. You did what you thought was right, your very best. No one can fault you for that, and most of all, you." She released his chin.

He looked away and stared at a shelf of books, lined up like soldiers on parade. "If anyone, of all the men, had a right to find fault with me, it was Doug. All of our lives were forever changed, but his especially." Hugh let go a puff of air. "That's why, when I knew I was called to the ministry, I had to see Doug."

"I don't remember this."

"I asked if things were all right between us. He was gracious to a fault. He said he never once blamed me for what happened. We were all just doing our duty. I made the best decision I could with the information I had at the time. He said that it didn't matter who made the decision, the result would have been no different. And I've had a special appreciation for him since."

"But you never said."

"No. It was between Doug and I, and our Maker. But that's enough of the past." Hugh put his hand on Berdie's thigh and gave a squeeze. "I could go another apéritif, love."

Berdie stood and took Hugh's glass. While pouring, she considered what Hugh had just unburdened. She almost deplored herself for thinking it, but she couldn't help it. Doug, Dave, Chad, Rollie, all of them wore wounds of one kind or another that were inflicted on Hugh's watch. Suddenly, Berdie saw Hugh's friends as possible threats. She shuddered. Had Doug truly never blamed Hugh? Was he that generous? "Yes," she whispered to herself. "Hugh believes he was. I want to believe it too." Just the thought of wrongful revenge made the back of Berdie's neck prickle. And she sensed something frightful lay ahead. If ever urgency pushed her to expose evil that lurked nearby, it was now. "My dear Hugh."

14

Lillie's voice croaked over the mobile Berdie held to her ear. "Why are you ringing me so early? I haven't even had my morning cup of tea. Is the sun up yet?"

"Just. I'm in the church back garden, Lillie." Berdie found herself competing with some squabbling greenfinches. She raised her voice just slightly while buttoning the cardigan she wore to keep the morning chill at bay. "I don't want Hugh to hear me." She paced before the memorial bench near the edge of the small pool that added such a sense of peace to the back garden. "All last night, I kept thinking about who may want to harm Hugh. I didn't sleep well at all."

"I should think not, but what can *I* do?"

"Help me." Berdie took a deep breath. "I don't want to believe it, but I think one of Hugh's chums may want to do him in."

"Why?" Lillie sounded more matter-of-fact than alarmed.

"I can't explain it all, but Chad, Dave, Doug, Rollie, and that fellow, Ennis, were all involved in a disastrous battle with Hugh in command. Each one suffered unimaginably. Ennis died. I don't know, but somehow, I think there could be someone who blames Hugh for it all and wants retribution, perhaps a settling of an old score."

"Have you talked to Hugh about it?" was

accompanied by the sound of an early-morning yawn.

"He thinks I'm off my chump."

"Well, calling me at this hour, I'm inclined to agree."

Berdie sighed. "What do you think, Lillie? Is it a reasonable assumption? Could someone be trying to get their own back on Hugh?"

"I don't know." Lillie exuded another yawn.

The greenfinch noise was becoming annoying. Berdie spied the offending birds. By the look of it, baby was squawking for breakfast from mummy bird and she was having none of it. The baby looked ready for flight, weaning age, yes, that was it, weaning. What a commotion.

"This horrible incident," Lillie offered, "the surviving fellows were all there, and they're all alive and breathing now. Right? Why then revenge?"

Berdie felt a sizzle in her brain. "They weren't there," she said to herself aloud.

"No, that's not what I said, Berdie. I said they were *all* there and they—"

"Oh, how could I have been so blind?"

"What?" Lillie sounded suddenly awake. "Blind?"

Berdie glanced toward the now-divested crime scene. "How absolutely diabolical."

"Berdie, what's going on?"

Berdie's thoughts were firing like so many lightning bolts, and along with it, scorching rage. Her knuckles went white from her tightening grip on the mobile. "Wretched, utterly wretched." She worked to collect herself and think with a clear focus. "I've got to ring up Matthew Reese," Berdie blurted.

"What's he got to do with this conversation?"

"How, how?" Berdie repeated.

"How what?"

Berdie snapped her fingers. "Just like the lock on Sundeep's door of the shipping container. How daring."

"Sundeep's lock?"

"The DIY lock he created for his door, in Slough, remember?"

"No."

"And where did he get the information? The library, of course. Why didn't I see it before?"

"Berdie, you're not making any sense."

"On the contrary, Lillie, I'm in full flow." Berdie glanced again at the greenfinches. "Bless those little darlings." Another thought struck her. "Little darlings." Berdie gasped. "Max and Emmy. Keep them safe. It's becoming clearer."

"OK, Berdie, you've completely lost me. Go eat breakfast and ring back later when you make some kind of sense."

"Right, I must call Rollie. And Chief Inspector Kent." Berdie became aware of Lillie's words. "Yes, breakfast. Go have your tea, Lillie. You've been wonderful."

"Have I?" Lillie rang off.

Berdie was beginning to see the puzzle pieces fit together. If she gathered the information she expected from the people she now needed to contact, a whole scheme of how to catch out the guilty party could be put into place immediately. She entered Chief Inspector Kent's number into her mobile. It felt hours before he answered.

"Kent" came in a raspy voice.

"Good morning, Chief Inspector."

"Is it?"

"Indeed. Listen closely, please. I believe I know who tried to murder Hugh. I have a few things to work out yet, but I haven't any doubt they'll try again, and I fear it could be soon."

"Who?"

"I can't say until I dig a bit deeper, and I know tomorrow is Sunday, but even so, what we need is a confession, and we'll need reliable honey, a substantial lure. Yes, and the sooner the better. Now, if you'd be so gracious, I believe, in an hour's time, I'll be able to give you 'the who' and a plan."

****

Berdie glanced about at Chief Inspector Kent and Hugh as they stood in the vicarage hall. The plan had emerged from Hugh's minor accident during rowing practice. The gravity of the moment hit her as they launched the daring scheme Berdie had developed. And now they were actually igniting the touch paper.

Berdie held the vicarage phone to her lips. "I'm so glad you're in." She labored to keep her voice even. "I was hoping I could ask a favor."

"Yes, what is it?"

"You see, Hugh's ankle began to hurt after rowing practice this afternoon following church. Quite sore—he's taking prescription medication for pain relief."

Berdie looked at Chief Inspector Kent, who glanced at Hugh. Hugh nodded.

"It's just that I've a commitment to speak at the women's guild over at Upper Winston this evening." That part was quite true, but Lillie had stepped in for her. "It will run quite late. I have someone who's staying with Hugh, but they must be home by nine this evening." Berdie swallowed. Another truth—CI Kent had called in Peter Brice, who would be at the house until nine, but still, she worked to maintain her composure. "I was wondering if you may see your way clear to look after him through the night."

"As a matter of fact, I am available."

"Wonderful." Berdie shuddered. "It shouldn't require a great deal of effort. It's just that I'd feel better if Hugh had someone with him. I'd be ever so grateful." Berdie's stomach churned.

"Don't worry. I'm glad to do it."

"Thank you so much." Berdie nearly choked on the words. "I'll see you tomorrow morning then, when I get back. Ta."

Berdie rang off. She felt an odd mixture of gratitude that the bait was taken so easily, but it was tempered with loathing and a touch of fear for Hugh's safety.

"Well done, Mrs. Elliott," Chief Inspector Kent commended. "Not an easy thing to do. I daresay they don't sound as if they suspect anything."

Berdie gave a quiet nod. "That's it then, everything and everyone in place."

"Now, don't worry, love," Hugh added. "It's a brilliant scheme, and it will all go like clockwork."

"I just want you safe, Hugh."

"And you've promised to stay out of the situation entirely, no heroics. You're nothing more than a hidden spy."

"Witness," Berdie corrected.

"You stick to that. Let Chief Inspector Kent and the others do their jobs, and I'll be fine."

"Besides which," Kent threw in, "if there's a hitch, the Yard will have my guts for garters, and that is *not* going to happen."

****

The small kitchen lamp which stood atop the collected stack of cookery books on the counter gave just enough subtle light to see what was happening. Berdie peeked through the tiny crack of the utility-room door that opened to the vicarage kitchen.

Tillie had just brewed a very special cup of chamomile tea, for Hugh, no doubt, when the back door quietly opened and a figure, dressed in black, slid silently in.

Berdie caught her breath.

The entrant observed what was happening. "Hello, Tillie."

The young woman nearly jumped out of her skin. She put her hand to her chest. "You gave me a turn. I didn't hear you knock."

"No, you wouldn't have."

Berdie focused to keep her breathing quiet and even.

"Why are you here, Chad?"

"I thought you'd appreciate a little help, Tillie." He smiled.

"Help?"

"Hugh, you know, taking care of Hugh."

Tillie rubbed her hand on her denims. "I'm doing just fine."

Chad moved closer to the young woman. "Come now, Tillie. I'm talking about *taking care of* Hugh."

"I don't know what you're on about."

Chad looked Tillie up and down, then grabbed an apple from the fruit bowl on the counter and rubbed it on his T-shirt, which made his strong abdominal muscles beneath noticeable.

Berdie could see Tillie's body relax.

Chad leaned against the counter's edge and took a bite of the red fruit. His tall, fit body seemed suddenly alluring and his dark eyes held a distinct magnetism.

"You helped me. In fact, I need to thank you. You did me a big favor, actually."

"Did I?" Tillie leaned against the counter. "How's that?"

"Although you didn't finish the job."

Tillie dipped her chin and lifted her eyes. She took a step toward Chad. "What do you mean?"

Chad took another bite, chewing slowly, keeping his eyes on the young woman. "You made him suffer, you tore his life apart, but the commander survived. Still, his world's in ruins, so well done."

"Chad, you naughty boy." Tillie's voice was velvet. She took another step toward him. "You've got a bit of apple, just there." She slowly slid her finger round the edge of his bottom lip and wiped the offender away. "Go on."

Chad didn't flinch. "Though it pleased me that the old fool got what he deserved, you didn't get what you actually wanted, did you?"

Tillie was close enough to Chad that he reached out and took her by the arm, then drew her close. "You and I are cut from the same cloth, aren't we, Tillie." It was a statement, not a question.

Berdie could just make out a low rumble of amusement that exploded into laughter from Tillie's mouth.

She leaned into Chad. "I knew you, but I didn't really *know* you. Not until the picnic lunch. You're not just a pretty face."

"Why a bomb?" he breathed.

"Why not?" She moved her lips alluringly close to Chad's face. Just as she did, he placed the red fruit to his mouth and took another bite.

Tillie pulled her arm from his grasp. Her eyes narrowed and she stepped back to her former place at the counter's edge and stared into the prepared tea.

"Tell me, Tillie, what gives you more pleasure? To dominate men or get away with murder?"

Berdie took a shallow breath. *Be careful, Chad. Remember, softly, softly.*

Chad tipped his head. "Such a beautiful woman and such a lust for vengeance." He set the fruit down. "Are you going after Hugh because of your father's injury?"

Tillie ran her fingers through her long hair. "If you think that's all it is, you're more stupid than I thought."

Chad lifted his chin. "I know how the commander ruined my chance for a decent career, a decent life."

Tillie pounded her fist on the counter. "Poor baby Chad. A decent career? What about maiming, death, destroying a family?"

Tillie yanked her scooped neckline downward, exposing her chest and the deep red scar that ran cross it, baring it for Chad's eyes. "A little souvenir from Daddy. Crazy mad one night, he thought I was the enemy and tried to slice me open."

Berdie squeezed her eyes shut and held back a gasp. *I thought as much.* She steadied her gaze again on the sad, sick figure of Tillie Devlin. Berdie fought her instinct to enter the fray.

"Ouch. That had to hurt."

"In so many ways. How many times did we huddle under the table, in fear for our lives, while my father wielded a firearm to attack the nonexistent enemy outside our door?" Tillie swallowed hard. "You've no idea."

Chad raised a brow. "Or maybe I do."

"And did you lose a brother?"

"Brother?"

"Marty, my little brother. My mother kept me with her. But she sent Marty away, for safety's sake, to stay with a mate of his from school whose single mum, unfortunately, drank too much. We didn't know. Neither of the boys had proper care."

Tillie looked wistful, eyes distant. The corners of her mouth sagged.

"Marty and his mate began to sneak out of an evening to run the streets." She took a deep breath and brought her eyes back on Chad. "He was struck by a car while chasing after his mate in the road. Marty died instantly." She looked away. "Probably a mercy in the circumstances."

Chad shifted his weight.

Tillie reclaimed the spoon to make rapid swirls in the chamomile tea. "Of course, my mother couldn't deal with it. She had precious little backbone at the best of times. I have to say she tried, but in the end the poor cow took solace in the arms of another man and left us."

"So it was all down to you. You had to nurse your father back to life."

Berdie watched the woman knit her brow, let go the spoon, and face Chad straight on.

"*I'm* the father. He's the child."

Berdie felt a cold shiver up her spine.

"How'd you make the bomb?" Chad appeared unaffected. "You should have asked me for help."

"Oh really?" Tillie crossed her arms. "Don't be idiotic. I couldn't trust you." She smirked. "If you must know, it was Kabil who was my supplier. We met when Avril first took up with him. He was into dark doings of all sorts. A shameless few moments of pleasure with him, and I got all the materials I needed.

"Lure him in, then blackmail for what you wanted?"

"A lot of men from his part of the world love blondes." She twirled a strand of hair in her finger.

Berdie's stomach churned. *Off comes another layer of the onion.*

"Oh yes?"

Berdie could just see the jut of Chad's chin. He was doing his best to maintain composure while Tillie went on.

"I felt bad for Avril; I really did, well, for about three minutes." Tillie dropped the hair strand.

"Cloak of Deception, that's where you learned to build the bomb. But you didn't learn very well, did you? I mean, it didn't do the job properly. He's still alive."

Tillie's face went red. "You trying to wind me up?"

"Yeah, maybe I am. You look good in that shade of pink."

Berdie wondered if Chad was pushing too hard.

But Tillie half scowled, half grinned. "Cheeky beggar." She leaned her back against the counter. "Actually, I was quite upset it was the commander who got it. I know what you think of him, but I rather liked the old boy. Had no idea he'd have that vile dog with him. Still, it bothered me at first, but then…"

"Bothered you that the commander got it, or that Hugh didn't?"

As if struck with her failure, Tillie's face darkened. She turned, stiffened, and seized the spoon from the teacup, then hurled it headlong into the kitchen wall with such force it sounded like cannon fire.

Chad clucked. "Now, steady on, Tillie."

"Don't *steady on* me, Chad. He made the call. The day of that ruinous hailstorm, Captain Hugh Elliott destroyed the father I knew and left me with a burned-out husk."

"Point taken," Chad spoke calmingly.

Tillie let go a long sigh.

"I know Doug has the occasional bout with depression and can be hard to deal with, but he's certainly more than a husk. He's gotten much better. Not trying to do you in anymore, is he?"

"And I'm supposed to be grateful?"

Chad didn't respond.

"My father never blamed Hugh, you know. Said it wasn't anyone's fault, things happen in war. Truth was: he had no bottle left in him." Tillie let go a quick breath. "So I had to take the responsibility, do the dirty work, to make Hugh pay."

"Like an avenging father would for a child. I know all about harboring the lust for revenge."

"Yes, I believe you do."

Reel this venomous woman in, Chad. Reel her in.

"You making tea then? I'm thirsty." Chad reached out for the cup Tillie had just made, but she placed her hand to shield it.

"No," she boomed.

Chad rocked back and grinned. "Ah. For Hugh, I

presume."

Tillie looked at the golden liquid and didn't respond.

"Just a few too many painkillers perhaps? Say, enough to put him permanently to sleep?"

Berdie watched Tillie smile.

The young woman, as if a penny had suddenly dropped, caught her breath and glared at Chad. "Hang on. You know too much."

Berdie froze.

"What do you mean? You know what they say about great minds."

Tillie turned her head to one side.

"They think alike, that's all," Chad asserted.

She regarded him thoughtfully for a few seconds. "Get yourself a cup, and I'll make some tea for you."

"Not with the same ingredients as Hugh's, I presume?"

Tillie's mouth bloomed into a half-smile. "Presume, if you wish."

Berdie strained to see Chad step to the cupboard, never turning his back. But for the instant he swung the cabinet door open, it blocked the view between him and Tillie, and Tillie moved quickly. Silently, she pulled out a knife from the large jug that held cooking utensils near the range, drew it down, and held it closely alongside her leg.

"My dear Lord have mercy," Berdie breathed.

Chad closed the cupboard door, cup in hand.

Berdie couldn't bear it. She had promised Hugh to stay protected, but this was deadly. Tillie was poised to strike.

Berdie had to do something, anything. Chad could take care of himself, but she had to warn him. How?

What could she do? Seconds felt like hours.

The utility room was just feet from the back door. The element of surprise? Berdie wrapped her hand round the utility-door handle, then made a fist with the other and beat upon the inside of the utility door, rapidly, several times. *Band, bang, bang.* In her best baritone voice, she shouted out the first words that jumped into her mind. "Vicar, special delivery. I need you to sign, please."

Berdie cringed. *Special delivery?* It had gone past ten.

A pounding raged, and it wasn't her fist. A miracle? She rapidly realized, a miracle all the same, there really was someone at the back door.

It burst open. The door smashed violently against the kitchen wall. Berdie caught sight of a black streak, a leather lead dragging after and an unidentified hand working to keep hold of it. The streak bumped a kitchen chair and came to an abrupt halt.

"Sparks?" *What's he doing here? He's certainly adapted to his cast quickly!*

A clatter resounded on the floor. A glint of metal was just visible at Tillie's feet. The knife.

Sparks launched into a barking tirade.

Tillie's scream nearly shook the roof. She grabbed Chad's arm. In desperation, she pushed him forward and wedged herself between him and the counter.

Chad grabbed the first thing he fingered on the kitchen counter. He thrust Berdie's summer canapé tray forward as a shield. "Get back," he shouted at Sparks, "back."

Berdie gasped.

There in the open doorway stood Milton Butz, legs spread, determination on his adolescent face. Avril was behind him.

"Sorry 'bout this," Milton apologized to Chad and Tillie. "He's a bit frisky tonight, getting his zip back," he announced buoyantly. He picked up the lead and held it taut. "Sparks, heel," he bellowed, but Sparks continued his exited tirade.

"Get him away from me," Tillie screamed.

Avril drew her hands to her mouth, wide-eyed.

An adolescent youth and fragile young woman were not a part of this evening's plan. Though Tillie's knife attempt was apparently thwarted, more needed to be done.

Berdie wrapped her fingers round a nearby broom. *Sorry, Hugh.* She yanked the utility door open. *Lord have mercy on us all.*

She leapt into the kitchen, broom at the ready, as if to sweep the frightful dog out the door. She stood back from the animal and motioned Avril to come stand behind her. The bewildered girl obliged.

"You!" Tillie screamed at Berdie.

Sparks lunged toward Tillie, but Milton held the dog steady.

"Mrs. Elliott," Milton announced with loud shock in his voice, "this place is certainly all go tonight."

The rumble of advancing feet and the impending reach of the law could clearly be heard.

Tillie struggled to pull away, but Chad pushed his back into her and held her captive, squeezed between him and the kitchen counter.

In an instant the whole of the kitchen swarmed with uniformed police, Chief Inspector Kent in the lead.

Milton's eyes became large as dinner plates as Sparks barked at the commotion. "Blimey."

"We'll take over now." Kent jabbed his index finger toward the back door. "Get that dog outside."

"Sparks, heel," Milton trumpeted. This time, the canine yielded. Both were soon out the door.

Berdie returned her broom to an upright position.

A policeman grabbed Tillie, who flung herself about as she tried to wrestle free.

"No," she screamed.

A second constable grabbed hold from behind, while a third one held Tillie's wrists together and applied the handcuffs he pulled from his belt.

"What's happened? Why are they taking Tillie?" Avril asked. Bafflement etched her face. "What's she done?"

"Evil" was all Berdie uttered. "Avril, we need someone to mind Sparks and Milton in the back garden until the police can speak with everyone. Would you, please? Milton can manage the dog. Don't be frightened."

Avril still stared at Tillie.

"Please, Avril? Outside?" Berdie knew the time would come for explanation, but not now.

The girl nodded and left out the door.

Tillie's angry gaze fell upon Berdie. "You wretched witch, I s'pose this comes down to you."

Berdie held the broom steady and straightened. "Though my broom is at hand, no, it's not true. I'm not a witch. But allow me a moment to tell you what is absolutely true." Berdie pulled her shoulders back. "Your father has more bottle than you'll show in a lifetime. He has forgiven everyone for all that has happened. He's understood the complexities of life on this planet, good and bad. That's why he can move on in his life, why he *is* moving on in his life."

Tillie's upper lip twitched.

"The real hero takes where he is and makes the best of it. Your pathetic revenge can't change that."

"How dare you." Tillie struggled against the restraints.

"Killing Hugh won't bring your father's health back, nor your mother, or brother. And it certainly won't give you peace. Letting go, Tillie, that's where peace lies."

"I'm tired of listening to your rubbish, you interfering cow."

Berdie eyed Jasper Kent.

"Matilda Margret Devlin. I'm arresting you for the attempted murder of Commander Cedric Royce."

Tillie, hair disarrayed, still struggled against the constable that held her in tow.

A uniformed officer poured the tea from the cup prepared for Hugh into a special laboratory container.

"And the attempted murder of Reverend Hugh Elliott, by the look of it," Kent went on. "You do not have to say anything, but it may harm your defense if you do not mention, when questioned, something you later rely on in court. Anything you say may be given as evidence. Do you understand the caution?"

"Get stuffed," Tillie snarled.

The constable grappled her from the kitchen to the hall, headed for the front door and the awaiting police car that would take her away.

Berdie was wrenched by a concern for Tillie and relieved that Hugh was safe, all in the same moment.

"Well said, Mrs. Elliott," Chad cheered. "That *rubbish* sounds familiar."

Chief Inspector Kent shook Chad's hand. "Mrs. Elliott said you were the man for the job. We could use someone like you in our organization."

"Thank you. I may take you up on that."

"Good work all round." The chief inspector was matter-of-fact. "Though we hadn't counted on company."

"Yes, I must apologize," Berdie offered. "I hadn't counted on that either. Avril's been staying over with her father at hospital. I hadn't any idea she was coming in this evening. Milton or Sparks either." Berdie perked. "But it seems to have helped our scheme. I think we owe a certain debt of gratitude to our four-legged friend."

"And his young caretaker," Chad added. "Not short of substance, that one."

"Yes, well, I'll be back in a shot. I want to just be sure my men get that she-wolf settled in the police vehicle securely."

"Yes," Berdie acknowledged.

The moment Kent left, Berdie moved close to Chad. She wanted to speak to him about a discovery she made while putting the picture together of what had happened in the past twenty-four hours.

"Have you read the book?" She studied Chad.

He shifted his weight and lifted his chin. "What?"

"*Cloak of Deception,* the exposé on intelligence operations by an author named S. N. Flow."

Chad looked away.

"You know, I recently had a revelation. The commander had a copy of the book on his bedside table in the guest bedroom. I studied the cover. *Flow* is an anagram. Look at it in the mirror and it spells *Wolf.*"

Chad swallowed and tapped a finger against his thigh.

"Switch the *S* and *N* and you have it. N S Wolf.

Ennis Wolf is the deserter who defected to the insurgents. It's he who penned this exposé."

"You have a fertile imagination." Chad's voice was quiet.

"You know it, I know it, and quite frankly, I think all the fellows know it now that they've read the book, including the commander. But no one speaks of it. When did you become aware?"

Chad stared at the floor. "Ennis has a family, children who are proud of him and his service."

"He betrayed all of you."

Chad took a deep breath and swallowed hard.

"You've known a long while he was the mole. He leaked his information to the gutter press, to be published on his death. Did you know that part?"

Chad frowned. "Would anyone in their right mind let information like that be exposed?"

"The commander got the wrong man when he made those unthinkable accusations toward you. I believe he knows that now."

Chad was poker-faced and still.

"Now, our conversation on this subject is done, and I'll not speak of it again. Whatever needs to be done is up to you and your fellows."

Chad sighed in obvious relief that this discussion was ended.

"It sounds like you may possibly have a job offer."

Chad smiled.

Chief Inspector Kent reentered the room, Hugh with him. "Now then, she's settled in for her free ride to the nick."

"And so she should be." Hugh sighed.

Berdie became aware of a very large presence at the back door.

"Reporting for duty, as you asked," Constable Albert Goodnight all but shouted, looking less than sharp in his wrinkled uniform.

"You're late," Kent rebuked.

"Yes, well, sorry about that, sir." Goodnight ran a finger down his uniform buttons. "It's just that the missus's sister needed a lift to the train station. Well, that and the fact that Tottenham's cup game went into extra time."

Kent's jaw fell.

Berdie almost expected as much.

Goodnight's cheeks bulged for smiling like a schoolboy on half term. "They won. One-nil."

"You're a Spurs supporter then." Chad was making light of it.

"Up the Lilliewhites." Goodnight bounced and rubbed his hands together. "So, have I missed anything?"

15

"Now, tell me again, Mrs. Elliott, how much are these going for?"

Mrs. Hall added her currant scones, one by one, to the other baked goods that graced the table while she squinted against the sun.

Berdie adjusted the large sign on the tent pole that read *St. Aidan of the Woods Parish Church Treats Available for Donations.* "All funds go to Help for Heroes."

"God bless our military. Yes, now I remember donations. I thought Mrs. Fairchild was to man this stall."

"I'm sure she'll be here soon," Berdie said with careful optimism. "The final boat race takes place soon."

"It's a beautiful day for our Whitsun Regatta, all the churches and their stalls offering such fun."

"Indeed, Mrs. Hall."

The woman finished her task and grinned widely, advancing the fact that she had made a full recovery from her dental surgery.

"And before I toddle off, may I say, well done catching that bomb culprit. Who would have ever suspected such a pretty little thing?"

"Yes, she had me fooled for a time too. But you know those old words of wisdom, Mrs. Hall. Judging books by their covers, and all that."

"I've wondered how she could have managed to plant a device on a vehicle in such a small village with no one seeing her."

"That's probably the tragic part of it, Mrs. Hall—we're a small village."

Mrs. Hall knit her brow.

"As a guest at the vicarage, she had fine village credentials, if you see what I mean."

"Oh yes, I understand what you're saying."

"I thought Tillie, who seemed so devoted as a caregiver, needed to enjoy the company of some people. So, when Matthew Reese mentioned he was having a party, I sent Tillie along. It was that night, the evening before the explosion, that she set the frightful device in place."

"And isn't that terrible?" Mrs. Hall clucked.

"She arrived home from the party near midnight, or so I thought, because I heard her come in. But once the wheels of suspicion began to turn in my mind, late in the game, I'm afraid, I called Matthew, who told me Tillie had left the party just past ten. What was Tillie doing out and about for two hours?"

"She had the explosive materials with her?"

"Originally, she carried them in her suitcase, and then buried the lot, we discovered later, on the edge of church property near your herb garden."

"Oh dear." Mrs. Hall put her hand to her cheek. Her camel eyes enlarged. "How absolutely frightful."

"Remember how Sparks delighted in digging in your garden? His damaged nose was a bit off, but there it is."

"Yes, quite." The woman still looked a bit dazed.

"And it's all behind us now, Mrs. Hall," Berdie reminded and encouraged. "You are safe as houses."

She brightened. "Yes, well, we can all breathe easier. We're all grateful, indeed for the work of the authorities, but especially for your part in putting it all together."

"I'm afraid a great deal of time and energy was spent chasing smoke, as Chief Inspector Kent put it, but we got there in the end." Berdie beamed.

"Yes, you did indeed."

Memories of questioning herself about her God-given capacities to investigate surfaced in Berdie's mind, and they got a good mental kick in the backside. "Thank you, Mrs. Hall. With God's help, I do my best."

"Well, must get on. I'm meeting my nephew at St. Matthew's booth, the Coconut Shy. Imagine. A dentist, and he still fancies trying to knock things off their pedestal to win silly prizes."

"That's what regattas are all about, Mrs. Hall. Who knows, perhaps you'll have a stuffed bear to take home with you in the end."

The woman giggled. "Do enjoy your afternoon," she offered and departed.

"God go with you."

The satisfaction of a village back in proper order filled Berdie. The commander was improving daily, Avril at his side, Sparks was regaining health, and thank God above, Martha and Milton were still caring for him. Villette had toned down her passing of unverified information, and the Raheems welcomed Sundeep into their home once again.

Berdie hummed the words that still danced in her head from yesterday's Whitsun Sunday Service.

"Come, Holy Ghost, our souls inspire, and lighten with celestial fire." She placed some especially sticky cakes smothered with pink icing to the front of the display

where passersby would be attracted. *"Thy blessed unction from above is comfort, life, and fire of love."*

Though the fabric canopy overhead covered the table, with some room going spare, Berdie stepped into the full sun, where she adjusted her wide-brimmed straw hat and relished the almost-summer warmth. She inhaled the lake air and briefly let her eyes, now adorned with her new tortoiseshell glasses, shut. "Lovely," she breathed.

But when she opened her eyes, what she saw wasn't lovely at all.

Albert Goodnight trekked before her as she had never seen him before. A bright blue shirt, awash with palm leaves and white flowers, topped Bermuda-style shorts that did nothing to glamorize his bulging, hairy knees. His face was nothing more than dark, oversized sunglasses and mustache. And trailing after was the entire family.

"You be goin' to a fire, Albert?" Harriet Goodnight, dressed in similar fashion as her husband, plus a beach hat, bellowed. She toted a cooler box that looked to weigh nearly as much as she.

Jonathan, the oldest Goodnight child, followed behind her, carrying several folding garden chairs under his arms. "Come along, you lot," the young man commanded the three little squealing Goodnights that came after. Dressed in swimming costumes, they played about, just keeping pace.

"On a beach outing then," Berdie said, just audible.

"Aren't they just?"

Berdie was so taken in by the sight of the parading Goodnight clan that she hadn't noticed Lillie's arrival.

"Has Presswood Lake become Brighton Beach?"

Lillie ribbed.

"For them it has," Berdie contended. "They're having a grand time just as they are."

The constable spotted Berdie. "Mrs. Elliott." He raised his sunglasses just long enough to take in the table of delicious treats she stood near. He plopped the black lenses back in place. "Come along, kids." He took steps toward Berdie, all Goodnights following behind.

"County congratulated me for job well done in resolving the bombing case."

"Did they?" Berdie couldn't hide her surprise.

"Well, me and the Yard."

Ah.

"It's my first real day off work in weeks," he announced.

"I didn't know village constables got days off." Berdie watched the youngest child catch up her father.

"Well, this one does today."

The young girl, for all the world a miniature Albert, minus the mustache of course, eyed the pink frosted cakes while standing next her father. Berdie could see from the youngster's stare what was next. The small child stretched out her hand.

"Mind our fingers," Berdie said too late as the little one plunged several appendages into the pink goo.

"Beani, get your hand out of that. Look what your daughter has done," Albert said to the now-arrived Mrs. Goodnight.

"We can't take you anywhere, Benicia Noreen," Harriet squawked.

As Beani put the cake to her lips, the two other children, who resembled their mother, also made a grab for a treat.

"Howard, Maisie," Mrs. Goodnight fired so loudly

that Howard dropped his goodie in the dirt.

"Beani got one," Maisie moaned and set her cake back on the table, while Howard commenced crying.

"Yeah," Jonathon added. "It's not fair. We should all get one."

Albert Goodnight took a raisin scone to hand. "Why not then?" He bit into his nosh.

Berdie refused to step back from the table while mass chaos ensued.

Howard grabbed the same cake as Jonathan, and a shouting match proceeded, which Lillie tried to moderate. Mrs. Goodnight retrieved Howard's dropped cake that had gone icing-first into the soil and, in vain, tried to wipe the dirt off. She mutely returned it to the table. Maisie grabbed a different treat than she had previously and chomped it to nearly half gone. And once Jonathon and Howard came to peaceful agreement, they each took a different treat while Beani stuck her finger into yet another teacake.

"Thank you, Mrs. Elliott," the off-duty officer said between bites of his scone and appeared to beeline for the shoreline.

"Constable Goodnight," Berdie flared.

He grinned as he looked her way.

She pointed to the donations sign. "If you please."

"Harriet," he barked and continued on his way like the Pied Piper and all his little pests following.

Mrs. Goodnight dug into her pocket, dropped two pounds into a provided bucket, and took a scone for herself on the fly. "Ta."

Berdie looked after the departing troop with dismay. "Two quid?"

Lillie gathered the damaged and fingered goods, and then abruptly tossed the lot into the rubbish bag.

"Oh, let them be," she mocked. "They're having a grand time as they are."

"Lock up the ice cream and banish the prizes."

Lillie laughed. "We're down by eleven cakes, and two pounds to show for the lot."

"At that rate our veterans will be dining on egg and chips every meal."

"Others will be more generous, I'm sure," Lillie forecasted.

"Yes, from your mouth to God's ear."

"Where's Maggie?" Lillie asked.

"I'm expecting her any moment, I hope. You're a bit late yourself."

Lillie sheltered a tiny yawn. "Out late with Loren last night."

Berdie watched the myriads of people enjoy the multiple stalls sponsored by churches from the surrounding area, as well as schools, businesses, and special-interest clubs. A small stage was set up near the dock at water's edge where boats readied for the final heat. Hugh and crew had qualified and were in high spirits.

"Mrs. Elliott, I'm here at last," Maggie Fairchild sang out. Her pink straw hat framed a lovely smile that sent her eyes into dancing quarter moons. "My ride was a bit late. And hello, Miss Foxworth."

Berdie found it impossible to charge the kind woman with the lateness of her arrival. "Welcome."

"Oh, two pounds already," she observed with glee.

Berdie didn't explain the details. "I should expect much more by this evening."

"Yes, indeed." Maggie planted herself in a garden chair near the table. "Don't let me keep you. I'm sure you both want to watch the races. Fingers crossed for Reverend Elliott."

"Thank you, Maggie. Guard the rolls with your life."

Maggie chuckled. She didn't know that Berdie was half serious.

Lillie took Berdie's elbow. "The final heat isn't for a while yet. Come with me to see Loren at the first-aid tent."

"Oh, Lillie, you do invite me to the most exciting places."

Lillie laughed as she and Berdie walked to the tent that displayed a large red cross atop the doorway.

When they arrived, Loren was applying a cold pack to a child's swollen eye. "He had an altercation with a tent pole," Loren explained.

"Looks as if the tent pole won." Lillie smiled at the rather embarrassed father.

He simply nodded.

"Keep that cold pack on for a while yet," Loren directed father and son. "Give him children's pain-relief medication as necessary. And a bit of quiet rest wouldn't go amiss."

"Thank you, Doctor," the father said and left with son in tow.

"My usual patients can't breathe, yet alone speak a thank you." He beamed at Lillie and Berdie. "Now, let's see what the doctor's diagnosis is for you two." Loren pointed at Lillie. "You need hot coffee to revive you from our late dinner last night." He looked at Berdie. "And you need rest for all the work your brain has done in bringing justice to our pretty little village. Right?"

"The doctor's always right," Lillie twittered.

"My brain is content with the outcome of its work. No extra rest necessary at the moment."

"Quite startling that Tillie was the avenging bomber," Loren went on while fingering the penlight in his shirt pocket. "When was it that you twigged it, Berdie?"

"Really, not until the end."

"I'm all ears," Loren said, cleaning up after his patient.

"I suppose it began in earnest when Lillie and I discovered the Limb family. I realized Hugh was the target. But it was when Hugh told me about the botched military attack where he was in charge that I began to turn suspicion onto his mates."

"That made you consider Doug Devlin?"

"Yes, all of the fellows, really. It pained me, but it was too much of a coincidence that they were all gathered when the attempt on Hugh's life was made. The greatest suspicion fell on Doug. Yet Hugh was adamant that Doug was not the culprit. He was sure there were no ill feelings there, and I had a certain amount of confidence in Hugh's trust."

"Still, how did you connect it to Tillie?"

Berdie took a deep breath. "All villains make mistakes."

Loren's eyes narrowed. "And what was her biggest, would you say?"

Berdie tapped her finger on her lips. "The book, I'd say. Well, that in connection with Sundeep's lock on his hideaway door."

"Sundeep's lock? Oh, come now, how's that possible?" Lillie almost scoffed.

"Remember it, Lillie? He created it after reading a library book on how to do it, he told me. That was the first wrinkle of thought that perhaps the poorly made bomb could have been made as a result of information from the web or perhaps from a book."

"The book, Tillie's mandatory reading?" Lillie tipped her head. "At the B and B. She said it was a mystery."

"No, Lillie, *you* said it was a mystery and she agreed. It was the perfect chance for her to dodge the whole question."

Lillie's eyes fluttered. "Oh. I made an assumption. It sounded like the title of a mystery."

"And it wasn't at all. *Cloak of Deception* is an exposé, written by an intelligence operative who defected. And do you remember, Lillie, Doug's reaction when he saw the book?"

"Somehow odd, if I remember correctly."

"Tillie told us she was reading it for a class. Doug could not recall her ever mentioning the class before, because she hadn't. She made him think his memory was failing, that she had told him and he forgot. She cast aspersions on Doug's ability to retain information, making me imagine he may have lapses in his thinking which could create great damage."

"She demeaned her father for her own protection and to lessen his capacities in our eyes." Lillie frowned.

"Well, look at the secret she was protecting." Loren arranged the materials in the first-aid box.

Lillie straightened. "Tillie appeared to be doting over her father when in fact she was manipulating him."

"Yes," Berdie scorned. "I think she loved him, but her whole being was consumed with anger, revenge, and such loathing that it skewed everything."

"How incredibly sad," Loren said slowly.

"And she made every attempt to point at Chad as a suspect. She paraded him to police that very first evening they were in my home, but then she alerted the entire community when having tea in the Copper Kettle. She talked about the terrible conflict Chad and the commander had. She dropped Chad right in it. I shouldn't wonder that she, not Villette, spun it into a life of its own."

"Too clever by half," the doctor summed up, "though demented."

"Then, when bits and pieces were not making sense with the commander as the target, Tillie floated the idea of suicide, which by then, others were considering. Sadly, I took enough of the bait to pass it on to Kent, which was her expectation. But when it came down to it, suicide didn't fit the commander's character.

Lillie raised a brow. "Devious."

"The greenfinches were the final piece."

"Greenfinches?" Lillie wrinkled her nose.

"I observed the little greenfinch family weaning their baby, and as we spoke of the firefight involving Hugh and his chums. Your words, 'not there,' put me on to Tillie."

"But, I never said 'not there,'" Lillie corrected.

"Are you sure?"

"But back to the book," Loren redirected.

"Oh yes. I didn't read it, nor did I want to from what I understood, but Rollie had, and Hugh started it after the commander finished it. So, I asked Rollie about the contents. He told me, among other things, it contained a formula for creating a bomb."

"That would certainly point a finger at her." Loren set cotton balls next to a bottle of antiseptic. "Still, there had to be other indicators."

"Of course, but in terms of a big mistake, fleeing the vicarage in haste and leaving the book there was a silly mistake not worthy of her cunning."

"What tripped her up?" Lillie asked.

"Once I began to put pieces together, I saw her anger and distress when she left the vicarage in a new light. I thought Tillie's anxiousness to leave was due to concern about her father, as she said. But it was the fact that she couldn't face her blunder, what she had done to the commander, plus her failure to do in Hugh. That's what drove her from the place in such high dudgeon."

"Poor Doug. Tillie used him for her own purposes."

"Then there was the scar," Berdie went on.

"Just below her neckline?" Loren ran a finger cross his upper chest. "I noticed that at the dinner party. It was just visible, as I recall."

"Yes, that's it," Lillie answered him.

"It was little Emmy and Max put me on to that. Why was it Mrs. Limb brought the little ones to the vicarage that fateful day?"

Lillie rolled her eyes heavenward, then back to Berdie. "To keep them safe, she said."

"Safe from what?" Loren asked.

"My thoughts exactly," Berdie continued. "We knew their father was having episodes. Was Mrs. Limb protecting them from the whole ordeal? Of course. But what if the children were somehow threatened? What could that mean?"

Loren rubbed his chin. "A delirious father harming his own. What a grim effect it would have on a child."

"Precisely." Berdie nodded. "Tillie never spoke of her scar or how it got there, but we all know now."

"It surely fed into her revenge, but she didn't really blame Doug." Lillie took a quick breath. "Did she?"

Berdie shrugged. "Consciously, unconsciously? Who's to say? It was a constant reminder for Doug too, and I believe Tillie used it to her advantage."

Loren wiped the dispensary tray with an antiseptic wipe. "All of this could have been corrected, or at least managed if they had sought treatment. There are more funds, more practitioners now than previously to look after those with posttraumatic stress disorders."

"Well, Doug's receiving professional help now, bless him. And the Limb's young Alec is also getting services. Hugh was a great encouragement that way. He assured them there was no shame in seeking help and that it actually facilitated good overall family health as well."

"Speaking of." Lillie nodded toward the distance.

Doug and Sandra, hand in hand, strode the lake's edge, engaged in conversation, and no wheelchair.

"He's adjusted so well to his repaired prosthetic, and quickly as well. He's quite fit, actually," Loren commented.

"Sandra's certainly been a tonic in all this. Doug's devastation over Tillie has had a healing touch with Sandra's presence in his life." Berdie couldn't help but feel a bit self-satisfied. "God bless them both and…"

A cry of pain interrupted her conversation.

Berdie saw Rollie, arms anchored around Chad and Dave's shoulders, wince as he hobbled with the help of his chums to the first-aid tent, Joan behind them.

"Blimey." Berdie said what she knew her companions had to be thinking.

"Get him settled here." Loren put on a fresh pair of gloves while the men placed Rollie on a portable examining table.

"Didn't I tell him before that last heat to pull out?" Joan directed to Berdie. "He was limping the moment he got out of bed this morning. Well, now he has no choice but to listen."

"You've been overworking your muscles and joints, no doubt," Loren diagnosed by a simple glance. After removing a shoe that revealed a blue-tinged, swollen foot, Loren's simple prodding produced yelps and gasps of air on Rollie's part.

Berdie couldn't believe this was happening. She knew how terribly let down Hugh would be, all the fellows for that matter. Committing to show up and crew, their many hours of practice, hoping to honor the commander, all gone for naught. *And things had been going so well.*

Chad and Dave took in the situation.

"That's bad, Rollie," Chad finally admitted.

"Doc, can you wrap it, give me painkillers, and get me going?" Rollie grimaced. "We've a race to win in fifteen minutes."

"This isn't Premiership football, Rollie. The only place you're going is to hospital." Loren examined the offending spot closely. "It's a sprain by the look of it, and a bad one. But you need a proper X-ray examination to make sure it isn't something worse."

"I'll pull the car round," Joan said firmly to her husband. "And that's an end to it." She pulled car keys from her pocket, brooking no disagreement.

"Do you want me to come with you, Joan?" Berdie offered.

"No, you've got so much on here, Berdie, but thank you."

Loren handed Joan a small white placard with a red cross on it. "Place it on your windscreen where it can be easily seen and Mr. Braunhoff will let you come right up to the tent."

Joan took it and departed.

"Blast," Rollie railed. "Sorry about this, lads." He gritted his teeth. "Stupid thing to do."

"You just take care of yourself," Dave admonished.

Within three minutes Joan was back. The men helped get Rollie safely in the car and on his way.

Chad's face reflected the disappointment felt by all. "I'll go let Hugh know we need to scratch the team."

"Maybe you can find someone to step in." Lillie's tone didn't sound at all hopeful.

"In ten minutes' time?" Chad sounded piqued. "Any idea who?"

"Me?" The words came from the opening of the tent, where Doug and Sandra stood.

"Doug?" Berdie caught her breath.

"I saw Joan bring the car round, and I knew it couldn't be good news. But hopefully, I can help."

Chad looked Doug in the eye. "Do you mean it? Maybe a better question is: have you got it in you?"

"I won't know unless I try." Doug glanced at Sandra, who offered a reassuring smile and quiet nod.

Dave looked at Loren. "Dr. Meredith?"

Doug stepped forward. "I use to row with these fellows. They're my team. And I'm decently fit."

"Your thighs are very well developed. You've got powerful shoulders, but..." Loren didn't get a chance to finish.

"I'm not saying we'll win, but one leg is better than none." Doug was absolutely keen.

"That's the spirit." Chad slapped Doug on the back.

"We need to let Hugh know what's happening," Dave urged.

"He's been helping Mr. Webb at the church's hospitality stall since the last heat." Berdie pulled her mobile from her trouser pocket and handed it to Dave.

"You're quite sure, Doug?" Dave asked.

Berdie watched Doug's eyes, no longer clouded with the haze of sedatives, blaze with more confidence than she'd ever seen before.

"I want to do it."

That's all it took for the crew to smile and make way to the boat, Sandra too, while Dave rang Hugh.

When the five-minute bell sounded, Berdie left the tent. She, Lillie, and Sandra, who had returned, made way to the shoreline along with families, singles, teens, tots, grandparents, bikers, pets, and all other sorts. It seemed the whole of Christendom, and then some, gathered near the lakefront finish line.

Sandra hugged Doug's prosthesis to her torso for safekeeping since Doug was more comfortable rowing without it. She whispered to Berdie and Lillie, "Some may say Doug's got a leg up on the race."

Lillie's eyebrows rose, but Berdie chuckled. She appreciated Sandra's sense of humor.

Chad as toe man, Hugh, Doug, and Dave faced six other crews who were just as eager to take the Whitsun Regatta Cup. From all appearances, there looked to be only two other crews that had the same kind of competitive edge as Saint Aidan's. Blessed Virgin Kingsford and Waterside Chapel were the boats to beat.

Berdie was amazed at how quickly Blessed Virgin was off the mark at the starter pistol. Waterside Chapel was a surprising second and St. Aidan was third, all others trailing.

Several supporters began to hoot and holler encouragement for their crews. And by the time the boats reached the far side of the lake and went round their buoys, Blessed Virgin was in the lead, St. Aidan second, and Waterside Chapel third. That's when the roaring commenced.

"Heave ho, St. Clement."

"Go, go, Waterside."

"Show us what you've got, St. Margret."

"Give 'em what for, Blessed Virgin."

Berdie chuckled to think what an unsuspecting visitor might make of the cheers. She watched Blessed Virgin surge, Hugh and his crew a half–boat length behind. But the first-place crew began to flag, and Waterside Chapel took the lead. St. Aidan kept a steady pull and release and within several strokes was nearly even with the Waterside crew.

Berdie swallowed and felt her breath go a bit rapid. Suddenly, "Go, Hugh," joined the cheers filling the air of Presswood Lake.

"That's it, Doug." Sandra added her voice. She squeezed the prosthetic leg to her chest and began thumping it with an open palm. "You're doing it, love. Keep stride."

"Ai-dan, Ai-dan, Ai-dan," rose as a chant from a group of the church youth, Lucy and Milton Butz flailing arms to keep the rhythm pumped up.

Berdie could now see the look of sheer determination on the two leading crews approaching, but none looked more committed than Hugh, grittier than Chad, more dogged than Dave, or more indomitable than Doug.

"Stroke," Hugh heaved.

Berdie put her hands into fists, shaking them up and down as St. Aidan began to edge forward. "Come on, St. Aidan, you can do it, chums!"

Grunts, red faces, power shoulders, and Divine strength put St. Aidan just even with Waterside Chapel.

"If boats have noses," Sandra yelled to Berdie above the roar, "that's what we'll win by."

The words no sooner left Sandra's mouth when exactly that happened. By the smallest of margins, St. Aidan edged past the other boat just as they reached the finish line and was declared the winner.

"We did it, we did it." Berdie could barely take it in.

Sandra grabbed Berdie's hand, Doug's artificial leg bouncing, while Lillie yipped and laughed.

Berdie let go a "Yes," thrust a fist into the air, and sprang about as the supporters of St. Aidan of the Wood Parish Church erupted into cheers.

When Hugh and Doug, who was helped along by Chad and Dave, climbed onto the small awards stage, applause exploded.

St. Aidan's flock shouted and whistled with exuberance until the Lord Mayor of Timsley, whose thin legs looked just able to keep his bulbous body upright with its weighty mayoral chain about his neck, waved his hand to beg silence.

He lifted a silver cup upward. "On behalf of the people of Timsley and all the surrounding villages"— he extended the cup to Hugh—"we present the first annual Whitsun Regatta Cup to the crew of St. Aidan of the Woods Parish Church."

Applause abounded. "Ai-dan, Ai-dan" came from the church youth as Hugh accepted the cup.

"Lord Mayor," Hugh said amidst sweat, wet silver hair, and face red from exertion, "on behalf of our crew, we thank you."

As Chad, Doug, and Dave offered smiles and waves, there was more applause and not a few hoots.

Hugh raised his palm to silence all, and the crowd went still.

"We would like to dedicate our win and this cup to Commander Cedric Royce, who is expected to leave hospital next week."

Cheers, whistles, and thunderous claps arose from the St. Aidan crowd.

Hugh waved his hand again and took a deep breath. "Also, with our win we would like to acknowledge all those who have served or are on active duty in the armed forces. May our gifts and talents bring great honor and give us courage to gladly face all our tomorrows. God bless us all."

Hugh handed the trophy off to Doug, who had one arm draped around Chad's shoulder to keep upright and the other free to take the cup.

Not just St. Aidan, but the entire crowd went ballistic with appreciation as the triumphant Doug raised the prize high in the air.

"That's my man," Sandra all but screamed.

"Far better than a scratch, they've overcome," Lillie shouted.

"They have," Berdie answered. "We all have, really."

"Is that gifted investigative nose of yours back in full flow now, no doubts?"

"Not a doubt in sight. I'm ready and willing to use what God has given me whenever the call comes. I can tell you this right now. Overcoming is what happens when people utilize their God-given gifts for the welfare of the community."

"Amen to that." Lillie twinkled.

And the hands of time seemed to stand still at Presswood Lake as the people's Whitsun spirit of celebration reverberated from shore to shore.

A note from the author

The story, *Enigma of Fire: A Berdie Elliott Pentecost Mystery*, has a festive Berdie singing a song to herself at the Whitsun Regatta while she waits for Maggie Fairchild. "Come, Holy Ghost, Our Souls Inspire," or rightly titled "Veni, Creator Spiritus" in the original Latin, was written in the ninth century and sung in the early church. John Cosin (1594–1672), Dean and Bishop of Durham, England, translated it into English. It is paired, to this day, with a surviving plainsong melody. Although it was originally sung at Pentecost, it is now also raised in song at ordination services of the clergy throughout England.

"Veni, Creator Spiritus"

Come, Holy Ghost, our souls inspire,
And lighten with celestial fire;
Thou the anointing Spirit art,
Who dost Thy sev'nfold gifts impart.

Thy blessed unction from above
Is comfort, life, and fire of love;
Enable with perpetual light
The dullness of our blinded sight.

Teach us to know the Father, Son,
And Thee, of both, to be but One,
That through the ages all along
This may be our endless song:

"Praise to Thy eternal merit,
Father, Son, and Holy Spirit. Amen."

Thank you...

for purchasing this Harbourlight title. For other
inspirational stories, please visit our on-line bookstore
at www.pelicanbookgroup.com.

For questions or more information, contact us at
customer@pelicanbookgroup.com.

Harbourlight Books
The Beacon in Christian Fiction™
an imprint of Pelican Book Group
www.pelicanbookgroup.com

Connect with Us
www.facebook.com/Pelicanbookgroup
www.twitter.com/pelicanbookgrp

To receive news and specials, subscribe to our bulletin
http://pelink.us/bulletin

May God's glory shine through
this inspirational work of fiction.

AMDG

You Can Help!

At Pelican Book Group it is our mission to entertain readers with fiction that uplifts the Gospel. It is our privilege to spend time with you awhile as you read our stories.

We believe you can help us to bring Christ into the lives of people across the globe. And you don't have to open your wallet or even leave your house!

Here are 3 simple things you can do to help us bring illuminating fiction™ to people everywhere.

1) If you enjoyed this book, write a positive review. Post it at online retailers and websites where readers gather. And share your review with us at reviews@pelicanbookgroup.com (this does give us permission to reprint your review in whole or in part.)

2) If you enjoyed this book, recommend it to a friend in person, at a book club or on social media.

3) If you have suggestions on how we can improve or expand our selection, let us know. We value your opinion. Use the contact form on our web site or e-mail us at customer@pelicanbookgroup.com

God Can Help!

Are you in need? The Almighty can do great things for you. Holy is His Name! He has mercy in every generation. He can lift up the lowly and accomplish all things. Reach out today.

Do not fear: I am with you; do not be anxious: I am your God. I will strengthen you, I will help you, I will uphold you with my victorious right hand.

~Isaiah 41:10 (NAB)

We pray daily, and we especially pray for everyone connected to Pelican Book Group—that includes you! If you have a specific need, we welcome the opportunity to pray for you. Share your needs or praise reports at http://pelink.us/pray4us